King

HAD THERE BEEN n   te Tanner would have lived their lives together as intimate friends, and secret lovers. But when the revolution convulsed America, it threw them down on opposite sides of history...

Five years later, Sam is a Loyalist refugee in London, penniless, bitter, and scrambling to survive amid the city's shadowy underworld. It's a far cry from his respectable life as a Rhode Island lawyer, and the last person he wants to witness his ruin is Nate Tanner—the man he once loved, the man who betrayed him.

The man he can't forgive.

Now an agent of the Continental Congress, Nate is in London on the trail of a traitor threatening America's hard-won freedom. But the secret mission of his heart is quite different. Nate longs to find Sam Hutchinson—the man he still loves, the man he lost to the war.

The man he can't forget.

When their lives unexpectedly collide, Sam and Nate are thrown together on a dangerous mission. And despite everything that still divides them, old passions begin to stir...

Can they seize this second chance at love, or is their past too painful to forgive?

Copyright notice

King's Man

Outlawed I

Sally Malcolm

Acknowledgments

THIS BOOK HAS been a long time in the writing and wouldn't have made it to print at all without the help of my friends. So my deep gratitude goes to Joanna Chambers for her generosity and encouragement, and for helping me pull it all apart and put it back together again, better. And a huge thank-you also to Laura Harper, for her brilliant editing and polishing services, and for reading versions of this story too many times, over too many years.

And finally, I'd like to thank Angela Lowry Bricker for generously providing a necessary American perspective on the characters and the story.

Needless to say, if I've trodden on anyone's toes it's because of my own clod-hopping feet.

Historical note

THERE ARE A couple of terms used in this book that may by unfamiliar to readers new to this period of American history.

Tory — used widely in Colonial America, this was a term of abuse for those Americans who opposed the War of Independence. These days it's used in Canada and the UK as a colloquial term for conservative political philosophies and parties.

Continental Congress — during the period in which *King's Man* is set, America was governed by the Congress of the Confederation which sat between 1781 and 1789 and followed on from the First Continental Congress and the Second Continental Congress. However, Americans at the time still referred to it as the Continental Congress and so that's what my characters call it.

This was a volatile period in the new country's birth. The Continental Congress was crippled by arguments about how to govern, the economy was spiraling downward, and disaffected citizens rebelled in the backcountry.

Meanwhile, foreign enemies stood ready to exploit the instability for their own ends…

Part One

Chapter One

August 13th, 1778
Rosemont, Rhode Island

SUNLIGHT FELL IN dreamy pools over the man drowsing at Nate Tanner's side, burnishing his tangled hair with flecks of gold, and picking out freckles on the smooth skin of his back.

Nate lay watching him in the aftermath of their love-making, the warmth in his heart fading fast, cooled by the gathering storm. He recoiled from the knowledge that this would be their last afternoon together, but they lived in a time of war and there was no room for sentiment left in the land. Reaching out, he smoothed his palm over his lover's shoulder and smiled when Sam blinked open his eyes.

"Well," Sam said in a smiling rumble. "That was some-thing."

"So it was." Curling his hand around the back of Sam's neck, Nate pulled him close enough to kiss his lips. "Quite something."

With a contented sigh, Sam rolled onto his back, re-arranging them both until Nate's head came to rest against his chest and Sam's strong arms wrapped around him. Nate snaked his own arm around Sam's waist and, for a moment, buried his face against his skin, breathing in the scent of him. Committing him to memory.

"Hush now," Sam said, stroking a hand over Nate's back. "And tell me what's had you jumpy as a cat all afternoon."

As always, Sam knew Nate better than Nate knew himself. *Amicus est tamquam alter idem*: a true friend is a second self.

Nate let his thumb run over the ring he wore — the ring Sam had given him two years ago, engraved with an abbreviation of those words: AETAI. Its twin felt warm against Nate's back as Sam continued his steady caress. "I can't come here anymore," Nate said softly. A shard of sunlight lanced up from the heavy armoire by the window and Nate watched the dust motes dance, unable to meet Sam's eyes. "It's too dangerous — our friendship is drawing too much attention."

Sam stilled to his bones. Only the accelerating thump of his heart beneath Nate's ear told him that Sam still breathed. Outside, a songbird trilled, and a distant carriage rumbled past. If he listened very carefully, Nate could hear the distant rush of the Pawtuxet River. Inside Sam's bedchamber, the silence grew thick. Nate levered himself up onto one elbow and Sam's arms fell away to lay slack at his side, eyes fixed on the ceiling. "How long must you stay away?"

"I don't know." Despite his best intentions, Nate's voice wobbled. "Until things calm down. The British are so close. People are afraid."

"Is this — ?" A painful pause. "Is this because of Holden?"

Amos Holden. The swaggering little shit had resented Sam for years. Holden's recent elevation to chairman of

Rosemont's Committee of Safety had only made his persecution more vicious. And Sam did nothing to mollify him. Quite the opposite in fact, the obstinate fool that he was.

Nate had to look away from Sam's distress before he answered, staring at his chest instead, at his own hand resting there and the golden glint of his ring. "Not just Holden, the whole committee are against you now."

Silence. Then, "And does that include you?"

"Of course not." Nate spread his fingers, tried to find Sam's heartbeat again. "But you're not making it easy for me to explain our friendship. Not easy at all."

Pushing his hand away, Sam surged upright and swung his legs over the side of the bed. "Oh, so it's my fault?"

"Well…" He suppressed his flash of exasperation. "It's your decision to refuse the loyalty oath."

"It's my *right* to refuse it. I'll think as I choose, and Holden's mob can go to hell if they say otherwise."

"His *committee*," Nate corrected, "are trying to keep Rosemont safe."

"From me?"

"Sam…"

"No, tell me." Angrily, he turned around. "Does he think *I'm* a danger to Rosemont, to the place I was born? To the place my parents were born? Where they're laid to rest?"

"Holden's a bully, we both know that, and he's using the committee to settle old scores. But the world has *changed*, Sam. And you must change with it."

"Must I? Why? Why should I change to suit Amos Holden?"

"Because —" Nate raked a hand through his hair in frustration. "Because a storm's coming. Hell, the storm's already here. And in a storm, you have to trim your sails or be wrecked."

"Storms pass," Sam said, stubborn as a damned rock.

"And this will pass, too. Things will go back to normal, you'll see."

"Normal? Sam we're at war. Whether you like it or not, we're at war with Great Britain."

"*I'm* not at war. With anyone."

"But America is! You can't pretend — Look, you don't have to mean it. Cross your fingers if you must, but for God's sake take the loyalty oath." Cautiously, he touched Sam's bare shoulder. "Keep your head down and your mouth shut, love. Keep yourself safe."

But Sam shook him off, standing up. "Surrender to the mob, you mean." He picked up his shirt from the chair where he'd flung it. "Tear up the law and let anarchy reign."

Nate closed his eyes, searching for patience. "They're not a mob, they represent the people of Rosemont —"

"By whose authority? Nobody elected them. Holden made himself judge, jury and executioner. And I'll be damned before I swear loyalty to him or any other self-appointed despot."

"Yes, you've made that clear. To the whole damn town!" Nate scrambled out of bed and began to dress, buttoning his breeches with irritable swiftness. They'd been over this a thousand times. Sam was determined to cling to the life he'd always known, even if it killed him — which it might. And Nate was determined to fight for a radical new world, even if it killed him. Which it might. They should be enemies. Yet Nate still loved him as deeply as he had these last four years. Loved him with a fierce, angry passion that he couldn't quell. "Damn it, Sam. Why can't you just… just *bend* a little?"

"Why can't you?" Sam fixed him with a heated look. "You didn't have to join the committee. You didn't have to be part of this. You could have kept *your* head down and *your* mouth shut."

"I don't want to keep my head down —"

"Neither do I!" Sam sucked in an angry breath. "For God's sake, can't you see what's happening? All over the country, men like Holden are trampling the law to get what they—"

"I'm not saying I agree with it all, but this is a crisis. We're fighting for our liberty."

"Liberty?" Sam's eyes flashed angrily. "Amos Holden keeps ten enslaved people on his farm. He can talk to me about liberty once he's freed them."

Nate's jaw bunched, but he had no answer to that. "It's not about Holden. God knows he's a prick, but this… It's bigger than him. Bigger than us. You must see that. It's impossible to turn away from this fight."

"I'm *not* turning away." Sam bristled in angry defiance. "But I had no quarrel with the way things were. America *should* be at the heart of the empire. That's where we belong. Hell, I bet we'll be running it from Boston one day. And whatever your committee says, that doesn't make me an enemy of America. It makes me her friend. A better friend than the likes of Amos Holden."

"For God's sake, Sam. It makes you a British sympathizer."

"But we *are* British," Sam cried in exasperation. "*And* we're American. We're both, that's my point. And abandoning the rule of law just to score a political point—"

"That's not what's happening, and you know it."

"Isn't it?" Sam leveled a finger at him. "Your committee banned me from voting. They tripled my taxes, and they barred me from practicing law. All because I refuse to support this war. Because I see a different destiny for our country. Well, let them do their worst; I deny their authority over me. It stems from threats and violence and, as an American, I will not bow before it."

"No more than I will bow before a king who has violated all our rights as Englishmen."

"There are better ways to defend our rights than with violence."

"None that the British understand!"

Angrily, Sam bit off his response. After a pause, and with an obvious effort at calm, he said, "And here we are again, at an impasse."

"So it seems."

"Maybe there really is nothing else to say" — his voice cracked — "except goodbye."

Even though Nate knew it to be true, Sam's clear grief pierced him. "This isn't what I want." He reached for Sam's arm, winding his fingers into the sleeve of his shirt. "I don't want this to end."

"And yet you're ending it."

"Because I have no choice." The risk of loving Sam had always been high, but in the last six months even acknowledging their friendship posed a danger. Amos Holden had eyes everywhere, and it was impossible for Nate to explain his continued friendship with an infamous Tory. "If Holden used our attachment against you…" He blew out a breath. "It's safer this way."

Sam didn't respond, just looked at Nate for a long, anguished moment, then pulled his shirt free of Nate's grip and turned away. "It'll take me some time to —" He cleared his throat. "To gather all the books you've left here. I assume you want them back."

That was designed to wound, and it did its job, sliding like a blade between Nate's ribs. Oh, the hours they'd spent together reading. They'd fallen in love over those books. When Nate found his voice again, he said, "Keep them. Take care of them until we can…"

His throat closed around the words, eyes filling with tears. Blinking them away, he finished dressing in silence. And in silence he made his way downstairs, avoiding the front door. Sam followed, and they stopped in the kitchen amid the scent of drying rosemary. How he'd leave, Nate couldn't fathom, and for a few slow ticks of the clock they stood and gazed at each other in agonized silence.

"There was a time," Sam said roughly, "when you'd leave by the front door, when you weren't ashamed of our friendship."

Not shame, never that. But exasperation and dread and a terrible aching regret that balled up into impossible frustration. "I just wish you could see that history is with us, Sam. Our cause is just. It's right. And we will prevail. I wish you'd join us."

Sam straightened, his expression changing from sorrow to something colder, harder. It made Nate shiver. "I wish *you* could see that tearing down the law and raising up a mob risks every liberty you claim to defend. And I wish your committee could understand that I have a right to voice my opposition to this damned war, and that my *opinion* doesn't make me a traitor."

Those were his parting words. Nate had no answer they hadn't rehearsed a hundred times. They would never agree, and more arguing was futile.

Opening the door, he stepped out into the sticky heat of the afternoon and walked through Sam's neglected kitchen garden to the dusty road beyond. He looked back once and saw Sam standing in the shadow of the doorway watching him leave.

Neither said goodbye.

Chapter Two

**Two months later — October 24th, 1778
Rosemont, Rhode Island**

"TANNER! TANNER, WAKE UP!"

Heart rabbiting in his chest, Nate sat bolt upright in bed. It was pitch black. The darkest hour of the night. And someone was battering at the front door of his lodging house.

"Tanner!"

Stumbling downstairs, he wrenched open the door. John Reed stood outside, the portly old gentleman wearing his coat over his nightgown and no wig beneath his hat. In the moonlight, his skin looked waxy and sick. "My God," Nate said with icy dread. "What's happened?"

"It's Sam." Reed gripped Nate's arm, grim as death. "They've gone up to his place, a whole crowd of them."

Nate's stomach pitched. "Holden?"

"They marched right past my house — thirty, maybe more. I couldn't see enough to count. But Holden was up front. Urging them on." His grip on Nate's arm tightened. "They were ugly, Nate. Ugly."

Yes, they would be. With the British camped so close, Rosemont had been seized by terror for the past two months. "I'll go," he said. "I'll…"

What? What the devil could he do? Amos Holden was no friend of his. Always a self-important prick, he'd become the very image of Sam's swaggering demagogue since he'd made himself head of the Committee of Safety. And he'd always been suspicious of Nate's defense of Sam.

And what's Hutchinson to you, Tanner? What makes him so different from any other traitor who refuses to defend his country? Or is it because you and he are such particular *friends?*

The truth was that Nate had grown afraid of Amos Holden. He was the sort of man to ferret out trouble if he got its scent, or to invent it if he didn't, and God knew Nate and Sam had plenty of trouble to find. So Nate had stayed silent and Holden's braggadocio had grown bolder. Tonight, Nate feared the consequences of his silence would be realized, and the thought turned his stomach.

"Go home," he told Reed. "I'll deal with this."

Racing upstairs, Nate wrenched open the drapes to dress by moonlight instead of wasting time lighting a lamp. Throwing on his clothes, he shoved his feet into his boots and ran out of the house, passing Reed as he too hurried towards Sam's house. Nate wasn't surprised the old man refused to hide at home; Sam was almost a son to him. John Reed wouldn't turn his back on him, despite Holden's threats.

The streets of Rosemont were quiet — it must be long past midnight — but up ahead Nate could hear the distant clamor of angry voices, and the sound raised the hair on the back of his neck. This had been brewing for weeks. Like a storm sitting far out at sea, he'd watched it draw closer day-by-day. Inevitable as winter.

Sam's house lay on the outskirts of Rosemont, a fine brick building first constructed by his grandfather and improved upon by his father. Much bigger than Sam needed, now that there was only him left. And Amos Holden had long regarded it with covetous eyes.

Nate's lungs started to burn, breath billowing in the chill fall night, his feet stumbling over ruts as he ran. He fell once, skinning his palms, picked himself up and kept going despite the sharp twinge in his ankle. From ahead, came the flickering dance of flame — torches, to light the way. And to intimidate.

Holden's rabble were already outside Sam's house, a rough arc of people crowding around the front door. Wild with panic, Nate shouldered his way through the crowd, every face familiar: James Adams, the blacksmith, Abe Milton who owned the bakery, the O'Keefe brothers, all six of them. And several of their wives, by the looks of things. Neighbors, all. Friends, once. But angry now; angry and afraid.

"Let me pass," Nate demanded as he pushed forward. "Let me see —"

He stopped dead when he reached the front, choking on his own breath.

Sam knelt on the ground outside his front door. He was half dressed, in breeches and a shirt — Nate had an unbidden, agonizing image of him dressing in fright as the mob surrounded his house — and his hands were tied behind his back. His feet were bare.

Amos Holden stood before him. A balding, ruddy-faced man of about Nate's father's age, he held aloft a paper. The loyalty oath, no doubt. Behind Sam stood Bill Mather, one hand clenched in Sam's hair, forcing his head back and up. Not that he needed to bother, because Sam's ferocious gaze was locked on Holden. Even in the dark, Nate could see the flashing fury in his eyes. And the fear, stark and sharp. All around them, the air stank of hot pitch and violence.

"This is your last chance," Holden shouted, waving the oath for all to see. "By order of the Rhode Island General Assembly, the Rosemont Committee of Safety demands that you, Samuel Hutchinson, swear as follows: *I believe the War, Resistance, and Opposition, in which the United American Colonies are now engaged, against the Fleets and Armies of Great Britain, is, on the part of the said Colonies, just and necessary. And I will defend by arms the United Colonies against every hostile attempt of the Fleets and Armies in the service of Great Britain.*"

A ringing silence followed his declaration, nothing to be heard but the spit and hiss of the torches, the heavy breathing of the angry crowd. Nate held his breath, heart clattering wildly. *Please*, he begged Sam. *Please just say it.*

Perhaps he made a sound of distress because Sam's eyes flicked to him, then widened in shock. It had been several weeks since they'd seen each other. Sam sagged back against Mather, as if shoved by an invisible hand, and Nate took a half step forward, then stopped, paralyzed by indecision. If he spoke now, would he make matters worse? Holden would be only too happy to snarl insinuations about their friendship.

"Well?" Holden spat. "What's your answer, Tory?"

For a moment, Nate thought Sam might concede. He sat slumped in defeat and Nate felt an awful, shameful relief. But what a Pyrrhic victory it would be. Yes, he wanted Sam to take the oath; he wanted Sam to be safe. But to see him like this, humiliated and forced to comply by a thug like Amos Holden? It was unbearable.

Then Sam's eyes lifted to Nate's. The fleeting contact was so fierce he feared everyone must see it, although there was nothing tender in that gaze, nothing of the love they shared. And nothing of defeat.

Sam's gaze was all ice and defiance.

He looked away, his throat working, and moistened his lips. It was the only sign of his fear. "I cannot swear your oath," he declared in a loud clear voice. "I wish no man ill, but I do not believe your war is just or necessary. I believe it is a mistake, and I cannot swear otherwise. My conscience forbids it."

"The Committee demands that you do," Holden said, playing to the crowd at his back. "We demand that you demonstrate your loyalty to us and to the American cause."

"And I don't accept that your arbitrary, self-created tribunal has any right to govern my conscience. Who are you, Amos Holden, to tell me what to think? My *opinion* does not make me a traitor, sir. I have a right to think as I choose — about this war or any other matter."

Nate closed his eyes, half in frustration and half in desperate pride. What a speech to make on your knees.

"And those," Holden said, turning to face the crowd in triumph, "are exactly the weasel words you'd expect from a King's man. Are they not? The British are camped just beyond the Pawtuxet, and this man" — he flung out his arm toward Sam — "this *Tory* calls our struggle a mistake! He refuses to fight for our liberty! His conscience forbids it, he says. I say, where will his *conscience* be when the British guns are turned on Rosemont?"

"Traitor!" yelled a voice from the crowd.

"Pig-fucking Tory whore!"

"What shall we do with him?" cried Holden, swaggering and strutting toward the pan of hot pitch. He lifted it up and the crowd cheered. "What will Rosemont do with this traitor?"

"Tar him!"

"Tar him!"

"Tar him!"

Nate watched in rising horror as two men broke from the mob to rip open Sam's shirt, tearing it off his back with such force Sam would have fallen had Mather not gripped his hair.

"Look at yourselves!" Sam shouted, twisting in Mather's grasp to glare at Nate. "This is your liberty? This is the country you want to be? Can't you see what —"

Holden struck him, hard across the face. And it was too much. The sight of blood on Sam's split lip was too much. Nate surged forward, ready to fight, but someone grabbed his arm and yanked him back into the crowd. He spun around furiously, fists up, and found himself face-to-face with John Reed.

"Think!" Reed hissed. "Think, Nate. Don't make things worse for him."

"*Worse?*" His eyes blurred with furious tears, his throat aching. "How could it be — ?"

"This will only hurt his pride. But get him out of here when they're done. Do you understand me?" Reed shook his arm. "If they put a flame to him…"

A flame? Jesus Christ.

He turned back to Sam in terror. Holden was already pouring the pitch, while Mather and the other two tried to hold Sam still as he struggled. The stink of the tar made Nate's eyes water. Viscid, it crawled through Sam's hair, down over his face. Sam screwed his eyes shut, pressing his lips tight together, nostrils flaring.

Nate stifled a cry, hand to his mouth, the shouts and jeers of the men and women around him drowning out his aching horror. Reed's hand tightened on his arm until his fingers dug into his flesh.

Sam struggled and bucked but he didn't shout, he made

no sound that Nate could hear as Holden tipped the hot pitch across his shoulders and let it run down his chest, the muscles of his belly quivering in humiliation and rage.

Nate's heart begged to go to him. It begged to turn away. Nate allowed himself neither comfort. Instead, he made himself watch, made himself bear witness as a bag of feathers was fetched and dumped over Sam's head, sticking to the tar on his face and body. The mob laughed and spat their contempt, and Sam coughed and retched until Mather let him go and he sagged forward over his knees.

Nate bit his lip hard enough to draw blood.

No one dies from a tarring and feathering, he told himself desperately. Once Holden was gone, Nate would scrape the tar from Sam's skin and hair, he'd kiss away his hurt. And harangue him into leaving Rosemont. If there was no other way to save him, he'd put him in a damn sack and carry him away himself.

But then Holden seized a torch from someone in the crowd. "Now what?" he hollered, walking in menacing circles around Sam with the torch held aloft. "What shall we do with the Tory scum now?"

Nate's skin flashed cold in sudden dread and Reed's hand bit into his arm. Around him, the mood of the crowd shifted. Growing uneasy.

Holding the naked flame close to Sam's face, Holden hissed, "I could make a torch of you, Hutchinson." Dancing firelight flickered over the tar dripping through Sam's hair. "I could watch you *burn*."

Desperate, Nate lurched forward, but Reed pulled him back and stepped forward in his place. "Stop this!" he shouted. "You've done enough, Amos. Stop."

Holden turned his head, his smile sly. "Ah, Reed. Come to defend your clerk?"

Fear turned Nate's stomach liquid as he watched Sam on

his knees, sucking in great wracking gasps, but he dared not go to him for fear his grief and terror would betray them both. He couldn't risk giving Holden that weapon.

"You go too far, Amos," Reed protested. "Would you make murderers of us all?"

Behind him, the anxious crowd shifted. Silently, they watched. Waiting.

"The British will do worse when they come," Holden spat. "They'll torch the whole town and—"

"Then we must be better! Otherwise, why are we fighting at all?"

A deathly pause followed, closing around Nate's racing heart like a fist. Holden glared, a wild light in his eyes, and Nate braced himself to fight. But then Holden barked a laugh and swung away from Sam, throwing his torch to the ground.

The nervous crowd laughed with him, the tension breaking, and Nate's knees wobbled in relief. But he hadn't even caught his breath before Holden shouted, "Bring the wagon."

"What?" Nate turned to see a horse being led into the pool of torchlight, a cart at its back. "Holden, what's this?"

Holden ignored him as Mather and his accomplices dragged Sam to his feet. His poor, bare feet stumbled forward as they pushed him towards the cart, his hands still bound behind his back. He didn't look once in Nate's direction, though he passed so close they could have touched. It pierced Nate's soul with grief.

Then they manhandled Sam into the cart, and he scrambled up onto to his knees, still defiant. His face was hidden behind the grotesque mask of tar and feathers, but his furious gaze glinted in the moonlight. Full of bravado, Holden set a lit lamp next to Sam in the bed of the cart, its naked flame a dancing threat. "There's no room for your kind in Rosemont," he snarled. "You aren't fit to call yourself an American."

The crowd cheered, the driver tapped the horse's flank, and the wagon lurched forward. Rooted to the spot, heart seared, Nate felt like a man trapped in a nightmare. Unable to move, unable to wake up. Helpless, he watched as the hooting, hollering mob surged around and past him, following the cart out of town.

At the last moment, Sam stood up, struggling to balance. A final act of defiance, perhaps. But, no, he had a purpose. His gaze roved across the crowd, searching for something, and Nate's pulse skipped when Sam's eyes found his for one last look of utter betrayal.

And Nate knew that everything had changed.

Their bond was broken, shattered by the implacable wheel of history that forged ahead, heedless of the little lives and loves it crushed along the way.

Part Two

Chapter One

Five years later — July 22nd, 1783
London, England

SAMUEL HUTCHINSON DRANK cheap gin because it didn't remind him of home.

And if he kept his eyes fixed on the door of the sordid little room, one hand on the burly shoulders between his legs, this wouldn't remind him of home either. But then the man — Sam hadn't wanted his name — took him in his mouth with a groan so resonant Sam felt it at the root of his spine and his head hit the back of the chair.

"No." He gripped the man's shoulder but couldn't quite bring himself to push him away. "Don't."

The stranger lifted his head. In the tallow light his eyes could have been any color, his hair a dirty straw, but his accent had a harsh London rasp. "I reckon you like that, Yankee." He said it with a grin, wet lips gleaming.

And Sam did like it. "I asked you not to."

"Maybe I want to?" He licked a lascivious line from Sam's balls to the tip of his cock. "I reckon you want it, too."

A slight shake of his head, but the denial was weak. He did want it. He yearned for it. "Just your hand."

"I ain't your whore," said the man, and took him to the hilt with an expertise that drove Sam's eyes shut.

"*God*," he rasped, helpless as the memories surged forward.

It was night, the cicadas sang in the grass, and the Pawtuxet carved a molten line of silver beneath the low-hanging moon. Nate reached the riverbank first, laughing as he stripped off his shirt and breeches, his skin pale and his sharp-boned face eldritch in the moonlight. "Come on!" he shouted and dived into the silver water.

Sam wasn't far behind, slipping into the river with more decorum — there were no neighbors for miles, but you never knew. You never knew.

And then Nate was there, his slender body slippery and irresistible as he wound himself into Sam's arms. "Fuck me," he whispered in his ear. "Right here in the river."

Sam clenched his fingers into the meat of the stranger's shoulder, helpless against the way his hips bucked up into that hot, anonymous mouth — helpless against the memories brewing like a storm. The man groaned, and the wet noise of his mouth was now supplemented by the flesh-on-flesh whisper of his hand as he pleasured himself. Forcing his eyes open, Sam tried to stay in the present, tried to stay in the humid room that stank of sweat and gin. But his body betrayed him, its cresting desire knocking down all his fragile defenses as it always did…

"God, Nate —" Sam arched up off the chair and came with a despairing sob, a wracking heave of emotion, and there was nothing beyond it but suffocating terror and darkness.

In the raw silence that followed, he dared not look at the man kneeling between his feet, though he could hear him catching his breath. "Oi," the stranger said, not ungently. "Who the bloody hell's Nate?"

Sam shook his head. What a pitiful sight he must make, sprawled on the chair, tears leaking from behind his eyelids like a child. "I'm sorry. Just go." And then, more wretchedly, "Please."

He heard the man stand, fabric rustling as he readjusted his clothing. "The room's yours another ten minutes," he said — a kindness — and left Sam alone.

With shaking hands, he wiped his face and fastened his breeches, reaching for the gin. He downed the rest of his glass in one go and poured another, swirling it around his mouth as if the taste could scour away the memories. But as the fleeting illusion of pleasure receded, it laid bare what skulked beneath — darker memories, best left buried. The terrifying fury of the mob, the suffocating horror of Simsbury Mine, and, worse, the agony of betrayal and loss that never abated.

For that reason, Sam rarely indulged his physical desires. Yet another thing the war had stripped from him. Another thing Nate Tanner had stripped from him, the coldblooded bastard.

Sometime later, a light rap on the door roused him. Knocking back the rest of his drink, Sam slipped out of the room, avoiding the men laughing and making love with a freedom that still shocked and amazed him. There were dangers, of course, but until he'd come to London, he'd never seen anything like a molly house — not even in New York. It was this kind of old-world licentiousness, he supposed, that had disgusted the pious old Puritans who'd first founded his country. Well, they could keep it. Sam liked it better here in this roiling, tumultuous city of sin and enlightenment. A man could disappear in London, forget his past and drink away his future.

What was left to do when all else was lost?

Slipping out of the White Horse through a discreet side entrance, Sam emerged into a cool London evening. Summer had been a sketchy affair, and, despite everything, he missed the languid heat of home.

But enough of home and grieving. That was in the past and the past must keep it. He had a new life now.

Covent Garden's arcades were no place to be walking alone on a dark night, so he stepped lively and kept one hand on his knife as he headed back to the St Giles Bowl. Crouching on the edge of the infamous slum, the Bowl boasted the dubious distinction of being London's most disreputable drinking hole.

And the place Sam now called home.

Once, not many years earlier, the condemned of Newgate Gaol had stopped at the Bowl for a final drink on their way to the gallows, and its patrons had not improved a great deal since. The detritus of humanity found their way to the St Giles Bowl, the discarded, the despised and the dispossessed.

People like Samuel Hutchinson, who had nowhere else to go.

He paused in the doorway to study the ratty clientele — rogues and ruffians all. A few eyes turned in his direction, men lifting their attention from their cups or dice, their scrutiny curious but not hostile. They knew him here, now. His once fine clothes, increasingly shabby, still raised an eyebrow or two but for most he was yesterday's news. Him and the thousands of other American refugees sloshing around London. Nobody cared about them anymore.

The man who ran the Bowl, a bright-eyed black man by the name of Moses Adams, stood behind the makeshift bar, gossiping with another of Sam's friends: Elias Cole. Like Sam, Moses had been evacuated out of New York when the British fleet left America for good. Unlike Sam, Moses had once been enslaved by a Virginia planter and had fought for the British in exchange for his freedom. Now, they were both equally poor and equally abandoned by the British government, who had little interest in those who'd given everything in their service.

But he and Moses had become friends in London and Sam lifted a hand in greeting as he wound his way between the rough tables to the small door at the back of the tap room. Unlocking it with a sense of relief, he stepped into the den beyond and lit the oil lamp on his workbench. Light bloomed, catching on a treasure trove of odds and ends — silver-plate, candlesticks, jewelry, pistols, linens, silks, and everything between.

People in St Giles, with their almost incomprehensible slang, called this place a 'fencing ken'. For Sam, it was a place of refuge. Here, it was possible to forget the reality of his life and immerse himself in the fine pieces of jewelry and art that came his way. All of it stolen, of course. But what did he care about that? If the past five years had taught him nothing else, it had taught him that the law was worthless. What was the point of it when a petty demagogue with a mob at his back could tear it all down and call it liberty?

No, the war had made Sam an outlaw and so that was how he lived, valuing stolen property in exchange for a safe place to lay his head and hot food in his belly.

Making his way behind his work bench, Sam pulled up his stool and bent to examine the fine pocket watch that had arrived this morning. It had been brought in by the man who called himself 'Wessex', purloined on Hampstead Heath from one Robert Milligan, a wealthy Scottish merchant. Wessex made a habit of targeting men like Milligan, whose money was stained by their abhorrent trade in African people. It was one of the reasons Sam enjoyed doing business with him. That and his exceptional taste — the watch would fetch a good price. Which was lucky because Wessex appeared perpetually in need of ready money.

Someone tapped on the door and Sam looked up. "Come in."

Moses slipped inside, closing the door behind him. He was a tall man, shabbily but neatly dressed, hair receding at the front and pulled into a tidy queue at the nape of his neck. "Any luck?" he said.

"What do you think? They said I need more evidence." Sam had been at the Loyalist Claims Commission all day, trying to get compensation for the loss of his father's house, now occupied by Amos Holden. "I guess I should have stopped to fetch the property deeds before they drove me out of town."

Moses made a face. "They don't want to pay, that's all. Tight-fisted bastards. They're just looking for excuses."

He wasn't wrong. With a sigh, Sam changed the subject. "Did you see this? Wessex brought it in."

Moses took the watch and examined it. "Very nice," he said turning it over in his hand. "Gold?"

"Certainly. Enough to feed half of St. Giles. Hal will be happy."

"And speaking of Hal…" Moses handed the watch back. "He's why I'm here."

"Trouble?"

Moses shook his head. "A job. You're to go to Salter's tomorrow morning at ten, to meet a client."

"Ten?" Sam's shoulders slumped. He was tired, enervated by his frustrating day waiting to see the commissioners. "I was planning to get plastered tonight and to sleep until noon."

Moses grinned. "Tell that to Mr. Foxe."

Which, they both knew, he couldn't. Hal Foxe was the Upright Man of St. Giles and ruled his territory with a benevolent hand wrapped in a steel glove. Both Sam and Moses lived at his pleasure — and were grateful for it. Landing in London as they had, dumped like flotsam by the British navy, Hal Foxe had taken them in, given them shelter, protection, and work. Unquestioning obedience was a small price to pay in return. He sighed. "Who's the client?"

"A gent." Moses gave him a weighted look. "American, apparently."

"A refugee?" London was awash with them these days, drifting aimless and angry as the war crawled to its disastrous conclusion. Sam counted himself among their number. "What does he want?"

"He wants you."

"Me?" He fumbled the watch and it clattered onto the work bench. "Me specifically? Did he ask for me by name?"

"He asked for the best lockpicker in London," Moses said, regarding him carefully. "And that's you."

Of course.

Stupid to think it might be *him*; Sam didn't even want it to be *him*. Ruthlessly, he repressed his pathetic disappointment, burying it beneath the smoldering resentment he tended with care. He'd been a respected man, once: a lawyer, a property owner, an upstanding citizen of Rosemont. Now, he was a larcenist for hire. That's what this bloody war had done to him.

It's what Nate Tanner had done to him.

Thank God he was thousands of miles away, building a new country on the other side of the ocean. Sam never wanted to see him again.

He smiled, hiding his bitterness from Moses. No point in looking backward, no point in wallowing in what was lost. Besides, God knew that Moses had lost more than Sam could possibly imagine.

"That's me," he said instead, curving his lips into a smile as sharp as his resentment. "The best lockpicker in London."

Chapter Two

FLEET STREET, ON a soggy summer evening.

A jumble of coaches vying for space on the muddy street, spraying mud and filth from the open drain that ran through the center of the road. People everywhere: hawkers of gingerbread and 'cherries ripe-ripe-ripe!' crying their wares, ladies lifting their skirts and lamenting the mud, bewigged lawyers hurrying along, heads down, and gangs of ragged boys running riot. A cacophony of noise and bustle, the beating heart of the world's greatest city.

Nate Tanner would have rather been anywhere else.

However, he'd received a note that morning from Colonel Talmach, and had no choice but to act on it.

Rainbow Coffee House, eight o'clock this evening. M meeting F. Report when done. Col. T

And so here he was, sheltering beneath the grand arch of Temple Bar, watching the street ahead through a misting drizzle that couldn't even muster the energy to fall as rain. Specifically, he was watching one man on the street ahead: Paul Farris.

One of Nate's fellow countrymen, Farris was a devout Patriot, a prosperous merchant, and — almost certainly — a traitor. With luck, this evening Nate would gather enough evidence to finally sail home with Farris in the brig.

And thank the Lord for that; it had been a long three months in London.

As he watched, Farris picked his way along the busy street, stopping just a hundred yards or so past Temple Bar to squint up at one of the many coffeehouses lining the road. Squashed between two modern buildings, its ancient gabled roof and white plaster and black wood façade marked it out as a relic — a survivor of the Great Fire that had ravaged the city over a hundred years earlier. The sign above the door read 'The Rainbow Coffee House'.

Checking his pocket watch, Farris stepped forward and disappeared inside.

Nate stayed where he was for another few moments, giving Farris time to get himself settled inside, then slipped out of the shadow of the gate and along Fleet Street. He took a moment to focus before he went inside, stooping his shoulders into the slightly hunched and diffident posture he adopted when he took on the role of Farris's browbeaten lawyer, and prayed that his days of groveling to the bastard would soon be over.

Warm air, rich with the aroma of coffee, greeted Nate as he pushed open the door, along with the lively chatter you'd expect in a place mostly frequented by lawyers and judges. Behind the long bar at the back of the room, a woman flirted as she took orders, while boys and girls wove their way between the tables with steaming cups of coffee, chocolate, or — for those flush in the pockets — tea. Nate handed over his tuppence at the bar and made a show of looking about for a free table. "You're busy this evening," he observed to the woman serving.

"Yes, sir. Always busy when it rains."

He imagined they did good business then because it had been raining in London all damn summer.

It didn't take him long to spot Farris, his braying laughter loud enough to carry over the clamor of conversation. He was a nondescript man on first acquaintance — eyes, hair, face all colorless — but his weak chin and threadlike top lip gave him an amphibian appearance that Nate, childishly, found comical. Fortunately, Farris's loathsome personality kept Nate's amusement in check.

Today, Farris was in his element, evidently proud to bursting to be in the company of the man who sat across the table they shared near the window. John MacLeod, properly addressed as Lord Marlborough, was a large man, broad shouldered and big bodied. Perhaps he'd been handsome once, but the years had not been kind. Now he looked like exactly what he was: an English aristocrat who'd spent too many years indulging himself beneath the fierce West Indian sun. Thick around the middle, tanned and leathery of face, he held himself with an arrogance that bordered on aggression. A man to whom violence came easily.

Nate loathed him.

Bracing himself, he made his way towards the two men. They were deep in conversation.

"…and now Massachusetts, too," Marlborough growled.

"I always said it would happen," Farris agreed. "I said, 'What's the point of overturning one interfering damned government, if you set up another one to poke its nose into a man's business?'"

This was a familiar gripe from Paul Farris. He was of the firm opinion that the thirteen new states should be left to their own devices now that the British had withdrawn, and that the new Continental Congress was a sinister organization intent on gathering power to itself.

MacLeod was about to reply when he noticed Nate's approach. His small eyes squinted into pinpricks. "I say, Farris, isn't that your man?"

"What?" Farris looked over. "Damn my eyes, Tanner, what are you doing here?"

"Sir," Nate said, offering a suitably obsequious bow. "Lord Marlborough. What an unexpected pleasure. I've been visiting an acquaintance in Middle Temple and stopped in for refreshment before returning to my lodgings. Allow me to wish you a good evening, gentlemen, but I shan't intrude upon your privacy." He turned to go, then made a show of being struck by a brilliant idea. "Unless you're discussing business, sir? In which case, please allow me to offer my usual services should you require any notes taken." He tapped his haversack with an ingratiating smile. "I'm quite equipped to work, and you know you can rely on my absolute discretion."

Farris puffed up as he always did when able to demonstrate that he had a lawyer at his disposal. "As it happens, we *are* discussing business matters. What say you, my Lord? Tanner can take a note of what we agree and put it into legal language."

Really, his vanity was too easy to manipulate.

"I have my own lawyer," MacLeod said, glancing at Nate with indifference. "Your man can draft something for him to look over, but it'll have to wait until I return to London. I leave for the country tomorrow. Viscount Rowsley and his set are joining me for a few days. Do you know Rowsley?"

"Only by reputation, my Lord." Farris made an impatient gesture for Nate to sit down. "But I hear he's quite the hellion."

"Oh yes. And he plays deep." MacLeod smirked. "Very deep indeed."

As they talked, Nate pulled up a stool and withdrew his writing materials just as one of the coffee boys brought him his drink. He tipped the lad a ha'penny, set the cup to one side, and got ready to work.

"Well then," Farris said, returning to the matter at hand, "we were speaking of the risk to your business, my Lord, presented by—"

"Not just my business. Yours as well."

"All business," Farris agreed. "Damned abolitionists are everywhere: Vermont, New Hampshire, and now Massachusetts. It won't be long before they start attacking the African trade directly. The New England interest is too strong in the Continental Congress."

"Congress," MacLeod spat. "Are they bent on ruining America? You've already got no effective currency and no access to the West Indies, or to the rest of the imperial market. If they try to strangle the African trade too…" He made a little explosive gesture with his fingers. "How long do they think the plantations will survive without a ready source of labor? And how long do they think America will survive without the plantations? Not long, that's for damned sure."

"The question is," Farris said, "what can we do about it?"

MacLeod was silent for a moment. "In the short term, we take matters into our own hands. You have ships, use them to break the British embargo. Damned if they'll stop me from sending my own damned rice from the Carolinas to my Antiguan plantation."

Farris inclined his head. "For a fair price, my Lord, my ships are at your disposal. I've always favored free trade."

"As for the long term…" MacLeod lowered his voice. "The Continental Congress is weak and disorganized. It's vulnerable."

Nate's pen froze. *This* was what he was after, this direct attack on their government. He dared not look up, tried to sink into his chair lest he do anything to remind them of his presence.

A tense silence had fallen, and Farris gave a nervous laugh. "Vulnerable to what, my Lord? Are you talking about another revolution?"

"You don't need a revolution to make a weak government serve your interests, Farris, you just need to know how to wield the whip." Now it was MacLeod's turn to preen, rocking back in his chair and folding his hands over his belly. "And my people could do just that."

MacLeod had boasted many times about 'his people', but only in the vaguest terms. And although Talmach was convinced MacLeod's network of subversives was a threat, Nate had his doubts. *What people?* he thought, pen poised. *Name them.*

He could have crowed when Farris said, "What people?"

"Good people. Important people."

"Here in London, or…?"

"Yes, in London. Plenty of angry men here who've had property and businesses stolen by the damned rebels. They're ready to strike a blow, mark me on that. But we have allies in America, too. Tobacco and rice planters, men with sugar interests in the West Indies, merchants like you… Men who stand to lose a great deal if the African trade is threatened." He smirked. "I have a list of names."

"A list?"

"A long list. Names, information — a lot of information. But it's secret, only I know who's on that list."

Gaze fixed on the paper, Nate made notes and kept his expression neutral. This was always the way with MacLeod: half-truths, brags, and lies. It would surprise Nate if this infamous list existed anywhere but in the man's over-inflated imagination.

"I keep it locked in my study at Marlborough Castle," he went on, "in an excellent strongbox. German made. But the men on that list, Farris? Mark me, they could bring the Continental Congress to its knees."

Startled, Nate's pen scratched over the paper, blotting it. He cursed silently, but neither Farris nor MacLeod seemed to notice. Christ Alive, *Bring the Continental Congress to its knees*? Surely MacLeod was exaggerating. It was an extraordinary claim.

"These men," Farris said doubtfully. "They're inside the Continental Congress?"

"What? No. Bugger the politicians, it's the backcountry that matters. There's trouble brewing there, and where there's trouble there's opportunity. A Congress fighting disorder at home won't have time to attack the African trade."

"A distraction?"

"Precisely."

"I'll drink to that, my Lord."

"The question is, sir, will you help me create it?" MacLeod set his hands on the table, flattening them. They were broad, short fingered hands. Perfectly manicured, but muscular and rough-looking. Brutal hands. "I have several crates of muskets in a warehouse on Hay's Wharf — I need them to enter Boston without attracting attention from the revenue men. I'll see you fairly compensated for your trouble, naturally."

Farris sipped his coffee. "The *Triton's* docked at Hay's Wharf, ready to depart for Benin in three weeks, and from there to Boston." He smiled. "If your people can load the cargo discretely, I'll ensure it doesn't appear on the manifest."

"Excellent. Leave it aboard when you dock in Boston, and my people will retrieve it and ensure it reaches the backcountry. And *then*…" He smiled. "Well, then the Congress will discover it has more pressing problems than the African trade."

Farris's frog-like mouth stretched into an eager smirk. "And be damned to any government that thinks it can control how a man does business, eh?"

"Quite so. Do we have an agreement?"

"We do." Farris lifted his coffee cup in mock salute. "Here's to trouble and opportunity."

Nate stared at his paper, fingertips whitening as he clenched his pen in dismay.

"I'll drink to that with something stronger, sir." MacLeod pushed to his feet. "Join me at my club, I've a mind to mark the occasion."

"Honored, my Lord." Farris rose and attempted to bow at the same time, resulting in an obsequious shuffling that Nate might have found amusing if he weren't so horrified.

But MacLeod was right about the growing unrest in the backcountry, much of it directed towards the tidewater elite believed to dominate Congress. The fact that MacLeod and Farris were plotting to stoke actual violence — to arm people — filled Nate with dread and dismay. He had to fight to keep his fury from showing.

"Tanner."

Struggling to maintain his blank mask, he rose and said, "Sir?"

"Write up an agreement to the effect of what we've discussed and bring it to me when you're done. I expect it tonight, put into nobody's hand but my own. Do you understand?"

"Yes, sir."

"I'll be at…?" Farris glanced at MacLeod.

"Boodle's," he supplied. "Give my name at the door and they'll admit you."

Nate bowed in acknowledgment. "Of course, Lord Marlborough. It'll be an honor."

He sat for a moment after the other men had left, watching from the window as a coach bearing the Marlborough coat of arms pulled up and both men climbed inside. Had he really just witnessed a plot to incite insurrection in America? He could scarce believe it, but there were his notes before him in black and white.

After MacLeod's coach lumbered away, Nate gathered his wits and his writing materials, tucked his notes into his coat pocket, and downed his cooling coffee. From the Rainbow, he made his way to Milk Street and Talmach's modest lodgings.

It was after nine o'clock, but still light, by the time he'd scraped the mud from his shoes and knocked on the door. He was admitted by a silent pale-faced maid called Clara. She knew him and bobbed a curtsy, and Nate handed her a coin to compensate for the trouble of calling so late. Then he climbed the narrow stairs to Colonel Talmach's rooms, rapped the requisite four times — two slow, two fast — and waited. After a moment he heard Talmach's uneven tread approach, accompanied by the tap of his cane against the floor.

"Tanner." Colonel Benjamin Talmach gave a slight bow as he opened the door. Formerly of the Continental Army and now, like Nate, an agent in the Department of Foreign Affairs, Talmach still wore his black hair pulled back into a military queue, accentuating the severity of his strong features. He was taller than Nate, which had the effect of making his gaze predatory, as if he were a great bird peering over his beak of a nose. "You received my note?"

"Yes, sir. I've just come from the Rainbow." Nate stepped inside and closed the door. "I think we have him."

Talmach's eyes glittered. "Tell me."

As succinctly as possible, Nate reported the conversation he'd witnessed, handing over his notes for Talmach to read. "The long and short of it is that they're afraid Congress will attack the slave trade, so they're planning to stir up armed revolt in the backcountry as a means of distraction." He shook his head. "It's difficult to believe Farris would get involved in such an overt plot against America; he called himself a Patriot."

"Farris was never a Patriot," Talmach said, still studying the notes, "simply an opportunist. And now a traitor." He looked up. "And you're to draft a contract that will put all this on paper?"

"I should be doing so as I speak. Farris is expecting me to deliver it tonight."

"Excellent." Talmach's lips curled into a cold smile. "That's evidence of treason no court could refute."

"Finally."

Talmach steepled his fingers, tapping his lips in thought. "But I'm more convinced than ever that we must have MacLeod's list of subversives. Tories to a man, no doubt. Still can't accept that they lost the damned war."

Nate doubted that. "They're more likely to be men like Farris — planters or slave merchants afraid that American liberty will spread too far. Most Loyalists have either had an abrupt change of heart or left the country entirely."

The latter causing him a great deal of personal pain.

Talmach grunted but didn't accept the point — his contempt of Tories was legendary. After a moment's thought he said, "Either way, I want that list."

Nate took a calming breath. Like a dog with a bone, Talmach had been obsessed with MacLeod's list of subversives since Nate had first reported it to him. "Colonel," he said, "it's the conspiracy, not the list, that's key. All we need to secure Farris's conviction is his contract with MacLeod, and that —"

"Yes, yes but if there are snakes in the grass at home, they must be rooted out. There's nothing else to be done. I must have that list before we sail for Boston — and you must steal it."

"*Me?*" Nate stared. "But I'm a lawyer, sir. I don't know

how to steal things."

"I'm aware of your limitations, Tanner." The colonel's air was that of a disappointed father. "That's why I've secured the services of someone with the requisite skills to help you break into MacLeod's strongbox."

It took some control for Nate not to reveal his alarm. He couldn't waste time on this wild goose chase when he had more important things to do in London. "Colonel, are you sure that's the best use of my time? Marlborough Castle is some distance north, I believe. Perhaps someone else — ?"

"What will you be doing otherwise, Tanner? Sitting on your thumbs while we wait for MacLeod to return and put his name to this contract?" His eyes narrowed. "Shopping for more novels?"

Nate was not ashamed of his penchant for novels, but that was not what he intended to do with his last few weeks in London. Trying a final gambit, he said, "How will I explain my absence to Farris? If he grows suspicious, he may not board the ship home. And we can't arrest him on British soil."

"Leave Farris to me. I'll ensure he suspects nothing until we have his signature on that document and his person aboard ship." Talmach curled his lips in something approaching a smile. "It's a shame we can't take MacLeod as well."

"I think we'd be overreaching, Colonel, to arrest an English peer in London."

"Ha! Well. Perhaps one day MacLeod will take a tour of his Carolina plantations, and then we'll have him, eh?"

"I think that unlikely." John MacLeod would never set foot in America again if it posed any danger to his person. "Why risk himself when he has men like Farris to scurry around on his behalf?"

"I dare say. And perhaps it's for the best. The fewer Tory bastards infecting American minds the better."

Nate bowed to avoid replying and tried in vain not to

remember gentle, gray eyes and a warm, wide smile. Or to wonder where in the world their owner might be. Ironically, hunting Loyalists was an obsession Nate shared with the colonel — with respect to one specific Loyalist, at least.

Sam Hutchinson was the principal reason Nate had volunteered to accompany Talmach to London, although his search had proven fruitless. Not least because nobody in the city's sizable community of exiled Americans would give an agent of the Continental Congress the time of day. And this pointless sojourn to MacLeod's estate would eat up the rest of his time. He shifted restlessly, unable to refuse the colonel's order yet afraid his last chance of finding Sam was slipping through his fingers.

If Sam was alive.

If he was in London.

If he wanted to be found.

"I should go," Nate said, abruptly. "I need to draft this damned contract and Farris will be unforgiving if I keep him waiting."

"Very well. Meet me at ten o'clock tomorrow morning, at Salter's. We've an appointment with the man who will assist you in retrieving MacLeod's list of traitors."

With that, Nate was dismissed. But despite his need to rush, he found himself lingering once he reached the dark street outside Talmach's lodgings. Thoughts of Sam and news of Farris's plotting made him heartsick, the night-time clatter of London scraping against his raw nerves. The damned city never stopped, was never quiet. Evenings here lasted until dawn and Nate didn't think he could bear to spend another one in the company of Paul Farris.

Dare he escape to his own lodgings instead and deliver the contract tomorrow? One of the few benefits of visiting London had been discovering its many book shops, and Nate had recently come across a copy of a scandalous new novel, *Les Liaisons Dangereuses*. The thought of spending a few hours alone, reading, was almost enough to tempt him into abandoning Farris for the night. But Farris was a man who measured loyalty in fingers of brandy, and Nate couldn't risk alienating him. Not now they had a means to entrap him.

No, he didn't have a choice. Enough families, friends and — God help him — lovers had been torn apart by the war. He'd be damned before he let Paul Farris undermine everything for which they'd fought. The revolution came first.

The revolution always came first.

Chapter Three

SALTER'S WAS A gentleman's club. But Tobias Salter was no gentleman, nor were most of his patrons. It was Hal Foxe's favorite place to do business, however, even though he rarely ventured into the club himself. Bad blood of some kind between himself and the proprietor, Sam had heard. Not that he cared; he went where he was instructed and asked few questions.

Nonetheless, he liked Salter's. The building was subtly impressive, located on St. James Street not far from the famous White's. But unlike White's, Salter's didn't advertise its location or membership to the fops of *le bon ton*, and the two discreet footmen on the door discouraged any unknown faces from approaching.

They knew Sam, however, and opened the door for him with a silent bow. Pausing inside, Sam blinked as his eyes adjusted to the dimmer light and let another footman take his coat and hat.

"Mr. Foxe has reserved the Blue Room," the footman said, face impassive beneath his impeccable powdered wig.

"Thank you," said Sam. "Much obliged."

That earned him an uncertain look. Sam still wasn't used to the English habit of treating their servants like furniture, and he hoped he never would be. So what if it betrayed his gauche colonial roots? To his mind, if a man did an honest job, he deserved to have it acknowledged.

With a parting nod, he took the stairs two at a time and stalked down a well-lit corridor, stopping outside the Blue Room. He took a moment to run his hands over his hair, straightened his coat, and knocked.

A deep American voice answered — not one he recognized. "Come."

Telling himself the sinking sensation in the pit of his stomach was relief, Sam set his expression and opened the door.

Inside, a man sat before a brightly dancing fire, struggling to rise with the aid of a cane as Sam entered the room. He had strong features and dark hair, pulled back severely, which matched his austere black coat and breeches. "My name's Talmach," he said. "I'm afraid my associate appears to have been delayed." From Talmach's stern expression, Sam suspected that he didn't tolerate tardiness. He made a mental note; it was never a good idea to irritate Hal Foxe's clients.

"I'm Hutchinson," Sam said, offering a polite bow. "Mr. Foxe sent me, sir."

Talmach's eyes glittered as he surveyed Sam. Nothing about his scrutiny was suggestive, he appeared rather more like a hawk eyeing a rabbit. "You're an American," he observed at last.

"Yes, sir."

"From which state?"

Not a fellow refugee, then, to use that word. "In these circumstances," Sam said neutrally, "it's best if we know as little as possible about each other." He bared a pointed smile.

"I understand you have need of a lockpicker."

Talmach's gaze didn't waiver for a long, silent moment. When he'd looked his fill, he eased himself back into his chair, leaving one leg out straight in front of him. "Very well, Mr. Hutchinson, take a seat and we'll discuss business."

There were three chairs around the fire and Sam took the one opposite Talmach. On a low table between them sat a coffee pot and three cups. He ignored them, leaned forward, elbows on knees, and said, "I assume you want something stolen."

"A document."

"From where?"

"Marlborough Castle."

Sam puffed out a breath, flexing fingers that had clenched in his lap. "I…don't know it." Which was odd; his time with Foxe had given him a working knowledge of all London's principle houses and their occupants.

"It's the seat of John MacLeod." Talmach sat back, smoothing a hand over the pristine fabric of his breeches. "The Baron Marlborough."

Now that was a name Sam *did* know and it was one often followed by bitter epithets; Marlborough did not treat his servants well, and ill-used servants talked freely. Sam folded his arms. "And where's his castle?"

"In the north."

"Of London?"

Talmach's lips sketched a thin smile. "Of the country. Near the port of Liverpool, I understand."

Sam let out a low whistle. Not far short of two-hundred miles to the north, if his English geography could be relied upon. "That's a week on the road at least, just to get there. Aren't there any lockpickers in Liverpool?"

"*I'm* not in Liverpool," Talmach said. "And this is not a matter to be conducted by proxy." His eyes gleamed bright as a bird's. "I cannot overstate the importance of secrecy and stealth. Lord Marlborough must not know that the document in question has been removed. Do you understand? Nothing can be disturbed."

"I understand. I assume you're meeting the cost of the journey?"

"The cost is not —"

A knock at the door.

"At last," Talmach muttered under his breath. Then, louder, "Come."

Sam twisted in his seat and watched as the door behind him opened. "Is this your associ —?" That was all he managed before his throat seized up, before his heart stopped beating, before the world staggered to a halt.

Frozen in the doorway, stood Nate Tanner.

Nate fucking Tanner.

Impossible.

He stared at Sam, eyes impossibly dark against his ashen face, lips parted as if to speak. Stiffly, like moving through a nightmare, Sam rose. Was this the moment where he was denounced? *Tory. King's man. Traitor.* He'd meet it on his feet, at least. But Nate said nothing, his colorless face a blank mask.

Ah.

Sam understood. It would be worse for Nate to acknowledge his connection with a Tory than to expose him. Tanner was nothing if not a political creature and he'd grown ashamed of their friendship long before he'd ended it. Clearly that hadn't changed.

"Don't dither, man," Talmach grumbled. "You're late enough as it is."

Nate jerked his gaze from Sam. "My apologies, sir. The traffic in this wretched city… And the mud!" A man who knew him less well may have missed the high tension in his voice. "Almost lost my damn shoes."

Talmach snorted. "Then wear boots, man. Not those dancing slippers."

Moving like an old man, Sam managed to sit back down and fix his gaze on the fire. Bile or rage or grief clogged his throat, making it impossible to swallow. All he could hear was the rush of blood in his ears. All he could see was Nate's beautiful, startled face.

He hated that his pulse was racing.

He hated that his breath was short.

He hated that Nate Tanner was here, in London. In this room. So close, Sam could have touched him. Or throttled him.

"Sit down, Tanner," Talmach ordered. "This is Hutchinson, the man Foxe sent."

Sam kept his gaze fixed on the fire, watching the coals spit, praying that shock had robbed his face of color so that Tanner wouldn't see his humiliated flush. That Tanner, of all people, should know how low Sam had fallen…. He wanted to climb out of his own skin.

After a lengthy pause, Nate sat down and said, "You're the… lockpicker?" His voice rose with poorly hidden disbelief.

"The best in London," Talmach said. "So I'm told."

Sam closed his eyes. If he fled, Foxe would have his skin. But Hal wasn't a cruel man, perhaps he'd understand if Sam explained… He almost choked on the notion. Explain that he couldn't do the job because the man he'd once loved, the man who'd stood silent and watched him assaulted and exiled, was the client? Christ in heaven, he might be down on his luck, but he had more self-respect than that. He'd not go weeping to Hal Foxe and he'd not give Nate Tanner the fucking satisfaction of seeing him broken.

Deliberately, he raised his eyes from the fire and turned around. He let no recognition show, hid his anguish deep.

He wasn't the same greenhorn boy Nate had seduced nine years ago, and he wasn't the same innocent who'd thought their love eternal. Just like he wasn't the same fool who'd trusted his friends and neighbors not to turn on him like dogs. He was a man re-forged, hardened by the fire. He let Nate see what had been shaped that terrible night in Rosemont. "At your service, Mr. Tanner."

A flash of emotion lit Nate's face, fleeting and swiftly hidden. Difficult to interpret. Nate opened his mouth, then closed it again, clearly at a loss for words as he offered a slight nod. Sam permitted himself a sour twist of his lips, barely a smile. Rendering Nate speechless was a rare achievement.

Rigidly, Sam moved his attention back to Talmach. "Tell me about the document you want lifted."

"It's kept in a strongbox in MacLeod's study. I understand locks are your particular skill."

"They are." He put his unexpected knack for lockpicking down to the hours he'd spent as a child taking apart his father's beloved clocks, cleaning and reassembling them. He'd developed an affinity for mechanisms, a feel for how they worked, which apparently extended to the byzantine locks deployed by the manufacturers of strongboxes.

He wondered what his father would have made of that turn of events.

He wondered what had happened to his father's clocks.

Had Holden kept them when he took Sam's home? Or had he destroyed them, made a bonfire of all Sam's precious possessions, and watched them burn? "Tell me about the document," he said roughly. "How am I to recognize it?"

"You won't need to. Once you've opened the strongbox, Mr. Tanner will retrieve the document."

The hair on the back of Sam's neck rose. "I'm not taking *him* with me."

"That's not negotiable." Talmach's brow furrowed, clearly a man used to obedience. "I told Foxe as much when I commissioned your services. Tanner will go with you."

Christ, no. A week — two weeks — on the road with Nate Tanner? Unbearable. Just these last two minutes in the same room had been excruciating.

"Perhaps there's someone else," Nate said tersely. "Another…lockpicker?"

"Foxe said this man's the best. We don't have time to hold a damn audition, Tanner, we sail for Boston in less than three weeks —" He cut himself off and fixed his eyes on Sam. "You'll do the job you've been hired for, sir, or Foxe will know about it."

And God knew Sam was in no position to refuse work from Hal. He shifted in his chair, painfully aware of Nate's gaze. It burned like hot pitch. "Very well, but it's at your risk. I won't be held responsible if he…betrays my presence."

Nate tensed at that deliberate choice of word, and Sam felt a vicious stab of pleasure at landing the blow. "I assume you'd like me to leave as soon as possible?"

"I would. Tanner has money for the journey."

"Seven o'clock tomorrow, then." As Sam rose, he flicked Nate a quick look and hoped he was still averse to early mornings. "Be at the Swan with Two Necks, on Lad Lane. We can get the stage from there. If you're late, I'll leave without you."

"I won't be late," Nate said, sounding as distant and urbane as when Sam had first known him. His fingers, though, were curled into fists so tight his knuckles were white. "I'm looking forward to seeing more of" — a beat — "the country."

Sam swung around to face him, braced for the impact of those deep, dark eyes, the narrow elegance of his features. His beauty. He wasn't disappointed; they hit like a punch, leaving him airless. Nevertheless, he found he could still hate the sight of him and didn't need to force his lip to curl into a sneer. "In that, you're alone. It's the last thing I want."

Without another word, Sam stalked out and let the door slam shut behind him.

It rang with hollow satisfaction.

Chapter Four

"SAM!"

Nate sprinted down St. James' Street, garnering several disapproving glares as he dodged through the crowd. After making hurried excuses about being late for a meeting with Farris, Nate had abandoned Talmach at Salter's and bolted after Sam. The startled footman on the door had pointed him in the right direction and he'd set off at a dead run. "Sam, wait!"

Still reeling from shock, he could hardly believe they'd met like this, that fate had landed such an impossible stroke of good fortune in his lap. Perhaps he was dreaming?

But no.

There Sam stood, not twenty feet away in a patch of watery English sunshine, waiting to cross the busy road. Nate's heart thumped hard, and not only from the run. He slowed to a walk, catching his breath. Cautiously, he called, "Sam?"

Startled, as if lost deep in thought, Sam turned sharply and drew back. His flinty expression licked across Nate's skin, making his gut clench. "What do you want?"

"I —" Nate's thoughts scattered in the face of this resistance, shards flying in all directions like sunlight through broken glass. "I had to speak with you. I can't believe you're really here."

Sam drew himself up tall and rigid. Nothing like the warm, open man Nate remembered. Older, certainly. Well, they were both past thirty now and Sam wore the years in the stern lines of his face. Even his eyes were harder, gray as a winter sky. "Where else would I be?" His chin lifted, a defiant flush staining his cheeks. "I'm banished from America."

He spat it like an accusation, like it was Nate's fault.

Recoiling, Nate said, "I meant that I can't believe chance has thrown us together like this. And in London, of all places."

"Well, I always did have rotten luck." Sam's lips curved into a contemptuous smile. "I notice you spared your friend the sight of our fond reunion. Still afraid of being connected to a treacherous Tory?"

"You're no traitor."

"Aren't I? That's what I'm convicted of."

His bitterness pinched Nate's heart. "You know I never thought that for a moment."

"Doesn't matter what you thought, does it? It's what you did that counts. Or what you didn't do."

Nate opened his mouth to defend himself, but his throat closed around the words. He felt papery thin in the face of Sam's anger, insubstantial. "I —" He had to clear his throat before he could speak, and when he did the effort of keeping his voice steady made him sound stonier than he felt. "The war's over, Sam."

"Not for me. It won't ever be over for me."

Despite his hostility, Nate ached for him. For them both. "But we have peace now. You can —"

"Peace? What kind of peace is it when I can't even go home?" His gaze darted past Nate and back again. "Looks like your friend is on his way."

"What?" Nate looked over his shoulder, appalled to see Talmach limping along the street towards them. Hell and buggery, he couldn't let the colonel know about his friendship with Sam. For any number of reasons.

His panic must have shown in his face because Sam gave a low, derisive laugh. "Don't worry, I won't betray your dirty secret. Better all-around if we forget what was once between us."

"I don't want to forget."

"And I don't give a damn what you want." Sam tugged his hat low over his eyes, tipping his face into shadow. "If it was up to me, we'd never meet again."

With that, he stepped into the road and disappeared amid the ceaseless London traffic, leaving Nate bereft and bewildered.

"Tanner?" The tap-tap of Talmach's cane approached from behind him. "No luck hailing a cab?"

Nate closed his eyes, trying to swallow the aching thickness in his throat. "I was about to walk up to Piccadilly," he said as he turned around.

"Don't bother. Look, here's one. We'll share." Talmach held out his cane and the driver touched his hat in acknowledgment, slowing the hackney as he edged his way through the flow of traffic to the side pavement where they waited. "I can drop you on Thames Street."

Mutely, Nate nodded, his thoughts too full of Sam to argue. Christ, but the man he'd met this morning was a dark shadow of the one he remembered. He couldn't imagine *this* Sam laughing or tender any more than he could imagine the old Sam living here amid London's squalor.

Sam, a lockpicker? A thief? Good God, no wonder Nate's

search had proven fruitless; he'd been looking in all the wrong places.

He'd half hoped, and half feared, that Sam had left America. Hoped, because it meant he'd be safe. Feared, because it meant he'd been banished. But either way, he'd imagined Sam comfortable. Practicing law, perhaps. It was a shock to find him so reduced and resentful.

A sharp crack of pain in his ankle startled him. Talmach set his cane back on the ground, frowning. "Where's your mind today, Tanner?"

"My apologies, sir." The colonel was a prickly sod, especially when his wounded knee was acting up. Which it had been the whole time they'd been suffering the damp misery of this English summer.

"Thames Street," Talmach told the jarvey as the hackney pulled up and he clambered awkwardly inside, favoring his stiff knee. Nate didn't offer to help; he'd learned that lesson the hard way. With a grunt, Talmach sat and stretched out his bad leg. "I was saying that you'll need to be careful around this Hutchinson."

Nate paused in closing the carriage door. "Careful, sir?"

"The man has the stink of a Tory about him."

"Colonel," he said lightly, "not every American in London is a Tory."

Talmach grunted. "Most of them. Besides, that man looked the part — shabby and prideful. Prickling with hostility."

Hostility was right, although the reasons were more complicated than Talmach could imagine. But Sam *had* looked shabby, worn and weary beneath skin that had paled during his exile. Nate felt a twist of guilt but repressed it hard. Sam had made his own choices and the consequences were not Nate's to bear. Yet the sight of him so… so diminished left him empty, desolate inside. "Even if he were a King's man once, does it matter? We're all Americans now."

"And some of us are more worthy of the title than others." Talmach flexed his hand around the head of his cane. "Men like him don't deserve to call themselves American. They forfeited that right when they refused to fight for their country. I always said we should have hanged the lot of them." An angry smile stretched his lips thin. "But at least we'll get Farris, eh?"

"Farris is certainly a traitor," Nate said stiffly. "I assume Sa —" He covered the error with a cough. "Pardon me. I assume Hutchinson doesn't know the nature of the document we're after?"

"No. I've told him nothing." The carriage hit a rut and lurched, making Talmach wince as his leg jostled. "If the man took the enemy's side against us in the war, you can be damned sure he'd strike a blow for the King now. And he'd certainly shield his fellow dissenters from discovery. You must keep the nature of your mission secret."

Nate didn't answer. Five years ago, he'd have sworn that Sam had no interest in political machinations. But Sam had clearly changed. He'd grown hard and bitter, and the truth was that Nate no longer knew him.

One thing *was* certain, however: Sam would never trust him, never again consider him a friend, if he knew that Nate was working with the Continental Congress to unmask political dissenters. Good God, Sam would think him no better than Amos Holden. He said, with real conviction, "You can be quite sure that Hutchinson will learn nothing of MacLeod's list from me."

"Good." Talmach tapped his cane thoughtfully on the carriage floor. "Something about the man's name. Hutchinson…"

A quicksilver flash of fear. "You're thinking, perhaps, of Governor Thomas Hutchinson of Massachusetts?"

"Perhaps. But that devil sat at the heart of a spiderweb and this man may well be part of it. A cousin, perhaps. Or some other relation."

"If the man's exiled here what business is that of ours? He's paid his price and our interest is in those plotting against us at home."

"Be wary of him, Tanner. *That's* the material point. The mission's success depends on your discretion."

Nate simply nodded. Nevertheless, his gut squirmed uneasily. He feared what the colonel might do if he uncovered the truth about Sam's Loyalist past. But realistically, what *could* he do? Nothing, surely. Talmach's hatred of Tories might be legendary, but Sam was beyond his power in London.

Even so, a niggle of conscience suggested that he should warn Sam. At least make him aware of Talmach's position and prejudices. But in doing so Nate would have to reveal his own position, and that —

No.

He dismissed the idea immediately. Because if he told Sam the truth, they wouldn't be spending the next two weeks traveling together. Most likely, he'd never see Sam again.

And that would be unbearable.

Pressing his hand over the ache in his chest, Nate felt the ring hanging on its cord beneath his shirt, the gold warm against his skin. Politics be damned, he refused to give up this chance at reconciliation.

Whatever the cost, he'd keep Sam's secret from Talmach. And keep his own secret from Sam. *Christ.* What a tightrope to walk.

"I'll be careful," he told the colonel.

But unbeknownst to Talmach, Nate had another mission now — a higher mission.

And only two weeks to see it done.

Chapter Five

OF ALL THE wretched reversals of fortune to befall Sam Hutchinson in his thirty-three years of life, this accidental meeting had to be the bitterest. A million souls in London Town, and fate threw him into the path of Nate Tanner.

Why, in heaven's name? Had he not suffered enough?

Half a bottle of the Bowl's vilest gin later and Sam still had no answers, nor could he drown the memories stirred up by the sight of the man. In his mind, all he saw was Nate staring at him with those deep brown eyes of his, fine dark hair slipping free of his queue and his expression an astonished mix of hurt and frustration, as beguiling this morning as he'd been the first day he'd breezed into Sam's office and overturned his world.

His gut cramped. God, how he *loathed* Nate Tanner.

"Just give me the bottle," he suggested when Moses refilled his glass for the... sixth?... time.

"I'd be happy to. I've no objection to taking your money. But our friend over there's been giving me the evil eye for the last half hour, and you know what Elias Cole's like when he's righteously indignant."

Sam turned, peering through the Bowl's gloom toward the back corner — Cole's habitual haunt. "Still hoping to catch Wessex red handed, is he?" Sam said, rummaging around for a smile.

Moses snorted. "Not a chance. But I can't think of any other reason he'd be lurking in the shadows, alarming people."

Once one of Hal Foxe's most trusted confidants, Elias Cole had turned his back on St Giles years ago and was now usually found at the Brown Bear — the informal headquarters of the Principal Officers of Bow Street, and of London's private thief-takers. Of which Cole was one. That was where Sam had met him, thrown into the Bear's lock-up after being brought in with several other gentlemen discovered enjoying each other's company at the Lincoln's Inn bog house. Cole had seen them all released and had sent Sam — who'd nowhere else to go — to Hal Foxe. Hal had provided both refuge and safer hunting grounds, saving Sam's wreck of a life, and for that Cole would always have his gratitude.

But that didn't extend to ratting on Wessex. There was, it turned out, honor among thieves.

Pushing away from the bar, Sam grabbed his glass and made his way unsteadily towards Cole, who sat at a small table with a jug of ale at his elbow and newspaper clippings strewn before him. Sam sank into the seat opposite without invitation. "He won't just wander in with you sitting here, you know. Wessex is a clever man."

Cole glanced up, unimpressed. "And who pissed in your beer tonight?" He was a handsome man with a quick smile. Sam might have enjoyed it more had his heart not been anchored in deeper waters.

"Good evening to you too."

"If it was a good evening, you wouldn't be half cut already."

Cole's thief-taker gaze narrowed. "What happened?"

"Nothing."

Cole just cocked his head, waiting.

"I just —" He sighed. "I ran into someone. Someone from home."

An appraising pause followed. "An old 'friend' by any chance?"

No one knew about Nate. It was a story Sam had never told, not even to friends like Cole who shared his tastes. The shame of being abandoned by his lover was difficult to admit. But he saw sympathy in Cole's eyes, a guessed understanding of Sam's pain if not the detail of his injury. "He was a dear friend, once," he admitted, horrified by the catch in his voice. "Before the war."

"Ah." Cole reached for his ale. "I'm sorry, then, but I ain't surprised. Men like us, Hutch, we ain't meant for having 'dear friends'. It's too dangerous. A tumble in the White Horse is one thing, but them mollies with their marrying rooms and 'my dear this' and 'my dear that'? It ain't going to lead nowhere but the pillory or the gallows."

Sam gave a tired smile. "You're a cynic, Cole."

"Realist. Just ask Hal Foxe how fast 'dear friends' disappear when the law comes a-calling." He lifted a curious eyebrow. "But I suppose you already found out."

And he had, in a way. It hadn't been a charge of sodomy that Sam had faced, but Nate had still abandoned him. Perhaps, had they not been lovers, Nate would have stood between him and the fury of Holden's mob. Instead, he'd stayed silent and watched Sam's destruction from the shadows. "Whatever he was before, he's nothing to me now. And I'd as soon stay out of his way, but…" He looked up miserably. "We're to travel to Liverpool together, for a job."

"A job?" Cole's surprise was obvious. "What kind of job?"

"A serious one. Hal set it up." Sam told him about his

meeting with Talmach and the unknown document he was to steal, although he kept MacLeod's name out of it. Cole *was* a thief-taker, after all.

After a thoughtful pause, Cole said, "Liverpool's a long way to go. Days of travel." An artful smile. "Plenty of time to talk on the way, you and your friend. Resolve your differences, perhaps?"

Sam bristled. "Differences? You mean how he stood by and watched while I was stripped of my home, my reputation, and everything I owned in the world?"

"Something like that, aye." Cole leaned forward to take the gin from Sam's hand, disturbing the newspaper clippings on the table and sending one fluttering to the floor. "What does your 'friend' have to say on the matter?"

Sam snatched his glass back. He didn't care what Tanner had to say about anything, but he didn't want to argue with Cole about it. Instead of replying, he reached down to retrieve the newspaper clipping from the floor. The headline read: *Highwayman 'Wessex' robs the Bristol Mail Coach.* "This is becoming something of an obsession, my friend."

"He's a slippery bastard, but I'll get my hands on him one day." Cole took the clipping from Sam's fingers. "You can tell him that, next time he pops in with a bauble or two to fence."

Sam lifted his cup in salute and downed the rest of his gin.

"I reckon facing this bastard will be good for you," Cole said after a moment. "I ain't saying what you lost is nothing, but, well, the way I see it, you either let the buggers break you or you get up and punch them in the face." He tapped the pile of newspaper clippings. "I can't bring my brother back, but I can bring villains like Wessex to justice. And every time I see one of the murdering bastards swing, I know I've done right by Will. It might be small, but it's something. And ain't confronting your friend better than chewing on it in silence for the rest of your life? Make sure he knows what he done to you, what you lost. It'll make you feel better, at least."

"But it's two weeks in a stagecoach. I'll probably kill him before the end of it."

Cole smiled and tucked the clippings into his pocket. "Well, maybe I can help you there. Why not borrow the Bear's post-chaise? It'll cut a couple of days off your journey each way."

"Is that possible?" He'd considered hiring a post-chaise from a public livery to speed up the journey, but that was the sort of mistake that got your neck stretched when you were on larcenous business. Anonymous stagecoaches were safer. A private hire, safer still. "Would Groves allow it?"

Cole's lips twisted into a grin. "You leave Groves to me. Just make sure it comes back in one piece. He'll have my guts otherwise, and I don't mean metaphorically."

"Not a scratch," Sam promised and offered a hand to shake. "You have my word."

"I wish you luck, my friend. With all of it. You deserve a change of fortune, that's for sure."

Sam snorted. "And since when did anyone ever get what they deserved in this world?"

To that, Cole had no clever reply.

Chapter Six

NATE SPENT THE night tossed and turned by stormy dreams.

First came the memory of Sam's tender smile and a rose moon above them as they lazed by the river, the warm taste of Sam's lips and the weight of his urgent body pressing Nate into soft grass. Then, Sam watched from the shadow of his doorway as Nate walked away that last and fateful afternoon. Finally, a nightmare conjuring: Sam on his knees before Amos Holden, eyes burning fiercer than the mob's rage. And Nate fighting through the jeering crowd, desperate to reach him, held back by Reed's bony grip on his arm.

You did this, Sam spat through the pitch and the feathers. *You did this…*

He woke with a gasp to a spill of damp daylight, feeling brittle and fog-bound and unfit for the day ahead. Not that he had any choice but to face it. He shaved and dressed, fidgety with lack of sleep and weighed down by last night's bad dreams. As often happened, his arm ached as if Reed's fingers still dug into his flesh and he rubbed at it absently, regarding himself in the mirror. His reflection stared back ghost-like, dark rings under his eyes, lips a sallow line.

Was that how Sam saw him? Could Sam see him at all beneath the shadow cast by that horrifying night, five long years ago now?

He would soon find out.

By six o'clock, he was picking his way through the warren of filthy streets towards Lad Lane. Despite its strange name, The Swan with Two Necks turned out to be a large and prosperous coaching inn. Even this early in the day, the inn's yard was bustling with people, coaches leaving for all corners of the kingdom. Nate tried not to feel provincial as he made his way inside. He'd traveled across an ocean, for God's sake. He'd spent two months in Paris. A common coaching inn shouldn't intimidate him.

But perhaps it was the prospect of seeing Sam again, rather than the coaches and horses, that had his pulse racing.

Glancing up at the inn's large clock, he was pleased to see that the time showed ten minutes before seven. At least he wasn't late. When they'd worked for John Reed, Sam had always teased him for his tardiness, but Sam had been a minister's son and had lived his life by the tolling of the church bells. Nate had been the sophisticate, the Bostonian with rakish city ways.

How provincial that seemed now that they both found themselves here, in the biggest most dissipated city in the world: the very heart of the empire. Boston was a village in comparison with London. And yet, in London they had found each other again. It was difficult not to consider it fate, even for a man with Nate's natural inclination towards rationality.

"Watch out, there!"

He jumped out of the way as a stage lumbered towards the yard's entrance, several passengers crowded on top. It would be a long and uncomfortable journey, no doubt, and only the thought of sharing it with Sam made the idea tolerable. Slinging the strap of his portmanteau over his shoulder, Nate started to pick his way around the edge of the yard, avoiding the mud churned up by the horses' hooves. How many must travel through such a place every day? Hundreds, probably.

On three sides of the yard rose a galleried building, men and women coming and going from their rooms, parcels and goods being loaded and unloaded, and the shouts of the working men mixing with the street calls of early morning hawkers as the great city stirred. Not that it ever really slumbered.

How on earth would he find Sam amid all this chaos?

A set of stairs rose to his left, up toward what appeared to be the ticket office. A likely spot for surveying the yard, but he'd only just set his foot on the first step when a young voice behind him called, "Mr. Tanner?"

He turned, not quickly because of his heavy luggage, and looked around. A scruffy street-boy stood a few feet away, peering up at him.

"I'm Tanner."

"Follow me, if you would, sir," said the lad, turning back towards the yard's entrance. "There's a gent waiting for you on the street with a post-chaise."

Nate looked in the direction the boy was walking and, sure enough, a smart-looking post-chaise sat by the side of the road with a postilion holding the bridle of the nearside horse. Leaning against the carriage door, ankles crossed and gazing down at his boots, stood Sam. A curl of gold hair, darkened by the morning's mist, was just visible beneath the brim of his cocked hat, a sliver of his profile catching the watery sunlight.

He looked achingly familiar.

Out of the blue, a memory stirred: they were standing in Sam's parlor, laughing and damp after running in through a sudden rainstorm. Nate brushed that same damp curl aside and kissed Sam's brow. Smiling, Sam called him a fool and kissed him in return, slowly at first, then catching light in a flare of heat and desire.

Nate's breath left him in a rush, face heating. As if sensing his thoughts, Sam lifted his head and their eyes met for a flickering second before Sam broke the contact. It felt like a snub; it *was* a snub.

With a deep sigh, Nate started walking. As he made his way across the yard, he watched Sam exchange a few words with the boy before ruffling his hair and handing him a coin. From the wide grin on the lad's face, it was a handsome reward.

"Good morning," Nate said when he reached Sam, wincing at the strained formality.

Sam peeled himself away from the coach, standing upright. They were nearly of a height, although Sam had always been broader. Now, though, he looked sparer than Nate had ever seen him. His clothes hung on him as if they'd been made for a larger man.

But Sam's lean body looked harder too. Like his eyes. They were granite as they ran over Nate from top to toe. "At least you're not too dandified for traveling."

"Dandified? I've never —"

"We can forego the pleasantries, Tanner. We've nothing to say to each other, so I suggest we spend the journey in silence." With that, he yanked open the carriage door and disappeared inside.

Nate stared at the door for a moment, then went to hand his luggage to the driver before climbing in after Sam. The chaise was large enough to seat four, but even so it was hardly spacious. Sam took the far corner, body twisted to gaze out of the side window, and Nate took the other. "It's alright," he said frostily, "you can uncoil. I don't intend to molest you."

Sam stiffened but didn't respond.

Sighing, Nate took off his hat and set it on the seat between them. He was still watching Sam's averted profile when the post-boy mounted his horse and the carriage lurched into motion.

As the day grew warmer, London's traffic and muddy streets slowed them to a crawl. By midday, the sun shone fully into the coach, clotting the muggy air, making the chaise humid and sticky even with the windows open.

From the corner of his eye, Nate watched Sam shift uneasily. His attention was fixed through the open side window, hair fluttering in the scant breeze. It looked blonder in the sunlight than it had earlier, more like how Nate remembered. But his face had a wintery hue, his shoulders hunched and rigid. And his silence had grown into a prickly thing, louder than the clatter of the wheels and the beat of the horses' hooves.

Nate didn't know how to break it.

Hours passed.

Eventually, the chaise picked up speed and Nate found himself gazing out over the sprawling skirts of London as the city thinned and faded. The England that took her place was green and verdant, with trees and fields aplenty. But there was no wilderness here, everything was hemmed-in and owned. Not like home, where the frontier stretched out forever. He wondered how Sam could endure this place of restriction when he'd been born in a freer land — he wondered whether Sam thought his principles worth the price of losing that freedom.

They stopped twice to change horses and post-boys, leaving the chaise only long enough to stretch their legs and use the necessaries, and at last, for a third time, to eat a meal at an inn called The Three Cups. It was in a busy little market town called Dunstable with a half-dozen coaching inns and a friendlier atmosphere than London.

Climbing out of the carriage, Nate took a breath of clean air and stretched his back, grown stiff from sitting so long in cramped quarters. Then, while Sam went to see about more horses and another post-boy, Nate headed into the inn in search of dinner.

The landlady was affable and showed him to a table in a public parlor, promising mutton stew and fresh bread. In general, the English were proving pleasanter than Talmach had predicted on their arrival in London. Several had even expressed their support for the American cause, and their hope that the spirit of liberty would spread to their own country. That had surprised Nate, and he wondered what Sam made of it, although — at present — it was impossible to ask.

Taking a seat, he pulled out his book while he waited for his meal. He'd learned many years ago that the swaying of the carriage did not suit his stomach, and that reading often made his nausea worse. Which was trying, given his passion for reading. A passion he'd once shared with Sam…

As if summoned by the thought, a shadow fell over him and Nate glanced up to find Sam dithering in the parlor doorway, watching him with all the loathing of a man regarding a viper in his bed. And yet, in his hesitation, Nate glimpsed something else — a hint of sorrow that suggested a heart still beat beneath that brittle shell. Hope made his breath catch and he had to clear his throat before he said, "Will you join me?"

Sam's top lip curled. "Are you sure you want to be seen keeping company with a flagrant Tory?"

"I don't see why not, if you can stomach being seen in

company with a flagrant Patriot."

With a snort, Sam pulled out a chair and sat down opposite Nate, chewing his words silently. Nate had once kissed that stiff jaw, been intimately familiar with its contours. He'd brushed his lips over Sam's delicate eyelids, from beneath which his flinty eyes now stared coldly. "And what would your Mr. Talmach have to say about it?"

Nate closed his book. "Well. Talmach has certain… prejudices about those who took the British side in the conflict. Ones I don't share."

"Don't you?"

"You know very well that I don't."

Sam grunted but didn't respond and silence stretched between them again, loud amid the clatter of the inn. Before Nate could think of anything else to say, a red-faced serving girl arrived carrying two plates of mutton stew.

Seizing the distraction, Nate attacked his dinner. He'd eaten nothing at breakfast and despite the situation, he was ravenous. The stew was hot and tasty, the bread soft and not chalky, and the meal went a long way to soothing his tension. But even as he ate, he was aware of Sam's brooding presence across the table. And once his immediate hunger had abated, Nate cast a surreptitious glance Sam's way.

The cuffs of his shirt were worn thin and his neckcloth hadn't seen starch in quite some time. Sam glanced up, caught Nate staring, and they both looked away. He hated to see Sam so diminished, but it made him angry, too. Sam had ruined himself with his damn fool mulishness.

Picking up his cup, Nate swallowed a mouthful of ale. "How is it that you come to be in this…new profession?"

"Needs must." Sam blotted gravy with the last of his bread and didn't look up.

"You're a good lawyer. Can't you practice here?"

"I choose not to."

"Why on earth not?"

"Because I've lost my faith in the law, Tanner. Turns out, anyone can overturn it when they have a mob at their back." A flat smile touched his lips, not in the least bit welcoming. "I'm an *outlaw* now."

Nate set down his ale. "You put yourself outside the law. You know you did."

Sam shook his head but let the subject drop and Nate was grateful. What was the point in rehashing that old argument? The truth was that the world had changed around Sam. He'd refused to change with it, and his intransigence had cost him everything. It had cost Nate something too, although Sam might not believe it. Another spiky silence grew, and Nate was considering escaping outside when Sam surprised him by saying, "This man, Talmach. He's your employer?"

"He's my superior, yes." It was a risk, but Nate was proud of his hard-won position and wanted to share it with his old friend. "My employer, if that's the right word, is the Continental Congress."

Sam glanced up sharply, fixing wary eyes on Nate. "Is that so?"

"It is, yes."

"And you're in England because…?"

Nate hesitated, but looking into Sam's suspicious face he knew he couldn't risk telling him the whole truth. At least, not yet. But he could tell him some part of it. "The British have embargoed American ships from their West Indian ports. I'm working with an American merchant, by the name of Farris, to negotiate a… a private arrangement on behalf of our Carolina rice planters."

Sam's mouth twisted into a bitter smile. "Not finding it easy to trade now you've cut yourselves off from the world's biggest market? If only someone had anticipated that consequence."

"It's a temporary problem," Nate assured him, tamping down a flash of irritation. "In time, the British will come to their senses."

"And meanwhile, it makes plenty of work for lawyers."

"There is that." Nate offered a tentative smile that Sam didn't quite return before dropping his gaze back to the table.

After a pause, Sam said, "You don't work for old Mr. Reed anymore, then?" He kept his eyes down, fingers tapping a tense rhythm on the table. "I hope he's well?"

"Oh. No, he —" Nate's stomach squeezed as Sam looked up in unguarded concern. They'd both been apprenticed to Reed; it was where he and Sam had met one glorious fall morning before the world turned upside down. He had to swallow before he said, "I'm sorry, Sam. John Reed passed away last year. I didn't — I didn't realize you hadn't been told."

"Who would have told me?" Sam looked sharply out the window, blinking at the setting sun, his mouth a taut line. "Poor old Reed. He was a good man."

"He was. One of the best."

"And Mary?"

"She's well. Still in Rosemont. Young John took over the business." Nate put up his hands at Sam's look of incredulity. "Last I heard, the firm was still prospering. Perhaps he wasn't as inept as we thought?"

A reluctant smile tugged at the corners of Sam's lips, quickly suppressed. "Perhaps not, but I see why you don't work there anymore."

But Nate had seen that almost-smile, and it lit something beneath his breastbone — a spark of warmth. Of hope.

"So, this merchant you're working with," Sam said. "Farris. Would that be *Paul* Farris? Master of the *Triton*?"

"It is. Do you know him?"

"Not personally." Keeping his eyes on the table, he turned his cup around a slow three-hundred-and-sixty degrees before saying, "But everyone knows what cargo Paul Farris traffics aboard that ship." He glanced up from under his brow. "Funny kind of liberty you practice in your new republic."

"Look, I despise everything about Farris." And, hell, if he could only tell Sam the truth. "But — But there are more important things at stake."

"Oh, there always were for you."

"That's not true."

"Isn't it?" Their eyes met across the table, intimate and terrible. The old connection was still there, Nate realized with a jolt, as if they could speak heart-to-heart without need for words. But where once it had been warm with love and trust, now it was frosty and unforgiving.

He looked away sharply.

After a moment, Sam got to his feet, scraping his chair across the floor. "We should go," he said, without meeting Nate's eye again, "or we won't finish the next stage before dark."

Without waiting for a reply, he turned and left the parlor, taking the last word with him.

Chapter Seven

OUT OF THE frying pan…

Sam had fled the inn to escape the turmoil of his feelings. Of course there was nowhere to go but the narrow confines of the chaise where he and Nate now sat with only betrayal, estrangement, and a scant foot of empty space between them.

Staring out the side window, Sam tried to pretend he was alone. Yet, in the periphery of his vision, he could still see Nate. And his eyes, treacherous devils, wanted to drink their fill. The longer they were together, the harder it was to ignore the stirring of feelings he'd hoped were dead. No, not hoped were dead; had striven to kill. But it was no good. Nate was here. Impossibly, he was *here*. And to Sam's dismay, his heart was responding the way it had from the first moment Nate walked into Reed's office — with helpless longing and desire.

The truth was that Sam had always found Nate captivating. Not ruggedly handsome but striking in a way that made his feelings churn with a sweet-sour sensation halfway between pleasure and pain.

God but he'd loved Nate fiercely.

Deep in his bones he still remembered how it felt to hold him in the afterglow of their lovemaking, overflowing with tenderness and the need to keep him safe. Once, he'd have thrashed anyone who dared raise a hand against Nate Tanner. Once, he'd have thought Nate would do the same for him.

History had proven otherwise.

Nate fidgeted. He crossed his ankles, re-crossed them. He opened a book — he still had his nose in a book at every opportunity — closed it again. Sighed. Shifted. Eventually he spoke. "I'd give my right arm for a slab of that gingerbread they sell down at the docks." His accent was the accent of home and it fell with distressing softness on Sam's ears. "Have you tried it? Best thing about London. Well, aside from the bookshops."

Sam didn't intend to reply, but his stomach gave a disloyal growl and Nate huffed a soft laugh. It jabbed like a dart, familiar and painful. "I avoid sugar these days," Sam said gruffly. "It's difficult to enjoy the taste when it's polluted by the blood and tears of enslaved people."

Nate inclined his head in acknowledgment, hands spread ruefully. "I buy free sugar whenever I can. But I admire your principles, Sam. I know you have a sweet tooth."

They both did. Back in Rosemont, they used to buy slabs of almond cake, sometimes honey cake, and eat it together outside the church in the half hour John Reed allowed them for breakfast. You wouldn't know it from Nate's slight physique, but he'd always eaten like a horse.

Sam closed his eyes against an unbidden flash of memory: that lissome back glistening in the moonlight as Sam moved inside him, the green scent of the riverbank all around them. He cleared his throat, shifting uncomfortably as his prick grew heavy. Dear God, and with Nate right there.

He made himself summon a different memory instead:

a dozen burning torches in the hands of his neighbors, the terrifying stench of hot tar, suffocating feathers clogging his mouth and nose. And Nate, silent and watching while the mob imposed their 'justice'.

"I looked for you," Nate said softly, as if plucking the thought from Sam's mind. "As soon as I could, I went looking for you. But the British line was so close…" Sam didn't know how to respond to that. Was he supposed to feel grateful? "After the fighting moved on, I traced you as far as —" Nate's voice faltered " — as Simsbury Mine. But beyond that, nothing."

"That's because I escaped. The bastards didn't know where I went."

"That's what I hoped." Nate smiled fleetingly, uncertain as butterfly wings. "I prayed for it."

That was something from a man with no real faith, but it only made Sam's hurt that much sharper. "No point digging all that up." He turned back to the window.

"Dig it up? It's hardly buried." The bench shifted as Nate slid closer.

Sam could feel the heat of him through his clothes. Or perhaps something more than heat — the life of him, the profound bond that had once held them close. "It's done," Sam said tersely. "It's past. Best leave it there."

A taut silence. "If we leave the past in the past, can't we be — Can't we at least *try* to be friends again?"

The clear longing in his voice coiled around Sam's heart with hot pressure. He hated that Nate sounded like home, he hated that the very sight of him twisted raw scars in his chest until they bled, and he hated that Nate wanted to pretend the past had never happened. "No," he said, blinking at his reflection in the window glass. "No, we can't."

"But the war's over."

"Says the man working for the Continental Congress."

Nate sighed. "That doesn't make us enemies."

"Maybe not. But I still —" Sam turned, and the words fell away unspoken. Hell, but Nate was close, leaning expectantly into the last splash of sunlight. Their knees almost touched, the space between them a raw gash of loss and want. A breeze from the open window set Nate's hair shifting, sunset lending more copper than was due to those errant strands. His mouth parted as if to argue or to kiss, lips pink and a little chapped, his warm brown eyes luminous with misplaced hope.

Sam imagined taking his face in his hands, the scratch of stubble against his palms, the way Nate would melt when Sam kissed him. He imagined pushing Nate backward, fingers curling into his coat —

And he imagined slamming him hard against the seat, shaking an apology out of him, howling his pain and fury until Nate understood.

You betrayed me. You abandoned me. You let them destroy me.

"You still what?" Nate prompted softly, ghosting fingertips across Sam's knee, stirring the hair on his arms, the back of his neck. "Sam? You still what?"

His fingers gripped the edge of the bench seat. "I still hate you."

Nate stared for a blank moment, then turned away with a sharp twist of his body and a flash of hurt in his eyes.

Hell, but that felt sweet — harsh and sweet like vengeance or victory. Or punishment. Sam didn't know whether he was ashamed of himself, or proud.

After some time, Nate spoke. "Well, that's a shame," he said in a strained voice, "because we were good friends once."

"Yes." Sam's voice scratched in his throat, rusty as old nails. "We were. Real good."

They rode the rest of the way in silence.

Chapter Eight

HATE. SUCH A hard word. Nate felt it like a punch to the heart, like the shock of diving into cold water. It stole his breath, even as it clogged his throat and stung his eyes.

He couldn't look at Sam, and avoided his gaze when they finally disembarked from the carriage to make their weary way into the bustling coaching inn. While Sam lingered outside, ostensibly organizing the horses for the morning, Nate secured two rooms for the night but declined the landlord's offer of supper. The last thing he wanted to do was sit across from Sam and try to eat; his stomach was in knots, a churning mash of hurt and anger.

I still hate you.

What right did Sam have to say that, to *feel* that, after everything they'd once meant to each other? It wasn't fair. And it hurt, deeply. Because Nate still loved Sam. Or, at least, he loved the memory of Sam, and of what they'd once shared.

But a memory was all that remained, and he was a fool to think otherwise.

Sam stepped into the inn just as Nate was making his way

towards the staircase that led upstairs to their rooms. They eyed each other obliquely, both slowing. It wasn't crowded, although a few people sat eating late meals, filling the room with quiet chatter. But Nate could easily hear when Sam said, "Did they have any rooms — ?"

"Yes, I secured two." Nate's voice sounded normal, no betraying hitch or catch. "Ask the landlord for your key."

Sam nodded, cleared his throat, and said, "Are you having supper?"

"I'm not hungry."

"You should eat."

He stared. "What?"

"You should eat something." Sam wasn't looking at him, he appeared to be contemplating the toes of Nate's boots instead. "I don't know when we'll be able to stop for breakfast."

And why do you care? He might have asked the question, had they been alone, but what he said was, "I dare say I'll survive."

Sam didn't respond, so Nate turned back to the stairs. He'd made it halfway up before Sam called out, "Tanner…?"

Gooseflesh prickled across his skin. Cautiously, he turned around to find Sam standing at the bottom of the staircase raking a hand through his hair. Their eyes met, clashing like struck flint.

For no good reason, Nate's heart began to pound.

"I —" Sam's voice cracked, and he cleared his throat. "I ordered the horses for seven. Don't oversleep."

It was a struggle to keep his disappointment from showing, but, Christ, what had he expected? An apology? With a curt nod, Nate said, "Alright. I'll be ready."

But Sam didn't walk away, he just stood there studying him with an expression difficult to read in the twilight. Did he expect Nate to say something? Well, he wouldn't. What was there to say? He'd made his case in the coach and Sam's response had been quite clear.

So why were they staring at each other in this excruciating silence?

Eventually, Sam shook himself and said gruffly, "Well, goodnight."

"Goodnight," Nate said, and watched with his heart still racing as Sam walked away.

THE FOLLOWING MORNING dawned bright and sunny, incongruous after a long and restless night spent contemplating Sam's hurtful words. At least there'd been no danger of oversleeping and Nate came downstairs in good time, bleary and unrefreshed.

Sam was already outside, loading his luggage onto the chaise while the post-boy drank coffee and checked the tack. As Nate picked his way wearily across the yard, Sam glanced over and then quickly away. Embarrassment? Irritation? Indifference? Hard to tell. Either way, Nate couldn't bear the thought of being trapped inside the coach all day with Sam's prickly, resentful silence.

So once Sam had settled himself in his usual corner of the chaise, staring morosely out of the side window, Nate jumped up onto the box seat and nodded to the post-boy to set off.

It turned out to be the right decision because, despite everything, the morning proved pleasant. Gentle sunshine in the east lifted his flagging spirits, the fresh morning air fragrant with summer. England may be falling into tyranny, but its sun occasionally shone, and its birds still sang. Even Nate couldn't deny the sweetness of the country.

At the next staging post — some place called Daventry — they stopped for a breakfast of good bread rolls and cold beef. And ale. Always ale.

While Sam disappeared inside to eat, Nate brought his breakfast into the sunshine and sat on a wooden plank set across two barrels that served as a bench. He watched the new horses being hitched and the post-boys swapping news, leaning idly on the fence of the paddock — gnarly little men, hard-boned and leather-skinned from so much time in the saddle. Then the bench shifted beneath him and he turned, surprised to see Sam sitting next to him, staring straight ahead while he finished his beer.

Well, well.

Hope flickered in Nate's chest, but he dared not speak in case he drove Sam off; things had been left so oddly between them last night. Sam didn't speak either, so they sat in silence under the strengthening sun until it was time to leave.

Nate decided to ride on the box again, allowing Sam his space. Besides, it was stuffy with them both inside the carriage and the day promised to be sunny and warm. But when he climbed up, he found Sam climbing up the other side of the coach. Their eyes made glancing contact, like stones skimming across water, just long enough for Nate to understand that Sam was choosing to sit with him.

The flicker of hope in his chest grew a little brighter.

Nate kept his hat low as they drove into the midday heat, and after a while pulled off his coat. Sam did the same and they exchanged a look.

To the devil with English manners, it said, *I'm not broiling for the sake of decorum.*

It was pleasant with the wind whipping through the linen of his shirt and Nate loosened his neckcloth too, just a little. They'd crested a crop of low hills earlier and now the land fell away before them, a gentle rolling slope of trees and fields. "It's pretty country," he said at last, the first words spoken between them all day.

"Does it — ?" Sam cleared his throat. "Does it remind you

of Rosemont? Sometimes I can't quite remember."

Nate couldn't see much of Sam beneath the brim of his hat, only enough to know his eyes were fixed straight ahead. "A little," he said, struck painfully by all that Sam had lost — even his memories of home were fading. "It's not so wild here, though."

"No."

He wished he could reach out and take his hand, to offer comfort and show that he was sorry for all Sam had lost. That was impossible — Sam would never allow it — but Nate smiled anyway because even that short exchange between them felt like a rapprochement after yesterday's harsh words.

He relaxed, uncoiling muscles held unconsciously tight, letting his shoulder bump against Sam's, the heat of Sam's arm pressing against his own through the fine linen of their shirts. So familiar, that touch. He swallowed but couldn't beat back a cresting wave of longing. It flooded through him in a rush and he had to suck in a quick breath, fighting the urge to turn his head and bury his face into the damp curls above Sam's ear, to breathe in his scent and savor the salt-sweet taste of his skin.

Christ, it was a special torture to sit so close to a man he'd once loved intimately and be forbidden to love him at all.

Sam shifted his long legs, cramped by the narrow seat, spreading them so that his thigh pressed against Nate's with a solid heat. Nate's pulse quickened, fluttering at the base of his throat. How easy it would be to rest his hand on Sam's leg, to run his fingers up the length of his thigh. The post-boy would never know. No one would know but them.

They'd done such things once, dangerous as wild lightning strikes: a touch here, a press of bodies there, a kiss stolen in the silence of Reed's file room with a promise of more, later. Once they'd started, they'd hardly been able to keep their hands from each other. Right up to the very last moments, before it all came crashing down, they'd sought each other out like that — even when their heads had been distant, their bodies had brought them close.

He wondered whether that could happen again, whether, beneath Sam's anger, he felt the same excruciating longing. Whether they could fuck without forgiveness, make only a physical reconciliation. Did Nate even want that? His head didn't know, but his body screamed 'yes' the longer Sam sat pressed next to him in the slow summer heat.

It would be a start, at least.

THE DAY DRAGGED on, stage after stage, the trundle of the chaise making the base of Sam's spine ache, much as the heavy silence between him and Nate made his heart ache.

His words had hurt Nate yesterday. At the time, in the moment of speaking, he'd relished striking the blow. But as the day had worn on, and Nate had sunk deeper and deeper into silence, Sam had begun to regret his harshness.

He'd wanted to wound, that was the truth of it. He'd wanted to make Nate hurt the way *he'd* hurt for the last five years — to ache right down to his bones for everything they'd lost. But Sam's father would have warned him that a man who lifts his hand to harm a friend harms himself the deepest.

And so it had proven.

Nate's hurt had been obvious last night, proclaimed by the miserable slump of his shoulders and the dousing of his fiery spirit. He'd looked so dejected as he'd trudged miserably to bed that Sam, fool that he was, had almost apologized. He'd resisted at the last moment, reminding himself of Cole's advice — *make sure he knows what he done to you* — and told himself Nate deserved the pain. What right did Nate Tanner have to feel injured when Sam was the one wronged?

No right at all.

And yet Nate's wounded expression and tentative glances ached like a bruise beneath Sam's skin, impossible to ignore. And today, in his need to ease his own discomfort, he'd relented. Too proud to apologize for his severity, he'd moved to sit with Nate on the box, allowed their legs to press together, allowed Nate's shoulder to brush his own, and let his body hum with remembered intimacy.

Upon reflection, that had been a mistake.

Because by the time the light began to fail and they stopped for the night at an inn near Solihull, Sam was mired in a confusion of feelings. Anger, desire, resentment, longing: how was it possible to feel it all at once?

The Greswolde Arms was a smart building for a coaching inn, and very busy. "We don't have any more rooms," the landlord apologized. "You're welcome to sleep in the hayloft or leave your chaise in the yard and sleep in there. Or you could try up at the Black Horse, but everyone's busy this time of year."

"I'll be comfortable enough in the hayloft," Sam said, throwing Nate a quick glance. "Mr. Tanner can sleep in the coach."

Nate's answering expression was inscrutable. "As you like."

Sam did like. He needed time away from Nate, time to restore his equilibrium. Time to reinforce his shaky defenses.

They ate in silence amid the noise of the crowded dining parlor, and Sam ordered himself a bottle of the inn's cheapest gin. Nate eyed it while they ate but said nothing. He was, like Sam, partial to a good Kentucky whiskey.

Eventually, the landlord appeared with blankets for both and another apology. "It don't feel right letting a couple of gents go without a room. I'd offer my own bed but the wife —"

"I can assure you," Nate said with a smile, "that Mr.

Hutchinson and I are both used to bunking in odd places." He met Sam's eyes across the table. "We used to go night fishing back home. Sometimes we'd just bed down right there on the riverbank."

The bastard.

The landlord's gaze darted between them, a slight lift of his eyebrows suggesting curiosity, but he only said, "Well then. I'll bid you a good night, sirs."

Once he'd left, Nate reached for Sam's gin and poured a large measure into his empty ale cup. He lifted it in salute. "A man shouldn't drink alone."

Sam grunted and refilled his own cup. "It's been a long couple of days." But the liquor was at least rubbing off the edges of his tension, his shoulders starting to unknot.

"And some long ones yet to come." Nate examined the rim of his earthenware cup, then lifted his dark gaze to Sam's. "Listen. You should know that MacLeod is a violent man. Vicious. If we're caught in his house, he'll take matters into his own hands. You need to be ready for that."

"What nice company you're keeping these days."

Nate conceded that with a spread of his hands. "Needs must when the devil drives."

"So speaks the great revolutionary. What happened to *Give me liberty or give me death*?"

Nate's lips tightened as he looked away. "Must everything come back to that?"

"Everything *does* come back to that. You made it so."

"*I* did?" The challenge in Nate's eyes, the flash of irritation, shouldn't have raised gooseflesh across Sam's skin, but he felt raw and dangerously exposed tonight. Vulnerable. "We both had a hand in it. We both had our principles and made our choices."

And there was truth in that, he supposed. Even if Sam's choices had been forced by men who refused him the liberty of his own conscience. But what was the point of still arguing? It was done now, it was over, and in a few days, Nate would be gone. There was no going back to what they'd once been, but this journey would be intolerable if they kept worrying at the past like dogs fighting over old bones. "Perhaps," Sam said cautiously, "we could call a truce while we're on the road."

"A truce?" Nate cocked an eyebrow. "We're not at war, Sam."

That was true. The battle was over, the land laid waste, and they were picking through the wreckage until they went their separate ways once more. With a sigh, Sam said, "I guess not."

A flicker of emotion lit Nate's eyes, chasing away yesterday's sadness. "Truce, then." he said, knocking his cup against Sam's and swallowing a mouthful of gin. "Christ." He pulled a face. "This is vile. Can you not get good whiskey in England?"

"You can. I prefer not to drink it."

"Why on earth not?"

Because it reminds me of you. "This feels more fitting to my current situation." He pushed the half-empty bottle toward Nate, standing up. "It's yours. I'm done and for bed. I hope you sleep well."

"Do you really?" Nate's gleaming eyes caught his; he was a little drunk, Sam realized. A little reckless. "You could help with that, you know."

Sam's mouth dried at the blatant suggestion because, yes, part of him wanted that. Some base, physical part of him responded to the invitation in Nate's eyes like sulfur to a flame. His whole body ablaze with helpless desire, cheeks burning.

But the rest of him rebelled in indignation that Nate could treat the subject so lightly. That he could be so frivolous about something that had meant so much to them. And Sam knew with absolute certainty that if he succumbed tonight, it would make his sadness all the harder to bear in the morning. "I should —" He turned away, knocking against the table and sloshing the gin in his haste. "Goodnight."

He fled to the jakes, Nate's hot gaze on his back.

Once he'd relieved himself, he crossed the yard to the stables, pausing outside to take a couple of steadying breaths. No doubt there'd be a few hands sleeping in the hayloft tonight, but, like Nate had said, he'd slept in worse places. The dark, dank pit of Simsbury Mine being the worst. And anything was safer than a night sleeping within reach of Nate.

He was just opening the stable door when someone grabbed his arm. Sam spun, fists up, only to find Nate standing there in the dark. His eyes gleamed with reflected moonlight, lips slightly parted, and he was breathing fast as if he'd run. Sam slowly lowered his arms.

No. He wanted to say it aloud. *No, I don't want this.*

But the words wouldn't come.

Putting a hand to Sam's chest, Nate crowded him around the corner of the stable into deep shadows. "Sam," he said, so close Sam could feel his breath on his lips. "Can't we put the past behind us?"

Sam wanted to push him away; he wanted to pull him closer. He did neither, just stood there in the darkness watching the glint of Nate's eyes, the shape of his mouth, needing but unable to take. Never had he wanted, and not wanted, anything so much in his life. The contradiction paralyzed him.

For a long moment they stood in silence. Heat from Nate's fingers bled through Sam's shirt, his dark gaze unfathomable. And then, with a frustrated growl, Nate surged forward and crushed his lips to Sam's in a fierce, desperate kiss.

Sam could do nothing but let him.

He tasted of cheap gin and desire, of love and longing and everything they'd lost. Sam's heart clattered painfully against his ribs as something big and ugly clawed its way up from inside, some base emotion that tore out in a raw sob. He hardly knew what he felt, only that it was too much. Overwhelmed, he drove his fingers into Nate's hair, knotting them there, forcing Nate's head back to deepen the kiss. To make it a punishment. But Nate only took Sam's face in his hands, too tender, too gentle, murmuring soft sounds that set Sam blazing.

Fuck, how he wanted him. How he *resented* him.

Desire like panic made him breathless, pulsed in his ears until the pounding of his blood was all Sam could hear. Everything was slipping out of control. With a grunt, he pushed Nate hard against the stable wall, pinning him there with his body.

"You bastard," he growled into the soft space beneath Nate's ear, tasting the salt of his skin, breathing in that delicious scent of home. Making Nate squirm. "You hell-born bastard. I *loved* you."

Nate gave a convulsive jolt and pulled Sam closer, hands fisting in his coat, his body arching. "Sam," he rasped, tugging at the fall of Sam's breeches, fumbling in his haste. "Let me show you…"

And Sam started to unravel, a world of fury and desire and fear unspooling at his feet. It was all madness. Glorious, blazing madness!

Until he couldn't breathe.

Until tar-stench flooded his nose and throat, choking him, terror leaping like flames toward his scorched skin. Hate-spitting faces loomed out of the dark — *Pig-fucking Tory whore!* The horror of Simsbury Mine squeezed his chest, its dank smothering darkness crushing his lungs. Cries and groans and madness. Panic like nothing he'd ever imagined, primal and humiliating. Unmanning.

"No!" Sam lurched back, blood pounding in his ears as he tore free of the memories. Dizzy, he tried to suck breath into his cramping lungs.

Nate watched him with wide eyes, half sprawled against the wall, chest heaving. After a moment he reached out a shaking hand, his face ghostly. "Sam?"

"I can't —" He stumbled back another step. "I don't want this."

Silence, broken only by their rasping breaths as they stared at each other. A distant bell tolled the half hour and eventually Nate lowered his hand. "I see."

"You let it happen." Sam's words crawled up from the dark, unbidden. "I loved you and you let them destroy me."

Nate flinched. After a moment, he pushed away from the wall and brushed trembling hands over his ravaged hair, tugging down his waistcoat. "How could I have stopped them?"

Sam didn't answer. He couldn't. There were no words to explain the howling agony of seeing Nate standing with the mob, watching in silence while Sam was humiliated, abused, and driven out of his home. There were no words for the pain of that betrayal, the pain of knowing that Nate simply hadn't loved him enough to try and save him. Maybe it wasn't rational, but that was how he felt and offering his heart, bloody and beaten, to the man who'd already crushed it was impossible. He couldn't do it.

Instead, he took a step back to give Nate room to leave.

He took the hint and moved away, toward the yard. "For what little it's worth," Nate said, pausing at the edge of the moonlight, "I wept every night for a month after you were gone. I thought I'd die of grief."

"I just thought I'd die."

Nate flinched but didn't respond, and after a moment he

walked away. Sam let him go, guts twisted into a knot of that sweet-sharp pain that was almost pleasure.

He told himself he had no regrets.

Chapter Nine

BETWEEN THE SWAY of the chaise, the stuffy air, and the rain pattering against the roof, Nate found it hard to keep his eyes open the following morning.

It didn't help that he hadn't slept much the night before. Which had nothing to do with the discomfort of sleeping in the chaise and everything to do with the man pretending to doze in the opposite corner of the carriage. Sam rested his head against the window, eyes closed, but the way his fingers were clenched in his lap told Nate that he wasn't asleep. He was just avoiding conversation.

They'd hardly spoken a word since last night's encounter, and Nate cursed himself — and the gin — for pushing things too far. Well, he'd paid the price for his foolishness. He wouldn't soon forget the way Sam had pulled away as if he'd found himself embracing the serpent in Eden.

The frustrating thing was that Nate knew Sam had wanted him. He'd felt it, and not just in the crude physical way a man's need became apparent. No, he'd felt it in his heart as the old connection had sparked back into life, rusty perhaps but still intact. Still linking them soul-to-soul. He'd felt his own longing reflected in Sam's desire, a building heat between them that fed upon itself, getting fiercer and fiercer.

But then Sam had pushed him away with a look of… Nate could only call it horror. At himself? At Nate? Perhaps Sam hated himself for still wanting Nate. It was an uncomfortable thought, but Sam's reaction had been eviscerating.

And it had felt painfully like loathing.

He sighed and stole another glance at his companion, pressed hard into the corner of the carriage as if putting as much space as possible between them.

Love. Loathing. Two sides of the same coin, so the saying went. But once the coin had been flipped, was it possible to turn it back to —

The chaise lurched violently, throwing Nate sideways as it tilted sharply downward with an alarming thud and a squealing protest from the horses.

"Christ!" Sam startled awake as Nate fell, half sprawling across his lap, and grabbed him before he fell through the door. The chaise juddered to a stop. And then they were a breath away from each other, a tangle of limbs and surprise, eyes locked. Hearts thumping. A thick curl of Sam's hair tumbled forward over his forehead. Nate fought the urge to push it back.

"Did we hit something?" It was a struggle to sound normal with Sam's strong hands on his body.

Up ahead, the post-boy swore imaginatively.

"A rut, most likely." Sam sounded gruff and looked quickly away from Nate. "We should get out."

It took a little maneuvering given the steep angle of the coach, but between them they got the door open without falling out and Sam clambered down onto the ground. It was much closer than usual and filthy deep in mud.

"Stay here," he warned Nate, eying his expensive boots.

"If we're in a rut, we'll both need to get out."

Sam shrugged his agreement and turned to squelch around to the back of the chaise. Nate followed as the post-boy came around from the other side and they met at the back where Sam was staring at their rear right wheel. It had sunk past its axle in a water-filled hole. "Hell," he said. "Cole's going to gut me."

The post-boy moved past them to examine the wheel, tutting and cursing the godforsaken roads. He looked about forty and was as tanned and wrinkled as a walnut. "Don't think it's broken," he pronounced, then eyed them uncertainly. "If you gents are willing to help push, we should be able move her."

Out of some old habit, perhaps, Sam glanced at Nate for his opinion.

He tried not to read anything into that unconscious gesture of confidence. "I think we're up to the challenge," he decided, taking off his coat. "Going to be muddy work, though. We might as well keep most of our clothes clean."

Sam grunted his agreement and the two of them stripped off their coats and waistcoats and went to set them inside the chaise.

It wasn't a warm day, but it *was* June, and the sun was strong when it managed to shoulder its way through the clouds. Nate could feel it against his forearms as he rolled up his sleeves. Around them sprawled a rugged heathland, distant woods crowning hills to the east. He'd not ventured beyond London during his time in England and this place was beautiful — it had something of the wildness he'd missed about the south. "Pretty country," he said to Sam. "Where are we?"

He peered about. "No idea."

Nate laughed. It was just a huff of breath, really — Sam had hardly cracked a joke — but Sam smiled a little in response and the ease and familiarity of the moment turned Nate inside out. God, they'd been so close once, co-conspirators in their secret love. Surely Sam didn't really hate him, did he?

"Come on," Sam said, brusquely. "Let's get this done."

While the post-boy started the horses pulling, Nate and Sam ducked in under the chaise to try and lift it enough that the wheel would clear the rut. They heaved and gasped for a good ten minutes, the chaise splashing back down after every attempt. Nate found himself soaked past his knees and sweating from the effort as the sun burned off the clouds and turned the clammy air steamy.

"We need to put something into the rut," he said, wiping his forehead after the umpteenth attempt had failed. "Planks or something."

"Planks?" Sam had removed his neckcloth and his shirt hung open at the neck. Nate tried not to stare at the familiar curve of his throat, the glimpse of muscle on his chest. "Where the bloody hell do you think we'll get planks from?"

Nate blinked the sweat out of his eyes along with the image of Sam's bare skin. "You sound like a 'bloody' Englishman," he said, in a poor attempt at the accent. "Very highfalutin."

Sam looked almost amused. "Highfalutin'? If I sound like anything, it's St. Giles."

"Who's he?"

"It's a place, you ignoramus." Sam sobered, as if struck by an unpleasant thought. "Home, I suppose." After a moment he added, "Maybe we can find a branch in the hedgerow that could help?"

He started making his way to the edge of the road, Nate following. This was the first time Sam had volunteered anything about his life in London and Nate wasn't about to let it go. "St Giles is a neighborhood, is it?"

"Of a sort." Sam tugged at a dead branch in the hedge, but it was well and truly stuck. "Hal Foxe gives me a room there."

"*A* room?" Nate failed to hide his dismay, his mind flashing back to Sam's beautiful house in Rosemont.

Sam didn't look like he was going to respond as he concentrated on dislodging the branch. But suddenly, he said, "I had nothing when I came here. They took —" His voice caught, and Nate's stomach swooped uneasily. "I lost everything. Stepped off the ship in London with nothing but the clothes on my back. The government promised to help, but — Well, there's thousands of us here, waiting on the Loyalist Claims Commission to compensate us for what we lost back home. And they hardly give out anything, just pennies, and only then if you have written proof of the property stolen from you." He tugged angrily at the branch. It scarcely moved an inch. "As if you stop to pack your papers when the mob's riding you out of town or burning down your damned house. But they don't think about that, do they? Because they've never been refugees. They don't know what it's like to…to…to lose *everything*. Even your country. So we wait. And they give us fuck all. And the devil take them anyway. So yes, Hal Foxe gives me *a* room and I don't much care what I do for it in return. If the Commission won't give me what I'm owed, then I'll damn well take it for myself." He yanked on the branch again. "Damn it, just —"

"Let me help." Nate stepped forward to grab the branch, but Sam whirled on him.

"I don't need your help!"

"With the branch," Nate clarified, hands up. "I meant, let me help you free the branch."

Sam didn't reply, jaw working as if he were chewing back an angry response. But neither did he object when Nate cautiously moved next to him and took hold of the branch, their hands side-by-side, so close their fingers were touching.

"On three," Nate said, and they hauled. With a wrenching crack the branch came free, sending them both staggering back so hard that Nate lost his balance, feet sliding in the slimy mud until, with an unmanly squeal, he landed on his ass. "Mary Mother of God!" he gasped. "It's cold!"

The bastard snorted, amused. Nate glared, picking at the mud that had splashed up onto his face, which only made Sam laugh out loud, his startling smile so familiar it completely overturned Nate's dismay.

And then he was chuckling too, hilarity rising like a bubble through the thick tension between them. "Damnation," Nate said, trying in vain to get up without having to stick his hands into the mud for leverage. "This is disgusting. I have mud — You don't want to know where I have mud."

"Here." Sam leaned down to offer his hand.

Nate stared at Sam's outstretched hand, his laughter fading. Slowly, with care, he reached up and clasped Sam's hand. Firm fingers closed around his, warm and strong and painfully familiar. He tried not to react to the sensation as Sam hauled him to his feet, but then they were standing rather close and Nate couldn't look away, couldn't let go. "Thank you," he said softly, gazing into Sam's clear eyes. Emotion shone there, but Nate couldn't quite decipher its meaning.

Then, as if suddenly recollecting himself, Sam tugged his hand free. "We need a couple more branches," he said. "I'll go look."

After taking a moment to compose his feelings, Nate followed, and they spent the next hour dragging dead branches out of the hedge and wedging them beneath the stuck wheel — or trying to. It was difficult to see beneath the murky water.

As a rule, Nate preferred not to get his hands dirty. It was why he'd studied so hard at the law — so he could earn his keep surrounded by books and ideas, not mud and shit. Yet here he was, up to his knees in both, and he found he didn't really mind all that much.

"We're ready!" Sam yelled to the post-boy, from where he had his shoulder braced against the chaise. Nate stood next to the wheel, ready to guide it onto the branches, soaked to the skin from reaching into the filth, his shirtsleeves pushed up and the rest clinging to him damply. The sun was fully out now, and hot. Not hot like home, but hot enough to dry the mud in his hair.

The post-boy urged the horses on, Sam grunted with the effort of pushing, and Nate hauled on the wheel. For a second — two, three seconds — it teetered on the brink and then suddenly it lurched forward, up and out.

Nate yelped, pulling his hands away from the heavy wheel, jumping clear of the branches as they squelched down into the mud. He whooped and Sam stumbled forward, lost his balance, and ended up on his knees in the dirt. "Hell!"

But he was laughing as he climbed to his feet, the post-boy bringing the chaise to a stop further along the road. Nate laughed too, grinning at Sam who, until he remembered he wasn't supposed to, grinned back.

"We should walk to the next stage and find somewhere to clean up," Sam said, eying the chaise. "Cole will drub me if we get all this dirt inside."

Nate peered along the muddy road ahead, the glare making him squint. "Besides, we might need to push her free again."

Sam grimaced in a way that didn't reach his eyes, panto-miming displeasure. Nate wondered whether, like him, Sam was enjoying the suspension of hostilities between them and didn't want the tentative truce to end.

They made a strange caravan, the chaise crawling along empty, Nate and Sam trudging behind like filthy footmen. It was difficult walking, the mud sucking at his boots, thighs burning with the strain of wading through the muck.

"Be thankful it's not still raining," Sam said, eying him sideways.

"At this point, I doubt it would matter. God's teeth, Sam, how do you live in all this mud?"

"I don't usually make a habit of wallowing in it. Besides, it rains in Rosemont too." He slid Nate a wry look. "Or has your Congress outlawed rain?"

"So they have," Nate said, catching Sam's light tone as carefully as he might a butterfly. "It's been decreed that the sun will always shine in America."

"The farmers won't be happy."

"Well —" The uncertain smile in Sam's eyes had Nate's hope rising. "Then the rain's only to fall on their fields. How's that?"

"About as plausible as the rest of your fantastical future, I suppose."

"Sam…" He couldn't stop the sigh. "It was your future too once, remember? We used to talk of — Christ!" His boot stuck fast and a moment later his stockinged foot slipped free and went plunging into cold, sticky mud. "Oh, for the love of…"

Sam snorted a laugh and watched Nate trying to pull his boot free. The damned thing wouldn't budge, and Nate's wet, slippery fingers couldn't get purchase.

"You could help," he snapped, wiping his hands on the shoulders of his shirt — the driest part of himself he could find.

"Suppose. But watching's more fun."

Nate glared, but Sam's grin popped his irritation like a soap bubble. He felt daring, suddenly, boyish in a way he'd not felt in years. "Is that so?" With a flick of his fingers, he sent a gob of mud right into Sam's face.

"You…!" Sam spluttered, gasping in shock, and Nate

sucked in an apprehensive breath. "You utter shit." Scooping up a handful of mud, Sam flung it right back. Nate ducked, but Sam's second shot hit him square on the arm.

And then it was war.

Nate was hampered by only having one boot, but he held his ground as they pelted each other with handfuls of mud, like children. He was laughing and breathless, and inside him something began to unspool — days of tension, years of regret and longing — all of it unraveling in this lunacy. He could see it in Sam too, in the sudden wildness unleashed between them, in his breathless laughter and glittering eyes. And when Nate charged forward to shove a handful of mud down the back of Sam's shirt, he found himself tackled around the waist and they both went down into the mud.

The breath knocked from him, Nate squirmed away. But Sam was too fast. He grabbed Nate's shoulder and hauled him in, flipping him over onto his back and straddling him. "Submit!" he demanded, one hand splayed on Nate's chest, warm through his sodden shirt, and the other holding a fistful of gloop high above his head. It dripped from between his clenched fingers. "Surrender."

Never! The word hovered on Nate's lips, but something in Sam's expression held him silent. Some need for victory. Until that moment, Nate hadn't realized that Sam might feel defeated, that he might consider Nate the victor in the conflict that had torn them apart. But, dear God, hadn't they both lost? His laughter failed and he held out his hands. "You win. I surrender."

He'd always surrendered to Sam, after all. It had been his joy.

Swallowing, Sam lowered his hand but didn't look away. He breathed hard, chest rising and falling beneath the mud smeared across his skin. And the heat in his eyes set Nate's heart pounding in hope, made his body respond. He saw

want there, certainly. Forgiveness? Something fonder still?
God, please…

"Damn you, Nate Tanner," Sam said, feelingly. "Damn you to hell."

He pushed himself to his feet and Nate scrambled up next to him, still missing a boot. It was sticking out of the mud some feet away. He reached out a hand. "Sam —"

But Sam was already turning away. "Come on, the chaise is halfway down the road. Let's get your damned boot and be after it."

With a frustrated sigh, Nate clambered to his feet and followed.

An hour later they reached the next inn, the sun high and the day approaching noon. Nate flaked dry mud from his arms as he trudged wearily into the yard, leaving Sam to make his way over to the inn to ask about a place for them to wash, and about a change of horses. The post-boy wanted to inspect the wheel for damage, so their stay promised to be lengthy.

He glanced around the yard while he waited, catching a couple of lads paused in their business of hauling water to gape. They probably made quite a sight, covered head-to-toe in filth. He hoped Sam had got something out of his system, throwing mud instead of insults, but feared it would take more than that to break down the wall between them. Perhaps they'd found a few chinks, but Sam appeared reluctant to look through.

After a few minutes, Sam appeared from around the side of the inn and beckoned Nate over. He had good news: a stream where they could wash ran behind the inn, and the landlady had offered to provide them with a meal when they were done. "And there are horses here, so we'll not lose too much time," Sam added. "The road into Stone is drier, apparently. We should go faster now the rain's passed."

Nate contemplated whether he considered 'faster' to be a boon or not as he followed Sam around the back of the inn, through a yard where a few chickens were scratching a living, and across a swath of grass to a sparkling stream.

A willow dipped its branches into the water at the point where the bank gave way to a shingly beach that was clearly used for washing and collecting water. Nate glanced around as he dumped his portmanteau on the bank and pulled out the cleanest clothes he could find. "I suppose the sight of two men frolicking in the stream won't bother anyone?"

Sam shrugged. "Dare say they've seen worse."

They shared an awkward glance before Nate turned away and started tugging his soggy shirt from his breeches. Reeds rustled on the far bank where the water ran deeper. "Looks like you'd catch some cotton fish over there," he said. "Do they have them in England?"

"Can't say I know. Haven't had much time for fishing."

"But you love to fish."

"London's rivers aren't exactly conducive."

Nate could believe that. There was more shit than fish in those filthy streams. "This looks like a nice spot," he said. "Shame we don't have longer."

"You're a fisherman now, are you?" Sam untucked his shirt, letting it gape, sunlight golden on his chest.

Nate looked away to keep from staring. "No, I don't fish. But I still read. Came across a copy of *Les Liaisons Dangereuses* in London." He risked a glance. "Have you heard of it? It's quite scandalous. I think you'd enjoy it."

Sam gave a huff and started working on taking off his boots. "So I'd fish, and you'd lay in the grass and read to me, just like we used to? And we'd ignore the bad blood between us and pretend like the world isn't a changed place?"

Nate sighed. "There's no bad blood between us, Sam. At least, not on my part. And maybe the world *has* changed, but a man can still go fishing with his friend. And read books."

"You think so? *I* can't even go home." With that he stood and strode out into the water.

The *Thanks to you*, remained unspoken.

After carefully taking the cord holding his ring from around his neck and tucking it safely into his portmanteau, Nate followed Sam into the water. He sucked in a breath at the cold and then dived under the surface to wash the mud from his skin and clothes. Once he was swimming, it didn't feel so cold and he scrubbed at his hair and limbs and then floated on his back, drifting beneath the willow and down past the reeds.

He stopped there. Sam stood a little distance away, head tipped back as he squeezed water out of his hair. He was breathtaking in the sunlit water — *that fair boy that had my heart entangled*. Nate sighed. Not even the poets could do Sam justice. He wondered whether Sam remembered the time they'd made love in the river, a hot summer night when they'd struck out past the edge of town in search of solitude and freedom. He imagined Sam did remember; the night had been unforgettable.

Standing up, Nate let his hair stream down his back, freed of the queue that usually held it in place. The sun was warm on his chilled skin, dappling through the leaves of the willow that hid them from the inn. His heart fluttered light and high in his throat. "I miss those days," he said to Sam, sending the words like fragile paper boats over the water.

Sam looked up from where he stood close to the bank. The planes and angles of his body were beautifully defined by the clinging linen of his shirt, rendered almost transparent by the water. He looked like a painting.

"I miss lying in the grass, reading to you." Nate walked closer, toes sinking into the silty riverbed. "I miss talking to you and debating with you. I miss —"

"Don't."

"I miss touching you." He flicked a glance over Sam's shoulder, but they were well concealed, so he put his fingertips to Sam's chest. "I miss *you*."

"For God's sake —" Sam grabbed his wrist but didn't pull Nate's hand away. "What the devil do you want from me?"

"Nothing." *Your forgiveness, your love.* "I just wanted you to know." Movement on the bank drew his eye. Two girls walked down from the inn, giggling and whispering, carrying a basket of food between them. Nate snatched his hand back. "I'm still your friend, Sam. I always have been." Then he let himself fall back into the water. "Looks like our meal is on the way."

They waited in the water while the girls — daughters of the innkeeper, perhaps — delivered a basket of food, ruddy-cheeked and laughing as they cast daring glances toward the river.

Nate raised his hand and waved. "Much obliged to you, ladies!"

That elicited another giggle and, from the bolder of the two, an extravagant curtsy, before they headed back toward the inn with several glances over their shoulders and explosions of laughter.

When they were out of sight, Nate made his way out of the river and he and Sam, backs carefully turned, stripped out of their wet clothes, set them out in the sun, and got dressed. Once they were dry and warmer, they sat on the riverbank beneath the willow and ate a meal of fresh bread, tangy red cheese, and early season apples that were as fragrant as anything Nate would have gotten at home. And more ale to drink.

"Honey cake," Sam said quietly. "Hot from the oven.

That's something *I* miss."

Startled, Nate looked up from his contemplation of his meal. "From Calder's Bakery," he said. "You always got the biggest slice because Miss Calder was sweet on you."

Sam shook his head and gave a wistful little smile. "Baked beans on a Saturday night."

"And after church on Sunday." Nate studied him, watched the way Sam toyed with the apple in his hand, the tension in the firm line of his jaw and around his eyes.

"Funny, the things you miss," Sam went on. "Sometimes, they're real small. Insignificant, seeming. Like honey cake, or the quality of the rain. But it's like a kick in the ribs, every time. It winds you." He tossed the apple in the air and caught it, tossed it again. "There's a place on Threadneedle Street in London called The New England Coffeeshop. Refugees gather there to read the American papers and talk about home. Reminisce, you know? I don't go there anymore. It's like scratching a mosquito bite — you get a little temporary relief but end up making it bleed." He set the apple back in the basket, adjusting its position carefully. "The way I see it, I'm better off keeping my eyes on the horizon and not looking back. There's nothing there for me anymore."

Nate didn't know what to say. It made him feel awful. *Guilty.* And he hated that. God knew, he'd tried to convince Sam to change his mind, or to at least keep quiet. That he'd chosen to voice his opposition to the war wasn't Nate's fault, yet he couldn't stand the thought of him sitting in a miserable London coffee shop pouring over old American newspapers, looking for a glimpse of home.

It hurt to imagine it.

"Looks like they're hitching up the horses," Sam said, and Nate realized he hadn't responded to Sam's confession. He tried to catch his eye a couple of times as Sam got to his feet and gathered his damp clothes together, but he was purposely absorbed in what he was doing and headed back toward the chaise without saying anything more.

Troubled, Nate followed.

And halfway across the swath of grass, Sam slowed and stopped. "I miss you, too," he said quietly, without turning around. "But that's just another reason not to look back."

Nate caught his breath, but before he could think of a response Sam had started walking again. Back straight and stiff, he crossed the yard toward the coach, leaving Nate to follow in his wake.

Chapter Ten

BY THE TIME they reached the Crown and Anchor in the market town of Stone, even the long summer evening was slipping into dusk. Sam figured it was past nine o'clock. They'd traveled late to make up time and were now within a day's reach of Liverpool. But Stone was full of travelers and the inn was very crowded.

He was lucky to get the last room.

"It's a large bed," the landlord said, offering them the key. "Comfortable enough for two gents, and not damp."

Sam took the key without comment, and they went into the tap room to eat a dinner of roasted beef and mashed turnips. The heavy brass key sat on the table between them like a threat. Sam could hardly look at it. As they ate, he glanced across the table and Nate met his eyes, unflinching. Unreadable. Utterly beguiling. He always had been, since the first day he'd walked into John Reed's office with his smart coat and glinting dark eyes and turned Sam's world upside down.

He was afraid he'd overturn it again if Sam let him.

Perhaps Nate saw something of that in his face, because

he offered a smile as he said, "The post-boy reckons we'll reach Liverpool tomorrow, if the weather holds."

"And from there to Marlborough Castle. How far is it, do you know?"

"Afraid not. We'll need to get directions at the inn. But no more than a day's drive, as I understand."

By unspoken consent, they lingered in the tap room until it got dark, which was late at this time of year. Sam still found it strange to see the sun dawdling above the horizon close to ten o'clock at night, but today he wished it would stay light longer still, putting off the inevitable moment; the thought of that one room and its one bed tormented him.

Nate sighed. "If you want, I'll sleep on the floor."

"Or I could."

A beat of silence fell between them. Nate said, "Or we could just behave like grown men."

Sam wasn't sure what that meant. He didn't ask, either, uncertain about the answer he wanted to hear. His resolve felt weak, after all that had happened today.

Truth was, he could have kissed Nate right there in the muddy road, pinned down, flushed and laughing. He'd wanted to. Or standing in the river with Nate's hot fingers resting against his chest. God, how he'd wanted him.

I miss touching you, Nate had said. *I miss you.*

Christ, he could still feel the bruising clash of their lips last night, Nate's heat and urgency, and the way his own body had ignited like tinder awaiting the fall of a spark. He hummed with it still, that incessant impossible desire that he couldn't smother. And daren't indulge.

When it could no longer be avoided, Nate paid for their meals and they hauled their luggage up to the room in silence. It was small, didn't fit much more than a washstand and the bed, although the landlord had been right about the bed — it looked big enough for two, even when one of them was as broad as Sam. Nate, he was a slender creature. In a bed like that, they'd —

The floor, Sam thought as his face flushed. *It had better be the floor.*

They washed and undressed in a difficult silence. Sam kept his back turned as he slipped off his boots and breeches, leaving on only his shirt for modesty's sake. And with each moment, the silence grew heavier. He could hear Nate moving around behind him, the rustle of his clothing, the thump of a dropped boot. Hell, was there anything more awkward than awkwardness where, once, there'd been none?

By the time Sam had folded his clothes into a neat pile atop his valise, dusk had faded to night. They lit no candle, but the moon was full. Its silvery light flooded the room, reminding Sam too much of the Pawtuxet and Nate stretched out naked on its banks. His cock stirred but he dared not pull the drapes. Ever since the suffocating dark of Simsbury, he'd needed to be able to see the night sky, to know he had a way out into the air. No, there would be no blocking out the moonlight or the memories tonight.

He took a pillow and a blanket from the bed, but the floor looked hard and cramped. While he wrestled with the decision, he glanced over at Nate washing at the basin. Bent forward, Nate scooped up water in his hands, splashing it over his face. His slender back and shapely ass were uncomfortably well defined by his fine lawn shirt, bare thighs as lithe as Sam remembered. His throat went dry, fingers clutching the thin pillow he held, and then something swung out from around Nate's neck to clank against the porcelain basin.

Nate cursed and tucked it back inside his shirt, but he was too late. Sam had seen the gleam of gold in the moonlight. With a jolt of recognition, he surged forward without thought and seized the leather cord that hung about Nate's neck, yanking out the ring he'd hidden away.

Nate reached for it too and ended up with his fingers curled around Sam's hand, the ring clutched between them. Then they were just looking at each other, Nate's eyes wide with alarm, droplets of water clinging to the tips of his lashes and the scruff on his jaw. They were so close Sam could feel the heat of Nate's bare leg pressing against his own, his breath washing over their tangled fingers. His whole body flushed with fire and fury. "Why do you keep it?" he rasped, chest heaving like he'd been fighting. "Why do you still have it?"

The ring was set with strands of his blond and Nate's dark hair, woven together as a token of their unbreakable bond. It felt like mockery now.

"You know why," Nate said, wrenching the ring back.

He looked angry and exposed in a way Sam hadn't seen for a long time. But he wasn't moving away, staring at Sam in heated defiance, breathing hard. A rivulet of water ran from the hollow at the base of his throat, seeping into the linen of his shirt. Nate swallowed, throat working. Sam tracked the movement, the rapid rise and fall of his chest. His skin smelled like soap and the lingering green scent of the river.

In the moonlight, he was beautiful. Angry and tempting.

Sam couldn't breathe for wanting him.

With a low growl, Nate moved, and their mouths came together in a furious clash. Less of a kiss than a fight. A flash-flood of desire. Legs tangled, bodies tussled, hands twisted into shirts. Wordless, noiseless but for their heavy breaths and Sam's snarl when Nate's hand slid under the hem of his shirt to find his prick. His knees went weak and he hated it, hated feeling so vulnerable. Pushing Nate's hand away, he grabbed him around the waist and ground into him instead, feeling Nate's rigid length hard against his own and watching with primal glee as Nate gasped, arching backward over Sam's arm in helpless surrender.

Submitting.

Through the fine lawn of Nate's shirt, Sam could see the hard nub of his nipples and bent over to taste and bite. Nate's cry was breathless, his fingers knotting into Sam's hair as he caught his balance.

But then the tug on his hair became a pull, then a push, and Nate seized Sam's shoulders, urging him up and backwards until Sam's legs hit the edge of the bed. Nate felled him with a shove that sent him half sprawling onto his back and was on his knees between Sam's thighs before Sam had time to catch his breath.

For a heavy moment, they eyed each other. Nate looked wild, loose hair cascading down to his shoulders, eyes wide and dusky, lips glistening. Neither spoke. To speak would break the spell. But Sam nodded once, and then Nate's mouth was on his prick, eager to please. Christ, he'd always been so eager to please in the bedroom.

Sam let his head drop back, terrified of the darkness boiling beneath his desire. Terrified of the memories it would stir up. But he couldn't make himself stop, he wanted it too much. "God damn you," he growled. "Fucking *hell*."

Nate made a noise, soft and desperate with pleasure, as his clever mouth made Sam see stars. God, but this was a familiar dance. Achingly, terribly familiar. Nate's shirt had slipped down, baring one shoulder, and Sam set his hand there, relishing the feel of smooth skin. Somehow, the intimacy softened him. Then Nate glanced up, eyes gleaming through his long lashes, and for an instant they were connected. Reunited, as one.

Sam's heart swooped like a bird on the wing.

And then Nate's eyes fluttered closed and he took Sam to the hilt, pushing him abruptly over the edge. With a cry, Sam's release swept up and through him, a bolt of summer lightning from a clear blue sky. It knocked him backward onto the bed, blazing white as pleasure overwhelmed him. Amidst it, Nate buried his face against Sam's thigh, his breath hot against his skin as he smothered a groan, the warmth of his release splashing against Sam's calf.

Breathless, Sam lay in the dark and waited for the memories to erupt: the tarpit stench, the flicker of the torches in the hands of the mob, and the dreadful despairing darkness of Simsbury Mine.

But those weren't the memories that came to him.

Instead, his mind drifted back to another night. To the night he'd given Nate the ring…

They'd been in the back parlor at home — what had been his father's home, before the typhus took his parents — with the fire burned down to ash and a single candle providing the only light. With the servants abed, Nate had lounged in Sam's arms on the settle and when Sam had fished the rings, a pair of them, from his pocket and shown him, Nate had laughed in delight. When he'd read the inscription — an abbreviation of *amicus est tamquam alter idem* — his eyes had turned liquid, lit gold by the dancing candlelight, and they'd kissed until Sam tasted salt tears on his lips. Nate had slipped the ring on that night and hadn't taken it off again.

"I lost my ring," Sam said after a while, watching the play of moonlight over the cracked plaster ceiling. "I used it to bribe my way out of Simsbury Mine." At the time, he hadn't thought it much of a loss, the ring already rendered worthless by Nate's betrayal.

"I'm sorry," Nate said softly.

Just that: *I'm sorry.*

But for what? The loss of his ring? The loss of his home, his friends, his country? Nate's silence when Holden's mob had come for him?

Or for simply not loving him enough.

There was so many questions Sam could have asked that

he found it impossible to ask anything at all, the words too heavy in his heart. He simply couldn't make himself speak.

In silence, Nate got up and washed himself again in the basin. The white of his shirt looked ghostly in the silvery light as, silently, he returned with a cloth and kneeled to clean Sam's leg.

A simple gesture, but it made Sam's throat burn.

When he was done, Nate lay down on the bed, staring at the ceiling. Hesitant, Sam collected his pillow from where he'd dropped it on the floor and set it on his own side of the bed, laying down again and mirroring Nate's position. Sam could feel his quivering tension through the mattress, but bit down hard on his absurd urge to pull him into his arms and comfort him.

What comfort did he have to offer? Nothing had changed; all they'd done tonight was muddy the waters.

Instead, Sam stared at the moon-dappled ceiling until his vision blurred and he sank into a restless sleep.

NATE WOKE AT dawn to the sensation of fingers in his hair, the lightest of touches brushing strands from his face. Warm, work-roughened fingertips ghosted across his forehead, achingly familiar.

He dared not move, tried to keep his breathing under control despite his racing pulse. From outside came the soft patter of rain and the opening bars of the dawn chorus. Concentrating on that, he followed the trills of birdsong to distract himself from the need to open his eyes and look. He didn't want the moment to end.

But what did this unexpected tenderness mean? After the blaze of desire that had ignited between them last night, Sam had been quiet and melancholy. Regretful, Nate had assumed. But now?

Another caress, Sam running Nate's hair through his

fingers like he used to years ago. Nate's heart squeezed. A sigh — the barest whisper of a word on Sam's lips. "Nate…"

He opened his eyes and Sam froze with his hand poised between them.

Neither spoke. For a long time, they just lay there watching each other, the steady patter of rain the only sound in the room. Nate wasn't sure what he saw in Sam's eyes — longing or reproach — and before he could decide, Sam turned onto his back and stared up at the ceiling. His skin looked wan in the half-light, tarnished gold curls spilling onto the pillow, a few clinging to his temple. Then, as if he'd reached a decision, he rolled out of bed, stripped off his shirt, and walked naked to wash himself in the basin.

Nate knew he shouldn't watch but he couldn't help it; Sam was still glorious, and it had been a long time since he'd seen anyone so fine. But as the morning light washed over the muscles of Sam's back, Nate caught his breath in horror.

A crosshatch of scars stretched across his skin, raised and knotted in a tell-tale pattern that made Nate's guts heave. Sam had been flogged.

Christ almighty, Sam had been *flogged*.

At first, he couldn't speak, didn't have the breath for words, his mind tripping over itself as he tried to understand how this could have happened. To Sam, to *his* Sam. He pushed up onto one elbow and, dry-mouthed, whispered, "God, Sam, your back…"

Sam stilled. Then, carefully, he reached for his old shirt, using it to dry himself as he turned around. "A memento from Simsbury." In the rainy light, his eyes were the same color as the dawn, a cool and inscrutable gray. "The first time I tried to escape, they caught me. They chose to make an example."

Nate opened his mouth, but no words would come. Because men fighting for the same cause as Nate had done this to him, and they'd done it in the name of liberty. They'd done it in *Nate's* name. And not just to faceless enemies, or saboteurs and spies, but to *Sam*. And if they'd done it to Sam, how many other good Americans had suffered the same fate? It was appalling. His mind shied away from the truth, because if he let himself imagine Sam's suffering, his pain and fear — His throat tightened, eyes burning. "I'm sorry," he said roughly. "God, Sam, I'm so sorry."

"Why?" His voice shook. "Why are you sorry, Nate? It was war. The British were close. Liberty was at stake."

Nate closed his eyes, marshaling his churning thoughts. "I'm sorry I couldn't keep you safe."

"Ha!" Sam snorted. "I don't remember you trying." He pulled a clean shirt from his valise and flung it over his head, hiding his scarred back. "All I remember is you watching. And that —" His voice cracked, and he said no more.

Through a thick throat, Nate rasped, "If you think Holden would have listened to me that night… Christ, Sam, he already suspected the nature of our friendship. He'd have used anything I said against you. And against me."

Sam grunted and began to dress in angry silence. Eventually, he ground out, "All you had to do was tell him he was wrong."

"Sam…" He knotted a fist in his hair. "All *you* had to do was swear an oath."

"Lie, you mean." Sam snarled the words as he pulled a clean shirt from his valise. "Appease the mob to save my skin."

"It would have kept you safe —"

"There are more important things than safety!" He flung his arms wide, looking like he might have shouted had the hour permitted. "And having the right to think as I choose is one of them. I'm surprised you don't see that."

"I do see that."

"Then why didn't you *do* something?"

"Because I was afraid!"

He startled himself with that blunt admission, but it was no less true for being blurted out in frustration. Taking a breath, he continued more steadily. "Reed came to fetch me that night — he'd seen Holden's mob heading for your house. But when I got there, they already had you on your knees. And I panicked. I didn't know what to do. The British line was so close, and Holden had everyone whipped up into a frenzy. The whole town was terrified."

"Of *me*?" Sam hissed. "*I* wasn't the enemy. I had a different vision of the future, that's all."

"But your vision left America enslaved."

"The devil it did!" Sam's face flushed as he pulled on his breeches and tucked in his shirt. "I wanted America at the heart of the biggest trading empire the world's ever known, not crouching alone on the fringes of the world. I wanted America *leading* the world."

"We *will* lead. We'll lead by example." Nate scooted to the edge of the bed but didn't quite have the nerve to reach out. "Sam, we'll hold up a light for liberty that the whole world will see!"

"Liberty?" Sam spat the word as he slung on his coat, leaving his shirt and waistcoat hanging open, his neckcloth scrunched in one hand. "Your liberty is the tyranny of the mob. Don't you see? You've torn down King George, but King Mob will take his place. And God help anyone who dares argue with *that* tyrant!"

"It won't happen, Sam. We'll —"

"It's already happened!" He threw up his hands in frustration. "What crime did I commit? Tell me that. Did I take up arms against you? Did I spy for the enemy? Did I plot against you? No. All I did was disagree and refuse to keep silent about it. And for that your arbitrary, self-created tribunal called me a traitor. For that, they stripped me of my God-given rights as an Englishman. And when I protested, they" — his voice cracked — "they took everything. They tarred me and beat me and sent me to Simsbury Mine to die."

"Sam —"

"*That's* your liberty. *That's* your future. A country ruled by men who wield the mob like a weapon and don't give a damn for the law. Men who think they *are* the law."

Nate thought sharply of MacLeod and Farris, of their plans to pull everything down, of the fragile Continental Congress and the simmering unrest in the backcountry. "We won't let it be that way."

"You already have. You already —" Sam faltered, his anger collapsing abruptly, leaving him stripped and hollow. "You already let it be that way when they came for me and you said nothing."

Nate went cold, heat leaching from his bones. "What could I have said? What could I have done that would have made a difference? Would you have had me condemn myself as well?"

Sam's gaze lurched to the floor, his fingers strangling the neckcloth in his fist. His mouth opened as if to reply, but then closed in silence, jaw working as he chewed on unspoken words. With a frustrated shake of his head, he moved to the door, then stopped with his hand on the latch. He paused there for a long moment and Nate waited with breath held. For what, he wasn't quite certain.

Eventually, Sam spoke. "I don't know what you could have done," he said. "I only know that I wouldn't have — I *couldn't* have — watched you suffer and done nothing."

With that he was gone, closing the door behind him, leaving Nate alone in a bed that still carried Sam's scent.

Chapter Eleven

LIVERPOOL LOOKED NOTHING like the twisting old city of London.

Clean and modern, it rose in homage to British mercantilism, the wealth of an empire on display in its sparkling buildings and neatly planned streets. The city seemed to grow even as Sam watched, rising at the behest of the men who owned the vast wharves and warehouses that towered over its docks.

But as the chaise clattered along Liverpool's broad streets, Sam realized it was not so very different from the capital. Poverty lurked here, too. Thin, hungry people poorly dressed, and every other house open for the sale of rum. Plenty of wealth, no doubt, but the wealth wasn't shared. As in London — as it was everywhere in England — most people labored under the yoke of their masters, for little gain. It was difficult not to contrast it with Rosemont, where men owned their own land and labored for their own benefit. But that happy vision took no account of the enslaved men and women who labored on the Narragansett plantations,

or whose sale had enriched generations of Newport merchants…

Perhaps Rhode Island was not so different after all.

He cast a glance at Nate, who sat gazing silently through
the side window. He'd been preoccupied all morning, and
Sam felt much the same.

Last night… Christ, but his body still glowed with the
aftermath of that conflagration, like embers after a good
blaze. Knock off the ash and he'd be burning still. But it was
their argument this morning that had left him off balance.
Nate's final, frustrated question had touched a point of pain
deep inside him. A secret, unspeakable truth.

Would you have had me condemn myself as well?

He'd been unable to answer, his thoughts too tangled.

Because *no.* Of course he wouldn't have wanted that.
He'd *loved* Nate, had wanted only his safety and happiness.
He couldn't have endured seeing him tarred and feathered
and thrown into the back of that wagon with its dancing,
dangerous flame. Deep in his heart, Sam knew that to be
true.

And yet…

And yet at the same time, *yes.* The unspeakable truth
was that a cringing, craven part of him *had* wanted Nate at
his side. *Had* wanted him standing between himself and the
mob. *Had* wanted them together in the back of that stinking
wagon. In the depths of Simsbury Mine.

Christ, what a shameful admission.

A dangerous one too, because it was difficult to blame
Nate for staying silent when his silence and safety were
exactly what Sam's rational mind would have demanded.
That contradiction ran like a fracture through the core of
his resentment, splitting it wide open. And without its iron
grip on his heart, he no longer felt anger when he looked at
Nate's tight, pensive expression. Rather, he felt deeper emo-

tions stir, as if freed from the dungeon into which they'd been cast. Feelings like tenderness, and compassion.

Hopeless feelings.

Because a gulf — an *ocean* — still divided them, and Nate would soon sail for Boston while Sam must forever remain in exile. Nothing had really changed, and all that would follow any softening of his heart was more misery.

With a sigh, he turned back to the window. The air was pungent with the salt-tang of the ocean that spread out beyond the western horizon toward home. Next to him, Nate sighed and crossed his legs…

Long lean legs that, last night, Sam had felt pressed bare against his own as they'd tussled for the ring Nate wore about his neck. He stole a glance at Nate's throat, as if he might see the leather cord beneath his neckcloth. All these years, when Sam had felt so forgotten, so forsaken, Nate had carried his ring next to his skin. Whatever he'd done — or hadn't done — when the mob came for Sam, Nate had not forgotten.

And that…that meant more than Sam could bear to admit.

"What's the matter?" He started at the sound of Nate's voice. "You're fidgeting like you've got fleas."

He looked over and Nate offered an uncertain smile. Sam returned it, just as tentatively. The carriage rattled on and their gaze held. Words flitted through Sam's mind, timid as butterflies unable to land, and after a moment Nate turned back to the window with a heavy sigh.

"This document we're stealing," Sam blurted, desperate to break the silence. "What can you tell me about it?"

Nate stilled, and when he turned back around his expression was tense. "No more than Talmach already told you: that MacLeod keeps it in a strongbox in his study."

There was more, Sam could see it in his eyes. Nate was

hiding something. "And you don't trust me enough to tell me what it concerns?"

"It's not that. But I'm afraid —" His lips pursed. "I'm afraid Talmach instructed me not to, that's all. I'm sorry."

It shouldn't dismay him, and yet Sam's heart sank. Because, really, what else had he expected? He was an outsider now, an enemy of America. Of course he wasn't to be trusted.

Briefly, Nate touched his arm. "If it's any consolation, I'm not entirely convinced the damned thing even exists."

"Well." Sam allowed himself a wry smile. "I'm glad we're not wasting our time."

After a moment, and rather seriously, Nate said, "I'll never consider this a waste of time, Sam. I'll never regret finding you again. It's what I longed for."

Helplessly, Sam's spirits soared, and he was on the verge of confessing something stupid when a sound from the street distracted him, raising his hackles in alarm.

Liverpool was not a large city, at least not in comparison with London, and they were close to the docks around which the buildings gathered. A forest of masts loomed over the rooftops ahead, but it was the babble of noise, of men shouting and arguing loudly, that set Sam's pulse pounding.

It sounded like trouble.

Uneasily, he glanced at Nate. He'd heard it too and opened the carriage window to lean out. Sam crowded in behind him so he could see better. They were passing a large square full of men shouting and gesticulating wildly. For a sickening instant, Sam thought they were a mob, but then he realized that the men weren't arguing at all but swapping flag-like tokens in a frenzy of friendly activity. It took him a moment to understand what he was seeing.

"It's a merchant's exchange," Nate said softly.

Sam hummed in agreement and they watched the spectacle in silence as traders and ship-owners went about their business, oiling the wheels of imperial commerce in loud, bold voices. After a while, Sam said, "You know what it is they're trading here? Or, I should say, who."

Although there were only a few black faces to be seen in Liverpool, this city, like London, was at the center of the transatlantic slave trade. And these men exchanging tokens were, in fact, haggling over human lives.

"It's repulsive," Nate said grimly. "In these days of enlightened thinking, it's absolutely repugnant that it's allowed to continue."

"Men want to be rich and they don't much care how they go about it," Sam said. "No amount of enlightened thinking is ever going to change that."

"But I disagree." Nate turned around quickly, and they were suddenly very close. Neither pulled back. "The world *is* changing. Men's thoughts are changing. Powerful men. One day the law will sweep this trade away."

Doubtfully, Sam said, "You mean in America, where all men are created equal? So long as they're free white men?"

Nate looked anguished but, for once, Sam didn't feel the urge to push the point. After a pause, Nate said, "I can't say change will happen right away. God knows plenty of powerful interests are resisting it, but we're trying. In Rhode Island, at least, we're trying. Pushing for it. And one day — one day soon — this trade will end."

"I don't suppose 'one day soon' is much comfort to the people whose lives are being bartered here," Sam said, looking back at the exchange as the carriage began to turn the corner.

Nate sighed heavily. "No comfort at all. I know it's not good enough."

His distress twisted Sam's heart, fool that he was, and he found himself saying, "But I hope you're right. I hope your revolution changes things, at home and here. I'd like to see a world where this vile trade is outlawed forever."

Nate's eyes brightened. "On that, we agree."

"Yes." Sam couldn't help smiling again, his lips curling without permission. "On that, we always agreed."

Not long after they'd passed the exchange, the carriage pulled into the posting inn where they left the chaise. They'd made good time and so Sam got directions from one of the stable hands to a livery where they could hire a trap for the drive out to MacLeod's estate.

According to the liveryman, Marlborough Castle was no more than six miles from Liverpool — an easy drive before nightfall. Nate tentatively suggested taking a room for the night in town, but Sam didn't dare risk the temptation. He knew, if Nate reached for him again, he'd be powerless to resist. And then he'd be entirely lost.

Besides, there was work to be done.

And so, after a couple of bone-shaking hours on narrow, rutted country lanes, the little trap crested a hill and Sam got his first sight of Marlborough Castle.

A heavy lumpen building, it squatted on the far side of a meandering river, deep in a shadowed valley, projecting all the menace a Norman keep could muster. "God in heaven," Sam breathed, reigning in the pony as the valley widened below them. "Do you think he's expecting a rebellion? Look at all those towers and ramparts."

"John MacLeod enjoys the trappings of aristocracy very much," Nate said dryly, "but I understand his father was only ennobled twenty years ago." He threw a sideways look at Sam. "In recognition of services to the West India lobby, of course." By which he meant the sugar and slave trades. "Lord Marlborough's descended from pirates, not nobility. Young adventurers whose riches came from Caribbean sugar instead of Spanish gold. He's as fake as his fake castle;

this ridiculous monstrosity is no older than you or me."

Sam snorted softly and twitched the lines, urging the pony on. "I want to look inside the place tomorrow," he said after a while, "and find MacLeod's study. I don't suppose you know where it is, do you?"

"No idea, I'm afraid."

"Well, I can't spend hours searching the house in the dark. I'll visit tomorrow on some pretext and see if I can —"

"You can't go in there alone."

The urgency in Nate's voice surprised him. "Why not?"

"Because MacLeod's a vicious bastard, that's why not. What if there's trouble? It's too dangerous for you."

Too dangerous for you.

Sam found his gaze fixed on Nate's earnest profile. Ridiculous how those words fell on him like rain after a drought, but until that moment he hadn't known how much he needed… What? Nate's concern? His kindness? Lowering, to need another man's attention so much. But maybe, when you'd lost everything, even crumbs of consideration felt like a feast.

When Nate looked over, Sam didn't dare meet his eye. "There's a track off to the right at the bottom of the hill," he said. "Let's try there for a place to sleep."

The track wound through the trees until it reached a small row of tumbledown laborers' cottages, backed by a stream that Sam could hear but not see in the encroaching dusk. There was no smoke in the chimneys, no light nor sound of habitation.

"Hello there?" he called as he drew the trap to a stop. No reply. He glanced at Nate, feeling another butterfly flutter of warmth as their eyes met. "We're in luck, perhaps? Better than a night under the trees."

Sam jumped down and Nate followed more cautiously. He looked uneasy and moved around to take the pony's bridle, keeping her still while Sam went to investigate the cottages.

They were crudely built and ill-repaired, rags at the windows shifting listlessly, a door creaking as it swung in the breeze. At the end of the row someone had built an animal shelter, but part of the roof had fallen in. The whole place reeked of abandonment.

"There's no one here," Sam said as he peered into one of the empty cottages. "I think we're safe to stay the night. The fireplace looks usable if we can find enough dry wood."

Nate eyed the place dubiously. "I hope there's no disease."

"No disease." Sam moved to the trap to retrieve their luggage. "This is what the English call progress, I reckon."

"Ah." Nate grasped his meaning. "These belong to MacLeod, then? He evicted his tenants before he enclosed his land."

"Probably." Sam shot him a glance. "London's full of folk turned off common land so that men like MacLeod can enrich themselves."

"If the British Parliament represented its people, instead of a handful of aristocrats and sugar barons, maybe it wouldn't allow these enclosures that impoverish them?"

Sam handed him his portmanteau. "There's plenty here who'd agree. You think only America understands liberty, Nate, but you're wrong. The British aren't sleeping, and they're not fools, either. But war and violence are no way to change a bad lot."

"Sometimes they're the *only* way." Nate put up a hand to forestall Sam's argument. "But it doesn't follow that they're always the best way. I agree." He smiled, cautious and — God damn it — sweet. "*We* agree, Sam. Again."

They looked at each other. "Maybe," Sam conceded.

"Just like we always did."

Until the end, until it had come to the crucial question

and they'd found themselves marching to the beat of different drummers. Sam sighed, turning his attention to the pony. "We should see to her while it's still light. At least there's water here and some grazing."

"So long as MacLeod doesn't catch her on his land."

Sam began unhitching the pony from the trap. "I don't think his reach can be quite *that* long."

"If it *is*," Nate said, "we'll have more to worry about than the damn horse."

Chapter Twelve

IT WAS ALMOST dark by the time Sam had finished settling the pony and pushed open the door to the ramshackle cottage. Nate had gotten a blaze going in the smoky fireplace, and Sam found him unwrapping the food they'd bought at the posting inn.

His stomach growled at the sight of the bread, cheese, and thick wedges of pork pie. Apples too. A veritable feast. He sighed in anticipation.

And then Nate looked up, smiled, and Sam froze.

Nate sat cross-legged on the floor near the warmth of the fire, shirtsleeves rolled up exposing his tanned forearms. Firelight gleamed against his hair, picking out coppery threads and turning his dark eyes liquid. He looked just the way he used to when sitting by the fire in Sam's parlor, all black and gold, vibrant and passionate and so very full of life. Sam missed him so badly it hurt.

"Come and eat," Nate said. "It's good."

Nodding, not risking his voice, Sam dropped down on the opposite side of the fireplace. Nate produced his knife and began to slice the bread and cheese into chunks, setting the pieces between them. They ate in silence, Sam concentrating on the sharpness of the cheese and the sweetness of the apples to keep from looking at Nate and remembering the passion they'd shared last night. Christ, his body still resonated like a struck bell. He was surprised Nate couldn't feel the reverberations.

But it had been the sight of him sleeping this morning, so beautiful and peaceful, that had truly undone Sam. His heart had damn near burst when he'd woken to the sight of Nate's tangled hair falling across his face and those elegant lips slightly parted. Rare had been the times they'd woken in the morning together, even back in Rosemont, and the moment had felt precious.

And had rendered him stupid.

To caress Nate like that, to permit himself any tenderness, had been foolish. Reckless, even, and he'd pay a heavy price. Yet he longed for more: another smile, another touch, another night.

It was like quenching your thirst with saltwater — entirely self-defeating. Because Nate was still Nate and Sam was still banished. Nothing material had changed.

He found himself cursing the times in which they lived. Fifty years ago, he and Nate might never have known war. They might have lived out their days in Rosemont, intimate friends in the way the world allowed. And quietly, privately they might have loved each other and been happy. Instead, the world had convulsed beneath their feet and thrown them down on opposite sides.

And it kept them there still.

From outside came the night-time hoots and rustles of the woods, inside there was only the crackle of the burning logs. In other circumstances it might have been peaceful. But tonight, the air was alive with tension. Every time Sam glanced up, he found Nate's gaze just slipping away from him, his bottom lip caught between his teeth.

He'd taste like apples, sweet and sharp. Like Nate himself.

Sam licked his lips and found Nate's eyes on him again, catching the firelight. Full of invitation, pulling Sam out like a dangerous tide.

He had to resist.

"You should stay here," he said, finishing his last slice of pie. "I'm going to survey the house."

"Now?" Nate looked alarmed. "In the dark?"

"We'll be escaping in the dark. It's best to reconnoiter in the same conditions."

"As every thief knows?"

"And every fugitive."

Nate considered that but didn't comment. "I'll go with you," he said. "For protection."

Sam paused in wrapping the remains of the cheese and stowing it safely in his bag for tomorrow. "I don't need your protection. I've walked the streets of St Giles at all times of night without coming to harm, I think I'll outwit a couple of badgers and a fox."

"I was talking about *my* protection," Nate said, eying the dark window. "I don't want to wait here alone."

"Don't tell me you're afraid of the dark."

Nate bristled. "Let's just say I'm not so fond of all this bucolic tranquility. As you may remember, I'm a born and bred Bostonian."

Sam gave a soft grunt. Of course he remembered. He remembered everything about Nate, starting with the day he'd walked into Reed's office with the crisp fall sunshine glinting in his hair, palpable tension in his lithe body, and an arrogant flash in his eyes. He'd looked so dazzling, so urbane and out of place, that Sam had wanted him even before he'd recognized his own desires.

Nate had known, though. Nate had known from the start. "I remember you didn't even know how to fish."

"But you taught me." Nate glanced up and they shared a long look. "And in return, I gave you Voltaire and Paine, Rousseau and Barnfield."

"Among other things." Like joy, companionship — and love. Most of all love. "Christ, I thought we'd always be —" His voice caught, and he stopped talking, embarrassed.

"I thought so, too," Nate said softly.

A log shifted in the grate, sending a fountain of sparks up the chimney. Into the live silence, Nate said, "Let me come with you tonight. It's better if we stick together."

Their gaze met and held. Neither said it was always better when they stuck together. Perhaps it didn't need saying. Or perhaps it was simply Sam's wishful thinking.

Either way, they finished packing away their food without further debate and headed back down the lane, walking in silence. When they reached the road, they stopped, regarding Marlborough's estate laid out before them. Lights blazed in the upper windows of the house, reflecting in the river that wound around the property. Out on the road, all was dark.

Sam said quietly, "I'm worried about that river."

"Really? Why?"

He glanced over at Nate but couldn't see much of him bar the gleam of his eyes and the moon-washed lines of his face. "See the bridge?" From their vantage point on the hillside, the road swept down and away to the left, past the entrance to Marlborough Castle. Its approach crossed the river by way of an ornamental bridge, all gargoyles and ramparts. "It's our only way over the river."

"You're concerned that we'll be visible."

"Yes. And if we need to make a run for it, that's the place they'll stop us. Put a couple of men on the bridge and we're trapped."

"Then we need an alternative escape route." Nate squinted into the distance. "What about up into the trees behind the house?"

"That's the obvious direction, but we'd still be on the wrong side of the river."

"Isn't it the only direction if we can't use the bridge?"

"Not if there's another way to cross. We can both swim…"

A sudden memory assaulted him: Nate, naked in the river, warm and slick in his arms. It was so visceral he could feel the slide of Nate's skin against his chest, the hot press of his lips against his throat.

"We can," Nate agreed with a look that suggested his thoughts were running in a similar direction. "But we'd be sitting ducks in the water — so to speak."

Sam cleared his throat, looking away. "And you'll want to keep your stolen papers dry."

"Don't worry about that. I have an oilcloth pouch to protect them."

"Alright. But a fording point would be safer. If there is one, I want to find it tonight."

When they reached the river, Sam found it wasn't as wide as he'd feared. He led the way along the bank, heading towards the bend where the river swung closer to the castle. That would be the shortest escape route.

Late as it was, lights still glowed in the castle's upper windows, but he was pleased to find the riverbank still swathed in shadows. Darkness would be their friend tomorrow.

He stole another glance at Nate. Sharp profile, slender shoulders, a lock of dark hair drifting loose from his queue: he looked so familiar tonight, as if no time had passed since that day Nate had kissed him on the banks of the Pawtuxet and changed his life forever. No cicadas sung in the grass here and the breeze was cooler, but it still sighed through the reeds and the green river scent still perfumed the air. Underfoot, the grass still sprung softly.

Sam fought a powerful urge to take Nate's hand and twine their fingers together. Instead, he tried to summon his terror of the mob and the suffocating darkness of Simsbury Mine, but the memories were distant. Tonight, there was only the burble of water and the feel of Nate walking so close their shoulders brushed.

"How about there?" Nate spoke quietly, pointing to a place where the river ruffled into foamy peaks. In the moon-light, his slim hand looked pale against his black coat sleeve. Sam wanted to capture it in his own.

"Looks possible," he said instead, heading down to the river. Nate matched him stride-for-stride. The water had cut into the bank on their side of the river, but on the opposite bank a sliver of beach lay exposed and there were one or two rocks poking up from the water halfway across. "I'll try it," Sam decided. Dropping down on the grass, he pulled off his boots and stockings, and took off his coat to keep the tails from getting wet.

Nate watched with unblinking attention, his intent gaze making Sam's pulse spike. "You're going to be short of dry clothes if you fall in."

"I'm not skinny-dipping, if that's your suggestion."

"Now there's a thought."

Sam tried to scowl, but it turned into an unwilling smile. "Hell, Nate." He swung his legs over the bank, felt the cold water catch at his feet and watched it running around his ankles. "How is this so easy for you?"

"Being with you was always easy. Easiest damn thing in the world."

Sam closed his eyes. Easiest thing in the world until it had been impossible. Levering himself off the bank, he slipped into the water, sucking in a breath at the cold, his feet squelching on the muddy bottom. But the water only came halfway up his shins. He rolled the legs of his breeches up a little higher.

"You should have taken them off," Nate called softly from the bank.

"Shut up." Feeling his way, arms flung out for balance, Sam inched through the water. It became stony and painful beneath his feet, the water running fast, but at its deepest it only reached his knees and after a couple of minutes he was up on the shingly shore.

Nate stood watching, a lean shadow in the dark. He looked a lot like the Nate of Sam's memory: the one whose eye he'd always wanted to catch, the one whose smile he'd always wanted to provoke. And for a moment he thought, *maybe.* Maybe he could wade back across, pull Nate into his arms, and let the resentment and loss flow away with the river. Maybe he could forget about everything else and let himself love and be loved again.

Maybe it was possible.

In the distance, a dog barked. Then another. Sam cast a wary glance over his shoulder. It was probably just MacLeod's hunting hounds in their kennels, but nevertheless he made his way back across the river.

Nate crouched on the bank, tension narrowing his eyes as he watched Marlborough Castle. "MacLeod's vicious," he said when Sam reached him. "He probably has vicious dogs."

The bank was higher on this side — which would pose a problem if they had to flee in haste — and Sam struggled to push himself up. He'd got one knee on the bank when Nate grabbed his arm and hauled him the rest of the way. "Some-one's there," he hissed. "Come on."

Sam grabbed his boots and coat, following as Nate darted back from the river toward the woods. In the distance the dogs still barked but Sam heard no sound of pursuit as they

ducked into the shadow of the trees. "Ow," he hissed, tread-
ing on something sharp in his bare feet.

Ahead, Nate stopped and came back. "Get your boots on,"
he said, scanning the riverbank. He was nervy as a cat, and
Sam wondered what he knew that he wasn't saying.

Shoving his feet into his boots and his arms into his coat,
he said, "Come on." When Nate didn't move, Sam touched
his wrist to draw his attention from the house. "Nate, come
on." And somehow that touch lingered. Somehow, Sam's
fingertips were tracing over Nate's knuckles. And somehow
Nate's hand turned beneath his own and their fingers tangled, threading together, pressing palm-to-palm. Nate's eyes
were very wide, full of questions that quickened Sam's pulse.
But all he said was, "We can cut through the woods to the
cottage."

He led the way and didn't release Nate's hand.

They'd been walking in silence for some time before Nate
said, "MacLeod *is* dangerous, Sam. He's a violent man, a
gambler and a bully. If he were to catch you…"

"I'm not afraid of him." Sam let his thumb trace Nate's
knuckles. He didn't ask himself what he was doing; it was
easier to ignore in the dark. "What can he do to me? I've got
nothing left to lose."

Nate made an exasperated sound. "You've got your life,"
he said, and stepped in front of him, putting a hand to his
chest to stop him. "If he caught you, I'd —" He gave a frustrated shake of his head.

Sam stared, intensely aware of Nate's warm fingers
against his chest. Every touch drove his good sense further
away. "You'd what?" he said roughly. "If MacLeod caught me,
you'd what?"

Nate took a step closer, spreading his fingers until his
palm lay flat over Sam's racing heart. Could he feel it beating,
pounding against his ribs? "I watched them hurt you once.

Do you think I could let it happen again?"

"I don't know—"

"Christ, Sam, of course I couldn't." He closed his eyes, and in a quieter voice said, "I wish I could undo that night. I wish none of it had ever happened. I wish—" His forehead dropped onto Sam's shoulder, his hand fisting into his coat. On a shivery breath, he whispered, "I wish you still loved me."

Those soft words pierced him. "Don't." He put a tentative hand on Nate's shoulder, feeling the tremor of his muscles beneath his fingers. "Please don't."

But Nate didn't move, he just stood there with his head bowed, shoulders shaking. And Sam couldn't stand it. Helpless against a deep rush of emotion, he put his arms around Nate and drew him close.

God in heaven, but it was a relief. He felt it in his bones, as if his whole body had been hurting silently for years and he only now recognized that hollow, persistent ache as longing. Longing for this, for Nate. For home. Tightening his arms, he buried his face against Nate's shoulder, and they clung to each other beneath the sighing boughs of the trees.

After a while Nate lifted his head and gazed into Sam's eyes, nothing but the rustling woods and the distant burble of the river filling the silence. Sam studied him. There were lines around his eyes that hadn't been there before, a sorrow in his face that only accentuated its sharp beauty. Sam lifted his hand to touch his jaw.

"You don't wish none of it had ever happened," he said softly. "The revolution is your passion, your *raison d'être*."

Nate's eyes glittered but he didn't deny it.

"You told me once that it was bigger than both of us, that our happiness didn't matter compared with the tyranny you were fighting."

"Maybe I was wrong."

"I don't believe you think so."

Jaw tight, Nate pulled out of his arms. "That doesn't mean I don't regret what it cost me. Or you."

"But it *does* mean you'd make the same choices again, if you had to."

Anguished, he scrubbed a hand across his eyes. "God, I wish we'd lived in different times, Sam. I wish we'd never known this damned war."

"And if wishes were horses, beggars would ride." Sam sighed, shoving his hands into his pockets to keep from reaching for him again. "Nobody wants to live in times like these. But here we are and all we can do is make the best of it."

"And what's that?"

"We had those years together. And we have our memories." His throat ached, thickening his voice. "Perhaps, if we can learn to look back on them with pleasure instead of pain, it'll be enough."

Nate stared at him. "It doesn't feel anything like enough."

"I know. But what else can we do? We are where we are."

In the distance, MacLeod's dogs started barking again, sending a shiver up Sam's spine. He looked back towards the river and Marlborough Castle, its lights gleaming faintly through the swaying branches. "Come on," he said, holding out his hand. "Let's go. One more day and we'll be on the road back to London."

And what then? Nate would sail for Boston, that's what.

And they'd have to say farewell forever.

Chapter Thirteen

THE NEXT MORNING, Nate found Sam down by the stream behind the cottage, shirtless and bootless as he bathed, sluicing water over his head. In the morning light, the scars on his back were less vivid, washed away by the brilliant sunlight. But still there. Those scars would always be there, on Sam's back and on his heart.

And on Nate's conscience.

"Sam?"

When he turned around there was none of that snapping resentment Nate had learned to expect. After their conversation in the woods last night, Sam's bitterness had softened into something gentler — more like melancholy — and Nate wasn't sure which was more painful to witness. Nevertheless, Sam smiled at him as he grabbed his shirt and used it to dry his face and hair. "Morning. Did I wake you?"

"I don't mind." In truth, he'd hardly slept, too alive with frustration and regret. Unlike Sam, Nate simply couldn't accept that the only thing left between them was memories. He refused to accept it. "I wanted to talk to you."

Sam's expression turned wary. "About?"

"Nothing bad." Dawn was a blush on the horizon, the sky turning from rosy to morning gray. In the soft light, Sam's damp curls looked dark where they fell forward over his forehead. "I've been thinking about today, that's all. About finding MacLeod's study."

"I've been thinking about it too," Sam said. "I reckon I should reconnoiter by myself. It's not worth the risk of MacLeod recognizing you."

"Well, I was thinking the opposite. What if I call on MacLeod?" He lifted a hand to forestall Sam's protest. "I'll tell him I'm there on Farris's business. With luck, I'll be admitted to his study."

"I don't like that."

"Why not?"

Sam gave him a speaking look. "He knows you, Nate. If you show up today asking questions, and tomorrow he discovers this document of his is missing…? I doubt he's a fool." His expression brightened. "Better if *I* call on him, like you said. He doesn't know me from Adam. I'll give him a false name and tell him Farris sent me to…what? You can give me a reason he'll believe. I'll find the study and look for a good route in and out."

Nate barked a laugh before Sam's indignant expression told him he wasn't joking. Schooling his face, Nate said, "You think you could convince MacLeod that you work for Farris?"

"Why not?" His eyes narrowed. "You're not the only lawyer in these parts, Nate Tanner. I know what I'm doing."

"I still think it's safer if I go."

"Well, that's not your decision," Sam said, straightening. "And it's not worth the risk of him linking you to the break-in when he doesn't know me, and I can go in your place."

Nate opened his mouth to protest, but there was logic

to Sam's argument that he couldn't ignore. It *would* be a disaster if MacLeod linked him to the theft. He'd tell Farris and that could expose Nate's identity, wrecking their entire mission. Talmach would probably drop him headfirst into the Thames. "Alright," he conceded reluctantly. "But I'm still coming with you. I'll pose as your servant and see what I can find out downstairs. Unless MacLeod brings staff down with him from London, which I doubt, his servants won't know me."

Sam lifted an eyebrow, amused. "You'll pose as a servant?"

"Why not? I can scrape a bow as good as the next man." He demonstrated, affecting a terrible London accent as he bowed over his leg. "Very good, Mr. Hutchinson, sir." He gave a suggestive wiggle of his eyebrows. "How can I serve you today?"

"You're a hell-born devil," Sam said, clearly fighting a smile. "And far too aristocratic to be a manservant."

"Aristocratic!" Nate feigned outrage. "How dare you?" But he grinned, delighted by the mischievous sparkle in Sam's eyes. He hadn't seen it in years.

"I guess we both need to spruce ourselves up if we're to pass muster," Sam said, gaze running over Nate's body with an interest that thrilled him. "And we'll need some breakfast."

Still smiling, Nate turned back to the cottage to fetch his shaving kit.

"Wait." Sam grabbed his wrist, tugging him back around. His mouth moved as if rehearsing words, but after a pause he dropped Nate's arm, fingers flexing at his side, and only said, "Be careful today."

Nate smiled, his heart full. "You, too."

AS THEY DROVE across the bridge some hours later, the great monstrosity of Marlborough Castle loomed before them as if torn from the pages of a Gothic romance. Gloomy even on this summer morning, Nate wouldn't have been surprised to see a ghostly figure haunting its faux battlements.

Imitation it might be, but MacLeod's castle still had the power to chill. That had more to do with the bastard who owned the place than any fear of malevolent spirits.

Sitting next to him on the trap, Sam nudged their shoulders together and they shared a quick smile as Nate drew the pony to a halt. They'd driven from the cottage, Nate posing as Sam's driver, and he stayed put while Sam trotted up the stone steps to rap on Marlborough's ostentatious front door — all gargoyles and grotesques. Sam tugged at his coat sleeves as he waited for an answer, the nervous gesture so painfully familiar that Nate had to smother a sharp pang of affection lest it show on his face.

"Mr. Hutchinson for Lord Marlborough," Sam said when the front door opened to reveal a lavishly liveried footman. "On a matter of business."

Nate held his breath as the footman looked Sam up and down, no doubt assessing his travel-worn appearance and threadbare cuffs. "I've come direct from London," Sam explained with his easy smile. "On behalf of Mr. Farris."

Oh, how Nate loved that smile.

Evidently it was enough to charm the footman because Sam was admitted into the dark maw of Marlborough Castle. At the last moment, he glanced over his shoulder just as one of MacLeod's men approached to direct Nate toward the stables. Sam turned away, stepped into the shadows, and was gone.

Nate swallowed his unease and reminded himself to focus on his own business. Sam could take care of himself, for heaven's sake. He'd been doing so for long enough. Nate's plan, such as it was, involved speaking to the servants and gleaning, if possible, any information that might prove useful.

To that end he handed the stable boy a coin in exchange for keeping an eye on his horse and asked the way to the kitchens. "I could do with some breakfast," he said with a smile.

"You'll be lucky." But the lad pocketed his coin, nonetheless, pointing him toward a small black door at the side of the house.

It opened with a creak into a scullery. Two girls were working hard, sweaty beneath their caps and up to their elbows in dirty, greasy water. They spared Nate a curious look but said nothing as he crossed the room and stepped into the heat and bustle of a busy kitchen. A dozen delicious aromas assaulted him at once — baking bread and roasting meat chief among them — and his stomach growled even though he'd eaten some of the leftover bread and cheese for breakfast.

"Can I help you, sir?" A girl looked up from rolling pastry on the large table that dominated the room. She wore a pale dress and white apron, her sleeves pushed up to the elbows and ruddy hands covered in flour. Nate guessed she was no more than fifteen years old.

He doffed his hat and sketched a bow, conscious that he was somewhat too well-dressed to pass as a servant. "I beg pardon for the intrusion," he said, hoping his accent would distract the girl from any other inconsistencies in his performance, "but my master's visiting his lordship this morning and I was hoping for a bite to eat while I wait."

The girl glanced toward the head of the table where a tall, broad-shouldered woman stood surveying the kitchen much like a general on the field of battle. The cook, he surmised. "I'd have to ask Mrs. Sturge, sir," said the girl

"I'd be much obliged if you would." He offered her a smile and was amused to see her blush as she wiped off her floury hands on her apron.

The cook — Mrs. Sturge — fixed the maid with a beady look as soon as she left her station, her quick gaze darting to Nate as the girl talked to her in low tones. He watched the woman straighten while she scrutinized him, no doubt taking in his too-gentlemanly appearance and cautious about what it might signify.

"My name's Reed, ma'am," Nate offered. "And I don't mean to put you to any trouble." He spread his hands and attempted to mimic Sam's charming smile.

Mrs. Sturge folded her arms, uncharmed. "We're not an inn, sir, and we're busy. We've house guests." Her expression tightened. "Viscount Rowsley and his retinue."

Nate regarded her carefully, noting her intelligent eyes and meticulous neatness of dress. This was a woman with professional pride, but not a woman impressed by Viscount Rowsley. Nate allowed himself a more honest smile. "Well, naturally the needs of a viscount must come before a man such as myself."

"Naturally." Her expression remained entirely proper, save the sparkling of her eyes.

"No matter which of us is the most deserving."

Mrs. Sturge's eyebrows rose but she didn't respond. Instead, she said, "You're an American, Mr. Reed?"

"Indeed I am. You recognize my accent? There's many who wouldn't." Few outside Britain's largest port cities would ever have heard an accent like his. "You've heard it before?"

Mrs. Sturge's expression narrowed and she looked away. "Sarah, fetch Mr. Reed a slice of ham and the heel of yesterday's bread. And a glass of beer."

"Well, thank you, ma'am," he said. "I'm much obliged."

The girl — Sarah — bobbed a quick curtsy and hurried to do as she was bid.

"We had a little American girl here once," Mrs. Sturge

said. "His Lordship brought her over as a… companion, of sorts, for her ladyship. From his South Carolina plantation."

An unpleasant and not uncommon story. "I see. Is the child no longer here? I'd have liked to meet her."

"No, she's gone." Mrs. Sturge looked away, getting back to her work.

"Gone back?"

"Nobody knows. One morning, she'd simply disappeared."

He didn't like the sound of that one bit. "What do you mean, disappeared?"

"Quite the mystery. His lordship was furious. Taylor took a beat —" She corrected herself, but when she looked up the sparkle was brighter in her eyes. "Taylor admitted he may have left the kitchen door unlocked that night and was punished for it. But perhaps the fairies took her."

"The fairies?"

One eyebrow arched. "We don't approve of enslaving people here."

"Ah," he said. "Well, plenty of Americans would agree with you."

While he ate his meal, set before him by the blushing Sarah, Nate pondered the fate of the child who Marlborough had brought over. By the sounds of it, his rebellious servants had conspired to free her and, while their actions were laudable, there was a hint of moralizing in Mrs. Sturge's expression that grated.

True enough, the British held few slaves in their own country, but they had plenty laboring on their West Indian plantations. And surely Mrs. Sturge knew how her master made his money? The money that paid her wages every week, the money that built Britain's fine ports and cities, the money that financed her empire.

Sugar money. Slave money. Blood money.

But perhaps out of sight really was out of mind.

"Ah, here's Taylor," Mrs. Sturge said. "He knew Milly best; she took a liking to him."

Taylor turned out to be one of the liveried footmen, sober beneath a gray, powdered wig that made him look older than his face suggested. In fact, Nate thought, he was about Nate's own age and appeared from a set of stairs Nate hadn't noticed. He carried a tray laden with used glasses and plates and set them down near the scullery with a blustery sigh.

"They're still bloody going," he complained, snatching off his wig to scratch his head, making his short hair stand up in spikes. "It's like Bedlam up there."

Mrs. Sturge cleared her throat pointedly and nodded towards Nate. When she told Taylor that he was an American, the footman looked over with interest.

"Oh, aye?" He set his wig on the table. "I took your side in the recent business, Mr. Reed. Followed it in the papers."

"Taylor," Mrs. Sturge scolded. "No politics."

"Why not? You know plenty of people felt the same."

Nate swallowed his mouthful, wiping away crumbs with the pad of his thumb. "You don't know which side I was on."

Taylor looked confused. "The American side, I assume."

And that was how it must appear to outside eyes. To some American eyes as well, no doubt. But Nate knew better than most that theirs had been a civil war, too, with all the pain and grief that entailed. "Of course. I supported the cause of liberty."

"Could do with some of that around here," Taylor said, and set about unloading the tray. "Fat chance with the likes of his lordship in charge." A stifled hush settled over the servants, a sense of all ears pricked and listening, of silences held. "What?" Taylor looked around. "I'm not saying anything you don't think."

"Perhaps the rest of us value our positions," said Mrs.

Sturge, with a wary glance at Nate.

He spread his hands. "Don't mind me, I've gone deaf all of a sudden." He offered Taylor a smile. "And I understand you keep all the doors locked at night, these days. Just in case of fairies."

"Fairies? Oh, aye." He grinned. "More than my life's worth to forget. I don't regret what happened with little Milly, mind. She's far better off where she is." Mrs. Sturge tutted, but Taylor just winked. "Wherever that may be."

A clatter of feet on the servants' stairs interrupted them and a maid rushed into the kitchen, looking rather wild. "It's Lord Rowsley," she gasped, catching her breath. "He's singing in the long chamber and…and…" Her face flushed scarlet. "Relieving himself in the fireplace."

Mrs. Sturge's lips tightened. "Very well, thank you Beth. Taylor?"

"For the love of…" He wedged his wig back in place. "This," he said, pointing at Nate as he stalked past, "is why you lot had the right of it. Bloody nobs, do whatever they like and bugger the rest of us."

Nate smiled but didn't comment, taking note of the fact that the servants loathed their master, and that the doors would be locked tonight.

"WAIT HERE PLEASE, sir."

The footman disappeared down a long corridor, his shoes clacking on the white marble floor, leaving Sam in a vast mausoleum of an entrance hall. Stone pillars edged the space, between which the dead-eyed gaze of austere marble busts regarded him with suspicion. MacLeod's esteemed ancestors, no doubt.

Pirates, according to Nate, ruthless young buccaneers who'd settled in the West Indies, discovered sugar cane, and amassed vast fortunes off the backs of enslaved laborers.

Now their descendants masqueraded as aristocrats. But perhaps all aristocrats were descended from brigands if you looked back far enough.

Opposite the entrance, a beautiful grandfather clock stood against the far wall, measuring out time with a patient tick-tock. A slow heartbeat in this dead space. A pair of matching footmen, no more than half an inch between them in height, stood sentinel either side of it, dressed in knee breeches, braided coats, and powdered wigs. Handsome, Sam noticed, if your taste ran to tall, athletic, and fair. A pair of human ornaments. He wondered whether it was Lord or Lady Marlborough who relished the sight of their well-shaped calves.

At the back of the hall rose an enormous staircase, sweeping up and around to an entresol overlooking the doorway. The lord of the manor could stand there and look down on his subjects like a king surveying his domain. As with every-thing about Marlborough Castle, it appeared designed to intimidate. And it told Sam everything he needed to know about its master.

Under the guise of gaping in awe, he attempted to create a mental map of what he could see. Double doors stood open to his left and right, through which he could glimpse more marble and opulence. An explosion of male laughter drifted through the doors on his left, from a more distant part of the house. This would be where MacLeod entertained, but his study would be part of the suite of rooms in which he conducted private business. Upstairs, more than likely. Sam eyed the sweeping staircase with distaste. It would be much too exposed to use when he came back tonight, but as he carefully scanned the hallway, he saw an inconspicuous door virtually hidden amid the walls' wooden paneling: the servants' stairs. These great houses all had them — passages and staircases that allowed the servants to move about the house like rats behind the wainscoting, hiding their honest work from aristocratic eyes. God forbid Lady Marlborough encounter a maid carrying her husband's night water downstairs.

But servants' stairs or not, Sam would need to see more than this damned entrance hall if he were to find MacLeod's study, and that would depend on whether he was permitted inside. Nate had assured him that Lord Marlborough was not so aristocratic that he left his business in the hands of an agent, but Sam was more skeptical. In his experience, men of MacLeod's position liked to pretend their fortunes were God-given, preferring to leave the unseemly matter of running their affairs to others. In which case, Sam would be taken to MacLeod's man of business who might be in the wrong part of the house entirely.

A door opened and the footman who'd admitted him returned. His expression was studiously blank, but Sam could see strain around his eyes and mouth. Tension, or perhaps fear. In London, MacLeod had a reputation among his servants for brutality, and Sam could see no reason why he'd behave any differently in the countryside. While there may be no slaves in England, men like MacLeod treated enslaved workers on their plantations with unspeakable violence and cruelty. Surely such savagery must scar their souls, must bleed into the ways they treated their servants at home?

"Lord Marlborough will see you now," the footman said. "This way, sir."

Hiding his surprise, Sam followed the man upstairs. At the top, he found a circular landing from which two corridors led in opposite directions. The footman took the one to the left, at the end of which stood a large door embellished with a coat of arms in gold leaf. MacLeod's suite, no doubt. But the footman stopped at another, smaller door, opened it and stood back to allow Sam to enter. "Please wait here, sir.

Lord Marlborough will be with you directly."

"Thank you," Sam said, catching a flicker of alarm in the footman's expression. God forbid anyone acknowledge the servants! And then the door closed behind him and Sam was alone.

Quickly, he looked around and couldn't believe his luck.

He stood in what was either a library or MacLeod's study. The walls were certainly lined with bookcases, although they were barren of actual books. Many shelves stood completely empty, and those that were filled contained only ledgers, a couple of atlases, and a selection of bibles. Neither novels nor poetry were to be found. Nate would consider it a travesty, Sam thought, but it was exactly what he'd expect of a man rapacious in the pursuit of money and with no love for anything beyond wealth, power, and status. Sam doubted MacLeod had read a book for pleasure in his life.

A tall window extended from floor to ceiling, an extravagant use of glass. Had this been a real castle it would have been defensively useless, but the window cast plenty of light across the huge desk that sat before it. Like everything else, the desk was large and commanding. It also appeared to be well used, which suggested Nate was right about MacLeod's involvement in matters of business.

He looked back at the door, listening, but all was quiet outside. Hurrying over to the window, he glanced out and saw a formal garden stretching out before him — the back of the house, judging by the angle of the sunlight. One floor below him a long balcony stretched the entire width of the house, onto which a set of French style doors stood open, letting in the warm summer breeze. That might be a good way in. Now, where was the damned strongbox? It must be —

Behind him, the door handle squeaked.

Sam darted away from the window and spun to face the door, hands clasped behind his back and heart thudding.

The footman reappeared. With a stiff bow, he announced, "Lord Marlborough."

John MacLeod didn't wait for his servant to move aside, barging past as he strode into the room. He was a big man, powerfully built with wide shoulders and a thick frame. Gimlet eyes and downturned lips spoke of a short temper, and an old-fashioned wig, yellowing with age, sat askew atop his head, giving his tan face a sallow hue. He was exactly what Sam had expected: a plantation owner playing at gentility with all the finesse of a hog taking tea. And he was dangerous. Sam didn't need Nate's warning to know that; he could see it in MacLeod's flinty eyes as they peered out from the fleshy folds of his face.

Sam bowed. "Lord Marlborough."

"And you are?"

"Holden, sir. Amos Holden."

"American?" MacLeod crossed the room to his desk, flicking out his coattails as he sat. "Damned business over there. Hang the bloody lot of 'em, I say. Damned traitors."

Unable to agree, Sam bowed again and said, "I'm come from London at the request of Mr. Farris, my Lord, to assure you that the contract has been drawn up and awaits your signature at your convenience."

Those were the words Nate had given him to say. Sam had held his silence about Nate's involvement in a deal between a brutish plantation owner and an infamous slave trader. In truth, he hadn't needed to say a thing; Nate's discomfort when he'd explained had been evident in the drawn line of his mouth and the slight flush in his cheeks. And it had served as a sharp reminder to Sam that Nate would sacrifice anything — even, apparently, his principles — in the name of the American cause.

MacLeod leaned back in his chair, regarding him with shrewd eyes. "A damned long way to send a man. I told him

I'd be back in London in a se'night."

"I have business in Liverpool, my lord, and was honored to oblige Mr. Farris in this matter."

"Is that so?" His gaze didn't waiver. "A friend of Farris, are you?"

Sam hesitated. "An acquaintance."

"What did you say your name — ?" A thud against the door and the muffled sound of an argument interrupted him. "The devil?"

Another thump, rather like a body falling against the door, made the handle rattle. Alarmed, Sam braced himself for trouble. Had Nate had been recognized?

Before he had time to worry, the door fell open and a panicked footman stumbled in, struggling to keep the very drunk man in his arms from collapsing. "My Lord," he was imploring, "you can't go in —"

"What the devil is this?" MacLeod roared.

The footman flinched, trying to turn and wrestle the other man out. "My deepest apologies, Lord Marlborough, I was attempting to —"

But MacLeod was already on his feet, storming around his desk. "I don't give a damn what you were attempting —" He stopped abruptly. "Rowsley."

The drunk pulled himself upright, hanging onto the doorframe with a nonchalant elegance that should have been impossible for someone so deep in his cups. But even foxed, the man was unspeakably elegant. Beautiful, in fact. Sam couldn't stop staring.

"Marlborough," Rowsley drawled, shaking back loose hair that fell in dark curls around his exquisite features. "What the bloody hell are you doing? We're still at cards."

MacLeod shoved the footman aside so hard he stumbled and fell, catching his chin on a sideboard as he went down and dislodging a vase of silk flowers that tumbled to the floor. Sam winced, but MacLeod didn't seem to notice, all his attention — suddenly obsequious — fixed on the newcomer.

"I've some small matters of business to attend to, my Lord." He took Rowsley's arm. "But you —"

"Business? Dear God, leave it to Cavendish. That's what I do."

"Very wise, my Lord." MacLeod's mouth twisted into what was probably meant to be a smile. "Perhaps you should — ?"

"And who's this?" Rowsley's gaze landed on Sam, flicking over him with an interest Sam might have found exciting in another man at another time. Here, it made him extremely uneasy.

"One of Farris's men, come down from London on some damned fool errand."

"He looks very obliging," Rowsley said, his gaze lingering. It appeared rather too frank to be wise, but Sam supposed that men like Rowsley could do as they pleased. "*Are* you obliging?"

"My obligation today, my Lord, takes me to Liverpool." He glanced at MacLeod. "If my business with Lord Marlborough is concluded?"

"Yes, yes." MacLeod was too occupied with Rowsley to give Sam a second look. "Tell Farris to call on me in London, Thursday next. We'll finish the business then."

"How sordid," Rowsley complained, yawning elegantly. Sam got the impression there was nothing the young man could do that would not be elegant.

MacLeod didn't seem interested in that, however, landing a meaty hand on Rowsley's shoulder. "Allow me to escort you back to the card room, my Lord. Cavendish will be —"

"You know, perhaps it's time for bed." Rowsley laughed, a brittle sound like the breaking of fragile glass. "Cavendish has taken enough from me for one night."

One *night*? It was the middle of the morning.

"Oh, come now," MacLeod said, guiding him out of the room, "your luck is sure to turn, my Lord. It must! Nobody plays whist as well as you…"

Sam, forgotten, stayed silent as MacLeod and Rowsley turned to leave, but the footman climbed to his feet with a murderous look in his eye. A gash had opened on his chin, bleeding profusely, and the poor man had cupped a hand beneath it to keep the blood from dripping onto the carpet. His expression was bleak, all humiliation and fury.

For a panicked moment, Sam thought he might go after Marlborough and God knew that wouldn't end well. "Here," he said, intercepting before the man could move and holding out his handkerchief. The footman stared at it as if a gentleman offering assistance was about as likely as pigs growing wings. Maybe it was, in this country. "It's alright," Sam said. "Take it before you ruin the carpet."

Still breathing heavily, clearly enraged, the footman took the handkerchief and pressed it to his chin. After a pause, he said, "I'm sorry for —"

"Don't you dare," Sam snapped. "MacLeod's the one who should damn well apologize. He's got no right to abuse you like that."

After a considered pause, the footman said, "Only an American would think like that. In this country, he don't need the right because he's got all the power."

"Even Lord Marlborough is subject to the law."

"Oh, aye? And who's the bloody judge, do you think?" The footman eyed him cautiously, still dabbing his chin. "But you know how it is, don't you? You lot know there's only so many times they can knock a man down before he starts fighting back. You showed 'em that."

The fire in his eyes was bright, just like Nate's. Just like Amos Holden's. Sam's gut pinched. "In my experience, violence rarely achieves anything but more violence."

"Perhaps. But it's the only language these nobs understand."

His words could have come straight from Nate's mouth and Sam felt his hackles rise. Yes, MacLeod was a bully and a brute, but that didn't mean his footman, or anyone else, could take the law into their own hands. Only anarchy and misery lay in that direction.

Maybe some of what he felt showed on his face, because the footman lost color, crouching to retrieve the fallen vase and scattered flowers from the floor. "I apologize, sir. I've spoken out of turn."

"No. Good God, you're entitled to your opinion." With the footman's back turned, Sam glanced over his shoulder at MacLeod's desk. Where the devil was his strongbox? "If I don't share your opinion," he went on, moving carefully towards the desk, "it's only because I've seen what... what violence and chaos can do to a people. I don't wish that kind of conflict on any country." He edged around the side of the desk. "And I believe — I hope — that change can be peaceful."

The footman grunted, setting the vase on the sideboard as he arranged the flowers back inside. "If you think this lot will change anything unless they're forced to it, you're fooling yourself."

"I..." He scanned the bookshelves and the floor. "I think the law is the only way to curtail a man's power, be he commoner or king." There! Hiding in the shadows under the desk. People always thought that was such a safe hiding place. "And if you trample the law to take power, there's every danger you'll trample liberty to keep hold of it."

The footman turned at that, words on his lips. They died there when he saw Sam, attempting to look nonchalant, behind MacLeod's desk. After a wordless silence, the footman said, "That's as may be, but I think I should show you out now."

Sam lifted his hands, to demonstrate that they were empty. "Simply admiring the view from the window, Mr....?"

A hesitation. "Taylor," he said, expression drifting somewhere between doubtful and rebellious. "Come on, his lordship won't be pleased to find you still here and I don't need another smack on the jaw today."

As he followed Taylor out and back down the stairs, he heard male laughter rising from one of the salons below. MacLeod and his friends, Sam supposed. Casually, he said, "Do they do this every night?"

"Viscount Rowsley and his companions are lively company, sir." Clearly, Taylor wouldn't speak so freely here, where he might be overheard. "And Lord Marlborough is generous with his hospitality."

"Which is lavish, I'm certain. No doubt the gentlemen make great use of his many salons and dining parlors?"

Taylor shot him a curious look. "They do, sir."

And Sam sincerely hoped the gentlemen *preferred* those rooms to the more intimate chambers upstairs. Even so, it would make his job harder tonight if the household were awake and cavorting instead of safely asleep when he slipped inside. Still, better to know it now than to find out later. He would need to be extra careful, that was all.

Taylor escorted him to the front door, click-clacking across the vast marble entrance hall, and fetched his coat and hat. The gash on his chin looked painful, swollen and bruised, but he met Sam's gaze with his servant's façade back in place. He offered a silent bow which Sam returned.

Then Taylor opened the door and Sam saw Nate bringing the trap around to the front of the house. His spirits rose in helpless relief and pleasure, and he could have kicked himself for being such a sentimental fool.

Nevertheless, departing Marlborough Castle with Taylor's eyes on his back, left Sam feeling disturbed. Wrong, in a way he couldn't define. As if a truth were flickering at the corner of his eye, hovering on the tip of his tongue.

A truth, perhaps, that he'd rather not grasp.

Chapter Fourteen

"ROWSLEY'S GOING TO be a problem," Sam said.

They crouched in a dark stand of trees just past the bridge, gazing at Marlborough Castle. Even after midnight, lights blazed in the upstairs rooms.

"If they're up playing cards, the servants will be awake, too." On Sam's instruction, Nate was tying a black silk scarf around his mouth and nose, to hide his face should they be spotted inside the house. It muffled his voice when he said, "And the kitchens will certainly still be in use. We can't get in that way."

"No, we'll have to break in elsewhere."

As he spoke, Sam jostled his shoulder against Nate's. The contact sent little sparks dancing over Nate's skin and he allowed himself to press back, to take comfort in the feel of Sam next to him. "That sounds risky."

"It is risky." Only Sam's eyes were visible, gleaming in the dark above the scarf covering his face. "Which is why you should wait here. Just tell me what I'm looking for and I'll fetch it."

Even if he'd been able to tell Sam what he was looking for, Nate would still have refused to wait outside. "What if you get caught? I won't let you face MacLeod alone."

Sam gave him a measured look but didn't respond, just adjusted his hat, pulling it lower over his eyes. With his face half hidden beneath black silk and shadow, he looked like a rogue, like a highway robber. Attractive in a way more dangerous than Nate had expected from the gentle man he'd known in Rosemont.

"Come on, then," Sam said, rising to a low crouch and starting to move towards the house. "Follow me and stay quiet. We don't want to set off the dogs."

Nate was anxious about the dogs and kept a nervous eye on the kennels. But Sam ran quickly and softly, and the dogs stayed quiet. He led Nate along the side of the house, bringing him around to the back. There, a grand set of stairs ran up to what appeared to be a long balcony across the breadth of the building, although on closer inspection Nate could see that there was another set of stairs leading down at the other end. At the mid-point stood a set of elegant French doors made up entirely of windows, which would lead onto the main floor of the house where MacLeod entertained his guests. Bedchambers and other personal rooms would be on the floor above.

The back of the house was dark, and he and Sam crept up the steps, keeping to the shadows until they reached the doors. Moving back, Sam scanned the floor above and then pointed to a dark window to the left of the door. "That's it," he whispered. "That's his study."

"Are you sure?"

"Yes." He flashed Nate a look that was barely a glitter of moonlight. "I've done this before, you know."

Which was still difficult for Nate to imagine so he simply nodded. "But we can't climb up the outside of the building."

He glanced at Sam dubiously. "Can we?"

A soft laugh. "No. But watch." Stepping forward, he pulled something from his coat pocket. It jangled quietly as Sam knelt by the door and inserted it — a key? — into the lock. After several moments of jiggling, he removed it, inserted something else, jiggled some more, cursed beneath his breath, removed that, and tried a third time. Nate glanced around, looking out at the dark gardens, ears pricked for the sound of footsteps. They'd be dreadfully exposed should anyone approach, with nothing but moon shadows to hide them. His pulse quickened as time stretched longer.

Sam swore again, fiddling with the lock, but finally there came a quiet click. "*Yes.*"

That triumphant hiss made Nate smile despite the way his heart thudded as Sam rose, turned the handle, and pushed open the door. It creaked. Both froze, waiting. Nothing happened. With care, Sam cracked the door a little wider, just enough that they could slip through the gap.

With a gesture, Sam indicated that Nate should follow as he drifted like a shadow through a room lit only by moonlight. Nate did his best to copy his stealth, but it became apparent that Sam had learned new skills since leaving Rosemont. It was difficult to reconcile his life as a criminal with the upright lawyer Nate had known in America, but that honest man had been made an outlaw in his own land and Nate could hardly fault him for acting the part in England. Especially not tonight.

Sam stopped at the room's door, put a finger to his lips and cocked his head, listening. From deeper in the house came the sound of carousing: male laughter and female giggles. He and Sam shared a look. With luck, the gentlemen — so called — would be too busy to notice the occasional creak of a floorboard.

Creeping from the room, Sam made his way along the

corridor to a discreet door at the end. He set his ear to it, listened, and then turned the handle. It opened silently onto a dark staircase and they both slipped inside. No carpets here. Nate's boots scuffed on bare stone because these were the servants' stairs. When he closed the door behind him, it was suddenly pitch black; they had no candle to light the way and no window to let in the moonlight.

Ahead of him, he heard Sam suck in a sharp breath. Then another. He sounded panicky. Blindly, Nate put out a hand and found Sam's arm, squeezing hard. A moment later, Sam's hand closed over his, fingers gripping tight. Nate moved closer, close enough to whisper, "What's wrong?"

After a long silence Sam said, "For a moment, I was back in the mine. It was very…" His swallow was audible. "Very dark and confined."

Simsbury. Nate's stomach clenched with a queasy mixture of regret and anger. He tightened his hold on Sam's arm. "Let's get out of here. Come on. Do we go up?"

"Up, yes."

Keeping hold of Sam's hand, Nate fumbled around until he found the banister and then led them up a narrow, turning staircase until he saw light bleeding beneath a door on the next landing. He stopped there, the scant light revealing Sam's shape next to him, all shadow and glistening eyes. "MacLeod could be up here," Nate whispered. "The lamps are alight…"

"Do you want to go back?"

"No. I doubt tomorrow will be any better."

"And at least the light will make it easier to find his rooms." Sam put his hand on the door, then paused, glancing back. "If there's trouble, get out anyway you can. Make for the fording point in the river, or up into the woods behind the house if you must. Avoid the bridge. We'll meet at the cottage if it's safe."

Nate's heart began to pound in earnest, cold fear prickling the back of his neck. Perhaps sensing it, Sam reached out and squeezed his hand. Nate squeezed back hard. Then, without another word, Sam opened the door and led them out into the hallway beyond.

After the dark of the stairs, it was bright, and Nate had to blink a couple of times against the glare. The hallway was wide and luxurious. A thick carpet ran along the center and there were lamps placed along the walls at ostentatiously close intervals. Had they all been alight, the corridor would have dazzled. But Nate wished more of them were doused; there were precious few concealing shadows. At least the carpet allowed them to creep along in silence.

They were halfway down the corridor when footsteps echoed from a large hallway ahead. Grabbing Nate's arm, Sam ushered them back against the wall. They pressed themselves flat. At the end of the corridor the house opened onto a wide circular landing, and Nate watched with breath held as a liveried servant crossed the space carrying a tray of empty glasses. If the man turned his head, he'd see them, and all would be lost. But he didn't, he walked straight past and disappeared. After a moment came the sound of his footsteps receding downstairs. Nate let out his breath as softly as possible, shoulders sagging.

In silence, Sam led him onto the marbled landing where they'd seen the servant. It stood at the head of a grand staircase and, beyond it, Nate could see a short corridor leading to an enormous door. Gold leaf gleamed on the elaborate heraldry carved around the frame: two lions rampant supporting a shield that bore the image of a castle, perhaps meant to be Marlborough Castle, topped by a knight's helm. Ridiculous.

Sam threw him an amused look. "MacLeod's bedchamber, at a guess."

"Or throne room. Where's his study?"

"Not far." They crept down the corridor towards MacLeod's monstrous bedroom door but stopped before they reached it. Quietly, Sam turned the handle of a less ostentatious door — it wasn't locked — and slipped inside. Nate followed, closing the door behind them. Only moonlight illuminated this room, but Sam moved unerringly around a huge desk that sat in front of the window and crouched down behind it.

Nate followed and saw Sam examining a large strongbox partially hidden beneath the desk. It looked impenetrable with a complex locking mechanism on its lid. Nate glanced uncertainly at Sam. "Can you open it?"

"Yes." Sam flashed him a look, difficult to read in the shadows, but perhaps a mixture of pride and shame. "But it'll take a few minutes."

From his pocket, he produced a roll of leather which he unfurled on MacLeod's desk. Inside were several tools which Sam took a moment to examine. Then, selecting one, he crouched down next to the strongbox and inserted the tool into the lock, leaning down with his ear pressed to the top of the box. Was he listening to it?

With nothing to do but watch and wait, Nate found himself all too conscious of the men and women carousing downstairs. And the possibility — the likelihood — that they'd repair to their bedrooms for further pleasures at any moment. The thought of capture made his breathing shallow and his head light. Deliberately, he held his breath for a count of four before releasing it and doing the same again, a trick Talmach had taught him one night when they'd been too close to the British lines for comfort.

A metallic click from the strongbox startled him and he saw Sam smiling, reaching for another tool before inserting it into the lock and bending to his task once more. The moonlight spilling in through the window turned him to silver and black, his hair steely and his face shadowed. But Nate could hear his soft, measured breathing as he concentrated, and it amazed him to realize that he remembered the sound. He'd heard it many times, in the quiet of the fireside as they read together. In bed while they drowsed in each other's arms.

It was quite a thing to know the sound of another man's breathing.

And standing there in the dark room, it struck him painfully that, once this brief interlude was over, he'd never hear that sound again. He'd never see Sam again. Their reunion was inescapably fragile and fleeting.

"Got it!" Sam's quiet exclamation jerked Nate from his unhappy thoughts, and he watched carefully as Sam turned the large locking mechanism on top of the strongbox. It moved with a gentle cascade of clicks before Sam, grinning, lifted the lid. "There you go."

"Impressive."

Rising to his feet, Sam stepped back. "Find what you're looking for and be quick about it."

Nate crouched, wishing he had a lamp but not daring to light one. The strongbox was well organized, at least, and he picked carefully through ledgers and papers, lifting them into the moonlight to read. Meanwhile, Sam went to stand sentry by the door. What they'd do if he heard someone coming, Nate couldn't imagine. Climb out the window? They were two floors up!

He shook the thought aside, refocusing on his search. Shipping manifests, correspondence with creditors and debtors — Nate noticed Rowsley's name cropping up frequently among the latter. Setting them aside, he discovered another batch of letters and shuffled quickly through them, skimming for anything of interest. And perhaps he wouldn't have recognized the letters for what they were had his eye not been snagged, as if by a fishhook, by one name: *Samuel Hutchinson, Rosemont, RI.*

Nate's breath caught, gaze shooting up to where Sam stood listening at the door. For an instant their eyes met and held before Nate looked down sharply. Pulse racing, he scanned the rest of the letter.

Samuel Hutchinson, Rosemont, RI. — Estate confiscated, tarred and feathered, imprisoned at Simsbury Mine (8 months, escaped). Evacuated to London. Impoverished. Open to financial inducement?

It had been sent by a man called Edward Cavendish in March of that year and contained a list of several men under the title: *Refugees sympathetic and potentially useful.*

Potentially useful for what? He remembered suddenly that MacLeod had told Farris of men in London keen to strike a blow against the government that had stripped them of everything. But not Sam. Surely not Sam.

Hurriedly, he looked through the rest of the letters in the bundle. Sure enough, they contained similar lists, some from this man Cavendish but many from other men. All naming names — known Loyalists, King's Men, and Tories. Men deemed sympathetic to MacLeod's cause.

Shit and damnation, was his network of subversives real after all? Only now, when he held the evidence in his hands, did Nate realize how much he'd hoped MacLeod's brags had been empty.

"Are you nearly done?" Sam hissed from the door.

With a jerky nod, Nate rolled the letters together and rearranged the inside of the strongbox to disguise their absence.

"Can you lock the lid?" he asked Sam. "The longer he's unaware they're missing the better."

Sam crossed the room and bent to relock the box, casting a curious glance in Nate's direction. Not knowing what to say — hell, not knowing what to *think* — Nate busied himself bundling MacLeod's letters into the protective oilcloth pouch in his haversack.

What did it mean that Sam's name was listed among these potentially useful contacts? He watched as Sam stood up, the moonlight casting stark light over his face. Had the war made him so bitter that he'd do harm to his country? That he'd be part of an insurrection against its duly elected government?

No. Impossible.

There was no world in which Sam would be part of any such scheme. Nate couldn't believe it. Sam hated violence; it wasn't possible that he'd do now what he'd sacrificed everything to refute five years ago.

Sam cocked his head. "I take it you found what you wanted?"

Hardly that. God, he almost laughed at the irony; this was the last thing he wanted. Out loud, he said, "I did."

Sam's gaze lingered, considering, but he didn't ask more. Nate was grateful. He didn't want to lie, but telling Sam he held a list of suspected Tory subversives in his hands — Sam's name among them — was unthinkable. It would endanger every tentative step toward reconciliation they'd taken, and Nate dared not risk it.

Saying no more, Sam touched Nate's shoulder as he moved around the desk, leading him back to the door. After listening carefully, Sam opened it and slipped out into the corridor. Nate followed. He took a moment to close the door behind them and spared a grateful thought for the servants who oiled the hinges so assiduously.

But just as he was hurrying to catch up with Sam, he heard the cold click of a door opening behind them. He spun around in fright, his breath hot and panicked beneath the scarf covering his face. Shit. *Shit.*

John MacLeod, Baron Marlborough, stood in the doorway to his room, backlit by a dazzling array of lamps, sans wig and wearing nothing but a shirt and breeches. Behind him, the wide-eyed woman in his bed gathered the sheets around herself. MacLeod's face purpled apoplectically. "What in the devil's name — ?"

Nate bolted.

Ahead of him, Sam, white-faced with alarm, stumbled briefly but recovered himself and sprinted out onto the landing. He didn't bother with the cramped servants' stairs, instead flew down the grand staircase. Still ten yards behind him, Nate's boots skidded on the slick marble floor of the landing as he tried to catch up, MacLeod's bellow chasing him down the corridor.

"Thieves! Stop them!"

The house exploded into life.

Nate flung himself down the stairs, but Sam had already reached the entrance hall below, dashing for the front door. A footman, panicked by the sound of his master's shouts, raced to cut Sam off.

"Stop the bastards!" MacLeod roared.

Nate jumped at the sound, almost losing his footing as he pelted down the stairs. McLeod loomed above him now, standing on the balcony overlooking the hall as he shouted. With a nimbus of lamp-lit gray hair around his head he looked like a mad Roman emperor.

"Stop them or I'll have your damned hides!"

The footman threw himself in front of the door, arms spread wide to block Sam. But his face was milky in the shadowy hall, his eyes distressed. And Nate knew him: it was Taylor, the footman he'd met that morning.

Sam didn't waste time on niceties. He launched himself at Taylor, trying to barrel him out of the way. But the man was strong, wrestling Sam to a halt. Running footsteps came from everywhere and as Nate leaped down the last of the stairs, he could see the shadowy entrance hall filling with servants in all states of confusion and undress.

Someone grabbed his arm and he lashed out, sprinting for the door. Ahead, the butler in his dressing gown lunged for Sam, who let out a yell and kicked the man hard, sending him stumbling back to land on his ass. Nate skidded around him, barreling into the footman still wrestling with Sam.

Taylor's hands were locked on Sam's coat, but his gaze shot up to MacLeod, raging at the top of the stairs, then back to Sam. Understanding passed between them. Nate saw it — a silent look, a moment of decision — and Taylor's hands fell from Sam's coat. Eyes wide with fear, he let Sam push him aside.

"You piss-bucket whoreson!" MacLeod charged down the stairs, something glinting in his hand.

Nate's gut pitched. "Shit. He's got a gun!"

A woman screamed; the sound cut off abruptly. Nate didn't dare spare her a look, his gaze locked on the wavering pistol as MacLeod strode across the hall towards them.

Towards Sam.

And there was only one thing Nate could do. "Go," he hissed as he stepped between Sam and the gun. "Run."

"Like hell I will."

"For Christ's sake." Nate lifted his hands in surrender, fixing his gaze on MacLeod's lumbering approach. "Will you save yourself for once in your goddamned life?"

Chapter Fifteen

THE DOOR STOOD open behind him.

Cool night air caressed the back of Sam's neck, stirring his hair. Blood thundered in his ears, it was all he could hear, yet even so he was aware of an airless waiting stillness among the servants. And he knew without doubt that they'd seen MacLeod wield this weapon before, that he used it to dispense arbitrary justice. It's what happened when a man's power went unchecked by the law, when he considered himself above the law.

"Who are you?" MacLeod demanded. "Show your face."

Nate said nothing. But Sam could hear the rasp of his breathing, saw the swift rise and fall of his shoulders. He was afraid, but he was not backing down.

"Tell me who —"

"Lord!" A bored patrician drawl drifted from between the marble busts that lined the entrance hall. "What the devil's going on, Marlborough? It sounds like a damned riot."

MacLeod's gimlet gaze twitched sideways. "Nothing to trouble yourself with, my Lord."

"Ain't it?" Rowsley emerged from between the sculptures as if a Greek god had been brought to life — one of the dissolute and disreputable ones. Afraid to look away from MacLeod, Sam still caught a glimpse of dark hair, a slender body, and a sensual swagger. "Have you caught yourself a highway man, Marlborough?"

"Thieves, my Lord. Or spies."

"Spies!" Rowsley crowed. "What the devil are they spying on up here? The number of tarts it takes to get a rise out of you?"

MacLeod's complexion darkened. "Go back to your cards, my Lord." The honorific dripped with contempt, his aristocratic veneer wearing thin. "I'll deal with this matter."

"Nonsense." Rowsley strode further into view, coatless and louche with a bottle of wine dangling from the fingers of one hand. His gaze flitted over Nate and Sam, then turned back to MacLeod. "Don't you have magistrates up here in the wilds? Or a man of business who can take care of this for you?"

"I prefer to conduct my own business," MacLeod said, the gun barrel dipping as his attention shifted to Rowsley. "And I *am* the magistrate."

Of course. The law didn't touch men like MacLeod. Here, as on his plantations in the colonies, he did as he pleased with impunity. And Sam realized with a jolt that MacLeod was exactly what Nate had taken up arms to resist: a petty despot, an autocrat. A tyrant.

"Well," Rowsley said, dry as a bone, "that must save time…"

MacLeod grunted, looking displeased and, for a moment, distracted. "Lord Rowsley, do me the honor of returning to the card —"

Sam grabbed Nate by the collar of his coat and yanked him backward towards the door. He caught a glimpse of

Taylor's grim face as he shoved Nate out ahead of him, sending them both stumbling down the steps. "Run!" he barked. "Now!"

Behind them, MacLeod began to roar. But they were already sprinting away from the house. "Not the bridge!" He wrenched Nate sideways, swerving away from the men on the bridge. Behind them came the crunch of running footsteps on gravel, shouts, and curses.

A gunshot.

Sam skidded, flinching, and looked back to see MacLeod staggering down the front steps, waving his pistol like a riding crop. "Whore-mongering thieving bastards!" he thundered and leveled the gun at them.

"No!" A blur of movement and Nate plowed into Sam, knocking him sideways as a second gunshot cracked the night, its echoes rebounding against the castle walls.

Sam staggered, momentum carrying him too far, and went down on his shoulder. Nate landed on top of him, pinning him in place for a moment before he rolled away onto his back.

"Nate?" Sam scrambled over to him, but there was no time to stop. Shouts of alarm rang out behind them and the gun fired for a third time.

"Jesus Christ!" That was Rowsley's cry, bright and horrified.

When Sam looked back, he saw a man sprawled on the ground. Motionless. Rowsley watched from the doorway, a hand pressed over his mouth, while MacLeod aimed his weapon again.

Cursing, Sam grabbed Nate under his arms and dragged him to his feet. "Get up! Run!"

With teeth gritted, Nate staggered forward. A riotous commotion rose behind them, and ahead ran the slick black line of the river. But Nate was lagging, slowing down, so

Sam grabbed his sleeve, propelling him forward. "Jump!" he barked and together they launched themselves off the bank and hit the water with an icy shock.

Deeper here than downstream, the current moved faster. Sam shot to the surface, but Nate came up slower, spluttering and struggling like something was dragging him down.

Sam hauled him up. "What the hell are you doing? Swim!"

"Can't —" Under he went, fighting back to the surface. "Arm…"

Breathless with cold panic, Sam turned Nate around, one arm locked around his chest and leaned them both back in the water. "Stop struggling," he hissed in his ear. "Nate, stop. I've got you. Let the river take us."

Gradually, Nate stilled, but he was panting hard, grimacing in obvious pain, and clutching his left arm. Sam's heart pounded hard with fear. If anyone came to the bank, they'd be seen — two pale faces staring up at the cloud-whipped sky.

But no one came.

"Nate," Sam whispered against his wet hair, "are you hurt?"

"Shot, I think. Left arm."

"Shit." Lightheaded with terror, Sam tightened his hold around Nate's chest and tried to stay calm. "It's alright. Just lay still until we get our feet under us."

Above, he saw the bridge, watched as they floated silently beneath it. Still no one looked. The men on the bridge were gone but he could hear distant cries, a woman sobbing — and the frantic sound of baying dogs.

Abruptly the river narrowed, speeding up where it looped around to the left. Sam felt a drag against his feet as the rocky bed caught his boots and, together, they scrambled upright, finding themselves chest deep in water near the fording point. Nate stumbled, woozy, and Sam clamped his arm around his waist. There were lights on the far bank, shouting and barking. Men searching with dogs.

He seized Nate's face with one hand, searching it for the truth. "Can you walk?"

A tight nod. "But we should go further downstream. They'll check the fording point — the dogs will track us…"

That was true, but Nate was bleeding. They'd have to stop soon, if only to bind his wound. "Come on," Sam said, keeping hold of Nate's arm as they waded through the shallows, sticking close to the bank. The water grew deeper again, up to his waist, the ground underfoot slippery and difficult to navigate in his waterlogged riding boots.

Nate stumbled, face ashy, and Sam hauled him up again. It was too dark to see the blood seeping through Nate's fingers, but the dogs would smell it bright as a damned beacon.

Marlborough Castle was to the left of them as they moved along the river, letting it take them behind the house. Lights on the bank moved, searching methodically. They should keep going, but Nate was slowing, losing his balance. Sam stopped, put a finger to his lips, listening. Dogs, men's raised voices — calling to each other, not shouting — the lap of the river, the shushing of the trees. Here, the bank was less steep, and the trees were closer, leaning their branches over the water. It would do.

Sam pushed himself up and out of the water with a grunt, the heavy weight of his sodden clothes making it difficult. Then he reached back down and helped Nate climb out, landing him like a fish on the bank. They lay there together for a moment, breathing hard, but Sam couldn't let them rest.

"Into the trees," he whispered, pushing to his knees. "Come on. Move."

With a groan, Nate got himself up and at a half-run they staggered into the woods. Only once they were deep enough into the trees did Sam let Nate stop and sink down with his back to a tree as he sucked in heavy breaths.

"Let me see," Sam said, crouching before him. "Nate, let

me see your arm."

"It's alright." Gingerly, Nate peeled his fingers away from the wound. "I don't think it's bad?"

"Yeah, well, I'll be the judge. Let me see."

Nate turned his head away while Sam checked his wound, looking back toward the castle through the trees. Dogs still barked. Lights still moved on the far bank. Beneath Sam's fingers, Nate trembled. "Did you see his face?" he whispered. "His… His arrogance, his complete disregard for…for common humanity. He'd have shot us like animals and thought nothing of it."

"I saw." Sam's hand stilled, watching the clench of Nate's jaw. He swallowed and added, "He looked like every tyrant who ever lived."

Nate's eyes gleamed in the dark. "Or every leader of a mob."

They shared a long look, Sam's breath quickening in a way that had nothing to do with MacLeod's pursuit. He felt a connection, or, rather, a reconnection. Something slipping back into place. It stole his breath.

A dog's loud bark made them both jump, Nate starting almost to his feet. Sam held him down. "Other side of the river," he murmured. "Let me bind your arm before we move."

Tugging free his neckcloth, Sam wrapped it around Nate's arm. "Grit your teeth," he warned, and tightened it hard. Nate clenched his jaw and didn't cry out, but all color washed from his face. Sam gently squeezed his shoulder. "That'll do for now. Can you walk some more?"

"As long as I don't try walking on my hands." Nate's grin looked wan, but it was enough to flood Sam with relief.

He offered his hand, Nate took it, and Sam pulled him to his feet. For a moment Nate swayed, bracing himself on the tree, but then he nodded. Ready.

They made their way through the woods, walking as silently as possible. There were other men in the trees now, down towards the fording point but on their side of the river. And they had dogs. Sam could hear their yaps and each time he did, Nate's muscles stiffened beneath Sam's fingers.

Cautiously, they made their way back towards the cottages. Sam needed a place to properly see to Nate's wound, and that was by far the closest. But he was wary. And as they drew nearer, the sound of voices ahead stopped him in his tracks. He could hardly see Nate in the dark but felt his vibrating tension next to him, his breathing short and shallow.

Sam crouched, drawing Nate down with him. Leaning close, he murmured against his ear, "Stay here. I'm going to investigate."

Nate didn't look happy, eyes wide with alarm, but he nodded and settled down in the undergrowth. Grateful for the rest, Sam imagined, although Nate would never say as much. Wrapping his scarf around his face again, making everything about himself dark, Sam crept forward until he could see through the trees to the lane and the row of abandoned cottages.

A young man stood there, a dog snuffling around his feet.

Suddenly, the door to one of the cottages — *their* cottage — banged opened and an older man emerged. Like the first, he was dressed rustically. A gamekeeper, perhaps. The dog ran over to him, jumped up and the man casually stroked its head with a murmur of affection. "Good girl. Get down now."

The dog obediently dropped back to her haunches, snuffling around again. Getting closer to the trees where Sam hid. Shit. He didn't dare retreat for fear of making a noise those canine ears would hear.

"Someone's been here," the man said, his accent thick and

difficult to understand. "Fire's still smoldering and there's a pony tethered down by the burn."

"Well, nobody's here now," said the man with the dog. "And I'm not staying up all night looking, not after what he done to poor Taylor. God rest his soul. Good luck to 'em, I say, if they stole from that fucking bastard."

Sam's heart lurched. Taylor was dead? Was he the man shot outside the house? Killed for allowing their escape. He felt sick with guilt, hands suddenly sticky as if with the man's blood.

"That fucking bastard's your master, boy," the gamekeeper said. "And he'll snuff you out like a candlewick if he thinks you're shirking."

"Then we'll tell the bastard they drowned."

Sam forced himself past the shock. Time enough later for self-recrimination, now he had to get Nate to safety. But this was a desultory search, he realized, by men who had no love for their master. How long would they keep looking? Fear might buy compliance, but it could never buy loyalty. That was a lesson the British had failed to learn in America, and it appeared MacLeod had made the same mistake.

But the damned dog was getting closer and suddenly she went very still, her whole body making a sharp arrow that pointed right at Sam.

Shit. Shit and fuck.

"He'd want to see the bloody bodies," the older man was saying.

"Eaten by fishes?"

A grunt of grim laughter quickly cut off as the game-keeper noticed his dog's posture. "Oh aye," he said warily. "What've you got there, Bess?"

"Probably a rabbit." The younger man shifted nervously, and Sam noticed he held a hefty club in his hand.

"Let's see, shall we?" The gamekeeper gave a short whistle

and the dog launched herself forward, heading straight for Sam. He couldn't run. Even if he'd been able to outpace the beast, he'd only end up leading her straight to Nate. Instead, he stood up. He'd at least meet his fate on his feet.

The dog jumped up at him, paws landing on his chest, barking, and Sam fell back, arms flung up to shield his face. But he felt no scratch of claws or teeth and at another sharp whistle the dog sank onto her haunches, watching him. Distantly, over the frantic pounding of his heart, he noticed that her tail was wagging furiously.

"Come out," the gamekeeper called, "or I'll have her pull you out by the balls."

Carefully, eyeing the dog, who eyed him back enthusiastically, Sam edged towards the tree line. Keeping his hands lifted, he stepped out into the lane.

The man with the club watched him warily, the weapon held loose at his side. Seeing him more closely, Sam realized he was a youth. Not even twenty, perhaps. Thin as a beanpole. And nervous.

"I don't mean anyone any harm," Sam said carefully, reaching up to tug the scarf from his face.

The gamekeeper said, "You're trespassing on Lord Marlborough's land."

"I'm leaving."

"Are you now?"

"If you'll let me."

The gamekeeper didn't answer, his gaze darting past Sam's shoulder. After a moment he sighed and said, "You can come out an' all."

Sam closed his eyes. Naturally, Nate couldn't damn well stay put.

The dog yapped, jumping to her feet, tail whipping backward and forward as she watched Nate emerge from the woods. He looked even worse than before. Bedraggled from the river, his face ashy and his eyes deep pits, he clutched his bound arm, cradling it against his chest. Sam's neckcloth was black with blood.

Instinctively, Sam went to him, putting an arm around his shoulders. "For God's sake, sit down."

Nate shook his head, eyes fixed on the dog.

The gamekeeper let out a heavy sigh, muttered an unintelligible curse beneath his breath, and called the dog to heel. To Nate, he said, "He winged you, then."

"Yes." Nate spoke through clenched teeth.

"Ah, bollocks," said the younger man. "I hoped you were poachers."

"We're leaving," Sam said. "We've done no harm to anyone, I swear it. And we won't be back. If you let us go —"

"If we let you go?" said the gamekeeper. "Lord Marlborough would have our balls for breakfast."

"Only if he finds out, which he won't."

Silence. The young man swung his club anxiously. He had a thoughtful, unhappy look about him. A boy who felt too much, perhaps. Who thought too much. Sam knew the type. "He's injured." The boy's eyes locked with the gamekeeper's and something passed between them. "If we take them back…"

The gamekeeper's jaw clenched. "I know."

"We could kip in the woods?" the younger man suggested. "And tell Marlborough we were out looking all night. He'll be none the wiser. He's got Rowsley and his lot to keep sweet after what he done to Taylor." Another silent communication. "He won't have time to bother with us."

"So you hope. But he'll be looking for someone to blame and I couldn't stand if he took that out on —"

"I know. Me neither. But if we take them in *knowing* what he'll do? That'll be on our heads, won't it?"

"Better that than —"

"Is it?"

They shared another long look, then the gamekeeper squinted up at the night sky. "Ah, fuck it, you're right."

The younger man hid a smile and said nothing more.

Sam risked a glance at Nate, but he was watching the two men with rapt attention. "We won't cause you any trouble," he said. "I swear it. We'll leave right away and not return."

The gamekeeper's eyes dropped to the ground, he scratched behind the ear of his dog. "We'll search further into the woods and come back at dawn. Make sure you're gone."

"You have our word," said Nate. "And our gratitude."

A grunt of acknowledgment, then a curt command to his dog who stood up, watching him. He exchanged another glance with the young man and together they walked up the lane, past the cottages, the dog trotting along at their heels.

Sam's knees felt suddenly weak with relief. And Nate sagged at his side with a soft grunt of pain. "Come on," Sam said. "Let's hitch up the pony and get the hell out of here."

Chapter Sixteen

DAWN HAD ALMOST broken by the time they reached Liverpool and Sam had secured lodging at an inn close to the docks — one used to merchants and travelers keeping strange hours.

Now, Nate sat on the floor of their small room in front of the fireplace, knees pulled up to his chest and his forehead resting on them. His injured arm hung slack at his side, his hand curled into a loose fist on the bare floorboards next to the rug, and the neckcloth that served as a bandage bloomed scarlet. The prospect of having to dig around and remove a piece of shot from Nate's arm left Sam a little lightheaded, but he'd learned enough at Simsbury about treating the wounds of others to at least feel ready. Bracing himself, he touched Nate's damp hair to rouse him. "Nate."

He looked up, blearily. "Ready?"

"Let's get your coat off first. On your feet." He offered a hand and Nate took it with his good arm, letting Sam haul him upright and steady him. "Alright?"

"Good enough." Nate looked pasty in the firelight, even

though he smiled. "Hurts."

Taking care not to jostle him, Sam untied the makeshift bandage, grimacing at the amount of blood.

"It's still damp," Nate reminded him. "Blood spreads in water."

"I know. Now your coat." He slipped it carefully from Nate's shoulders, but Nate still hissed when the sleeve dragged over his injured arm. A long hole sliced the fabric, a tear the width of Nate's bicep. The same was true of the shirt beneath, the blood black in the firelight. "You'll need a new shirt," Sam said, trying to smile as he helped Nate to sit back down.

He lay Nate's wet coat out near the fire and put his own with it to dry, then turned back to him. Nate sat cross-legged, peering down at his arm. "It took a chunk out," he said in a faint voice.

"Don't look." Sam kneeled in front of him, batting his hand away. "I'll just, uh —" He gestured at Nate's shirt. "This needs to come off." It shouldn't have been awkward, but they'd undressed each other many times and the echoes of that past tenderness resonated in this very different intimacy.

The look in Nate's eyes told Sam he felt it too. Without comment, he began working on his neckcloth one-handed, but the cloth was soggy and uncooperative. After watching him struggle for a moment, Sam reached to help. Their fingers brushed, tangling, and Nate gave a breathy laugh, letting his hand fall away. He didn't drop his gaze though. Sam could feel the weight of it as he worked to undo the knot, unwind the neckcloth, and unbutton the two fastenings at the throat of his shirt, letting it fall open.

Beneath, he glimpsed the leather cord holding Nate's ring. It rested against his clavicle, disappearing under linen that stuck damply to his chest. Helpless against the impulse, Sam reached out and touched the cord, tracing it with his fingertip. Nate said nothing, hardly drew breath, and when Sam looked up, he found himself watched. Feeling foolish, he drew his hand back. It was hardly the time for sentimentality. "Waistcoat," he said, and Nate closed his eyes, letting Sam fumble open the buttons.

Moving around behind him, Sam slipped the waistcoat over his arms. Nate didn't flinch this time, which either meant Sam was doing a better job or that he wasn't the only one with other things on his mind. Setting the waistcoat aside, he found himself caught by the shape of Nate's back through the clinging linen of his shirt, the way his hair fell loose, freed from its queue by the river.

The way the blood stained his sleeve.

From this angle, Sam could see that the shot had struck from behind — Nate had put himself in front of the bullet — and had torn a path across his bicep. With luck it hadn't penetrated the muscle.

"Your shirt," he said, embarrassed by how rough his voice sounded. Nate just nodded and reached down to tug it free of his breeches. Sam helped haul it up over his head, setting it aside with his damp waistcoat. Then he stopped, the supple curve of Nate's bare back as he curled forward making Sam's blood surge. He wanted to smooth his palm along the length of Nate's spine, feel the flex of his muscles, the heat of his skin.

He made himself focus on the wound instead. "It's not bad." He bent closer to get a good look. The shot had plowed a furrow through his arm, deep enough to bleed profusely but — thank God — it hadn't lodged in his flesh. There were some grazes along the top of his shoulder too, probably from when he'd fallen, but nothing too serious. Sam felt his stomach unwind in relief, a real smile finding its way to his lips. "I think you'll live," he said, resting his hand on Nate's shoulder. "Let's get this cleaned out."

Nate nodded and leaned his head on his knees, staring into the fire. He was probably afraid of passing out. Nate had never been a bear-wrestling kind of man, happier with his books and ideas than so-called manly pursuits. Sam felt a rush of fond feeling and permitted himself a squeeze of Nate's shoulder, a brief comfort to them both. Then he took the cooled boiled water the landlady had provided and used it to flush out the wound and wipe away the blood.

Nate tensed under his ministrations, muscles bunching, but he didn't make a sound. He just sat with his head bowed, hair falling forward to hide his face. Sam resisted the urge to sweep it back, to press a kiss to his temple. The faster he did this, the better for them both.

Once the wound was clean, he started applying a tincture of myrrh and turpentine.

"God's *teeth*!" Nate hissed, jerking away. "What's that?"

"Hush." Sam took firm hold of his arm. "It'll help. My mother swore by it."

"Hurts like the pissing devil."

"I know." Leaning down, he succumbed to temptation and pressed a kiss to Nate's shoulder, then ruthlessly applied the tincture, took lint from his bag to pack the wound, and covered it all with a strip of bandage.

Sam was sweating by the time it was done and sat back on his heels in relief. Nate turned to look at him through a fall of damp hair. "I'd make a terrible soldier." He managed a wan smile. "Not very brave about pain."

Sam's answering smile felt equally shaky. "You had a terrible nurse."

He put out a hand for Sam. "I had the only one I wanted."

"Lucky for you, then." He took Nate's hand in his, threading their fingers together. "Nate, this bullet was meant for me."

"For you or me," he agreed, softly. "What's the difference?

Amicus est tamquam alter idem."

A true friend is a second self.

Sam nodded, his throat tight, and gave Nate's hand a squeeze. Then he picked up the tincture again and cleared his throat. "Let me see to your back, there's a couple of grazes…"

With a groan, Nate dropped his head back onto his knees and Sam moved behind him, dabbing at the scrapes, feeling Nate flinch at each touch. "Shhh…" Sam set his hand on Nate's shoulder, running the pad of his thumb over the top of his spine to sooth him while he worked.

But he didn't stop once he'd finished, kept his thumb moving back and forth, back and forth. Then he spread his palm flat and smoothed it across Nate's shoulders, listening as his breathing slowed, feeling Nate's knotted muscles relax beneath his hand. In the firelight, Nate's skin gleamed golden, still kissed by the American sun. Three freckles, like beauty marks, ran in a line down his back. Familiar to Sam as the constellations, he let his fingers follow the path from one to the other and back again, and then all the way down the curve of his spine and up across the cage of his ribs. Touching him like a lover would, like he had when they were lovers.

Sam found his breath quickening and Nate gave a low sigh, curling further forward. In the grate, the wood shifted, sending a flurry of sparks floating up the chimney. The firelight was dimming but that didn't matter because dawn already grayed the sky. Barely four o'clock in the morning, but English summer nights were fleeting. They would have to leave soon; MacLeod would still be looking for them.

Nate's hair had dried into clumps and Sam reached out to thread his fingers through it, revealing the soft spot at the nape of Nate's neck that Sam longed to kiss once more. He looked to the window, to the paling sky, and took his hand away. He shouldn't —

"Don't." Nate glanced over his shoulder, dark eyes gleaming. "Don't stop."

"You're hurt."

"I don't care. Sam —" He turned around so that they were face to face. Nate's ring rested against his breastbone, at once standing between them and binding them together. "God knows what's going to happen next, Sam. Can't we just have this?"

"It's not safe here."

Nate laughed. "When has it ever been safe for us?" Lit by the dawn and the dying fire, he appeared once more that dazzling young man Sam had fallen in love with so many years ago. "I could have died tonight. Either of us could. Or we might both, tomorrow." He looked reckless, wild in a way that fired Sam's blood. "Sam…" Nate reached for him, fingers grazing his chest, bare where his neckcloth should have been. "Now. While we still can."

While we still can…

His heart sank. Nate might have been talking about MacLeod's pursuit, but Sam suspected he meant something greater. Whatever else lay between them, they still stood on opposing sides of history and this thing — this glorious, aching love — would always be sacrificed to that greater story.

He wanted to sob. Instead, he reached out with both hands and captured Nate's face, pressing their lips together. They kissed like the world burned, like floods were rising and the heavens falling. Like nothing else mattered but the slide of their mouths, the slow exploration of lips and tongues. And then Nate sank back onto the hearthrug, bare-chested, with his hair gleaming copper in the firelight. "Sam," he said again, in invitation, in offer, and held out his good hand. "I want to feel you everywhere."

With a wordless noise, Sam stripped, his gaze never leaving Nate's watchful eyes. And then he did the same for Nate, fingers unsteady as he undid the fall of his breeches, exposed his glorious stand, the lean expanse of his thighs, the sharp curve of his hipbones that Sam so loved to kiss.

"God, Nate, you're…" *Beautiful. Glorious. Mine.* He couldn't find the word.

"Impatient." A slow smile curled Nate's mouth and he held out his hand again. "Come here."

Sam lay down next to him, afraid of hurting his arm, and leaned over to kiss that smiling mouth. The rug was rough beneath his skin, but Nate was all warm lean muscle and soft skin and Sam lost himself in sensation and memory. They kissed as Sam ran an expert hand over Nate's chest, skimmed a nipple and felt him gasp, followed the line of muscle to his waist and lean thighs, fingertips trailing across the softness of his belly to the rigid silk of his cock.

They kissed on, an endless slow delight. Sam swallowed Nate's whimpers of desire, propped himself up on one elbow and slipped one leg between Nate's, groaning into their kiss as his cock met Nate's hip and Nate's stand pressed into his belly. They started to move, the rhythm easy and familiar, their bodies working together without conscious thought.

"Sam…" Nate pressed up into him, head thrown back, and face deliciously flushed. His eyes were shut, his lips parted. Breathtaking.

Sam hid a kiss beneath Nate's jaw, licked his tender skin and felt Nate buck and groan. "Still like that, huh?"

"*Christ*, yes." He clutched Sam's back with one hand, fingernails scraping his skin.

Sam nipped at his neck, sucked until Nate cried out again, then smiled and kissed him there, moving down to his collarbone. And there he found the leather cord holding the ring. It lay flush across Nate's throat, the ring itself on the floor behind his shoulder. Sam wanted to rip it off the damn cord, to slide it back onto Nate's finger and see it there forever.

But they had no forever, he knew that. They had only now.

Closing his eyes against a swell of pain, he buried his face against Nate's neck and kissed him until Nate was writhing and begging and Sam could feel nothing but desire and the onrush of release.

Nate was close too; Sam still knew him well enough to feel it. They were masters of this, of pleasuring each other's bodies. Perhaps God had built them solely for the purpose of loving each other? The space between them was hot, slick with sweat and their own eagerness. Nate's fingers gripped his shoulder, his rhythm faltering, breaths catching in his throat. Sam pulled back to see his face, to watch him shatter as he thrust up, back arching off the floor as he spent between them with a bark of despairing joy.

The sudden slick heat was all Sam needed. His own release swept over him, washing away the world for one blissful moment of silence, leaving nothing behind but peace. And then he fell, down into the gray dawn, and Nate was there to catch him and hold him and whisper impossible promises against his skin. Screwing his eyes shut against squally emotions, Sam buried his face in Nate's hair and lay still.

They rested there for a time, their slowing breaths filling the room, Sam's head on Nate's shoulder, Nate's fingers drawing patterns on his back. Through the window, the sky turned from gray to eggshell blue. Eventually, as Sam's body cooled and a shiver made its way across his skin, Nate spoke. His voice sounded heavy, but his hand still traced shapes on Sam's skin. He said, "My ship sails in a week."

Cold words for a summer morning. What could Sam say in reply?

"Would you — ?" Nate's hand stopped moving, his voice a rough whisper. "Sam, come with me. Come home."

Hell, but that sparked a searing pain. His throat tightened. "I can't. I'm attainted of treason, Nate. You know what that means. I'm banished forever."

"But —"

"I'm not welcome in America." He had to close his eyes against the hurt of that. It never went away, the pain of being cast out by your friends and neighbors, of being branded as *less* for daring to disagree.

Nate pressed a kiss into Sam's hair, but didn't argue. It was the truth and they both knew it. There were tens of thousands like him — men, women, and children from all walks of life — driven out of their homes, disowned, and disavowed by their countrymen. No, he couldn't go home. But another idea slipped into his mind like a sneak cracking a house.

You could stay. You could stay here, with me.

But he couldn't ask that. Forging this new America meant everything to Nate — more, Sam knew, than it did to him. It always had. It always would. And Sam wouldn't ask him to choose between them. Not again.

Chapter Seventeen

THEY MADE THE drive through Liverpool to the livery in silence.

Both were tired, Nate supposed, and their lovemaking had ended in melancholy of his own creation. Stupid, to ask Sam to come home with him when he knew it to be impossible, but the thought of leaving him behind had felt intolerable. It still did. He wondered whether he might be able to procure Sam a pardon… Yet even as the thought crossed his mind, he remembered Talmach and his hatred of men like Sam.

And he remembered MacLeod's letters.

He sighed and shifted on the hard seat of the trap, pressing in a little closer to Sam. His arm throbbed like the devil now he had no other distraction, and the jostling of the drive wasn't helping. Neither were his river-damp coat and boots. But at least the day promised sunshine and he hoped they'd dry on the road back to London.

They'd slept a little in the tiny bed at the inn, and left the docks by mid-morning. Nate wouldn't have been surprised to find MacLeod's men looking for them in the city. In truth, he'd half expected to encounter MacLeod himself stalking along the wharf, waving his pistol above his slapdash old wig, outrage purpling his face. He shivered. It would be a long time before he could rid his mind of the image of MacLeod leveling his weapon at Sam, the flash of the muzzle in the dark. His own stark terror.

He glanced behind him, just to make sure MacLeod wasn't there, and Sam cocked a curious eyebrow. "I thought we might have seen MacLeod's men asking questions," Nate explained.

"I hope it's a good sign that we haven't."

"What else could it be?" A thought occurred. "Damn. Do you think it means he recognized me?"

Sam shrugged. "We don't know what it means. Maybe he has other things to worry about, considering he killed a man last night."

Possible, although Nate doubted the law could hold MacLeod to account. Not even for murder. But Sam was right, there was no point in borrowing trouble. He shifted again, cradling his injured arm to ease the discomfort, somewhat regretting his refusal of Sam's offer to make him a sling. MacLeod must have seen him fall, though, and might have people looking for a wounded man. He didn't want to appear to be one.

Sam spared him a glance. "You know MacLeod better than me. What do you think he'll do?"

"That depends." If he discovered the missing letters, he'd assume that his network of subversives had been compromised and erupt into a rage. Rightly so, because Talmach would be dogged in his pursuit of the men named in those letters. Rooting out the enemy within was the colonel's *raison d'etre.* Far more than a simple duty, it was the man's obsession. Not that Nate could tell Sam any of that. "If

MacLeod recognized me, he'd go to Farris and accuse him of sending a spy. Which would scupper their deal, for sure." And that would jeopardize Talmach's whole case against Farris. The colonel would skin him alive. "Months of work ruined."

"For the love of God," Sam exclaimed, "*that's* what you're worried about? MacLeod killed a man last night. And he'd have killed us too if Rowsley hadn't blundered into the middle of things. How can you still want to trade with him?"

"I don't. But it's —" The truth hung on the tip of his tongue. After the tenderness they'd shared last night, it felt wrong to have secrets between them. Yet telling Sam the truth was too big of a risk. In only a matter of days, they would part. But at least now they would part as friends. Better still, they could hold out hope that one day, one glorious sunlit day, they might meet again as lovers on the grassy banks of the Pawtuxet.

Why endanger that dream for a truth that didn't even matter?

Because there was no way Nate was giving Talmach the letter containing Sam's name. No way he'd allow the colonel, or anyone else, to do Sam harm. And therefore, no reason for Sam to know anything about it.

Which was why Nate only said, "It's more complicated than you realize."

"Of course it is."

"What does that mean?"

"Never mind." Sam tugged his hat down against the morning sun, plunging half his face into shadow.

"Sam —"

"It doesn't matter." He sounded more resigned than angry. "I don't think MacLeod recognized you, Nate. He'd have said so if he did — loudly. So, don't worry, Farris will still get his deal."

"It's not about Farris —"

"I know!" Sam took a breath, then more calmly added, "I know America needs him, or needs this trade deal. It's all about the greater good. I understand."

Frustrated, Nate sighed. "You're right, in a way. It is about the greater good. We're trying to build a new country and sometimes we have to make compromises."

"That's what you call them?"

"Sam —"

"Look, I know how important this is to you. I do." Sam hunched forward as if he were closing ranks, sparing Nate a sad smile. "I always did."

Nate gripped his arm, looking for last night's connection in Sam's eyes. "It's not the *only* thing that's important to me. It never was. Not by far."

But Sam shook his head and pulled away, shifting until a cool slice of air separated them. "Look," he said, nodding toward the end of the street, "there's the livery. Let's get on our way quickly."

Nate made a wordless noise of agreement. He could do no more than that because those few empty inches Sam had set between them opened up a dull space in his chest, illustrating exactly why he'd hidden the truth from Sam.

And why he must hide it still.

ONCE THEY'D RETURNED to the posting inn and picked up the chaise, they made good time back to London, paying the post-boys extra to travel through the night despite the risk of robbery. Nate had decided that highwaymen were a lesser danger than the risk of John MacLeod reaching London ahead of him.

For the first day, they both sat on the box seat to dry off in the sun.

They didn't talk much and dozed a great deal, the long

sleepless night catching up faster than MacLeod. Once, Nate woke with his head on Sam's shoulder, held in place by an arm around his back and his hat resting safely in Sam's lap. He feigned sleep a little longer just to enjoy the closeness, to hold off the looming shadow of their parting. It worked for a while, but when he eventually stirred, Sam let him go with a regretful smile that only hollowed Nate out further.

The next morning, after they'd stopped for a quick breakfast, they sat on a bench in the inn's yard and Sam changed the dressing on Nate's arm. "No sign of infection," he said, examining it in the bright morning sunshine. He sounded satisfied, but he retrieved the infernal tincture from his bag nonetheless and Nate could only grunt his thanks through gritted teeth.

When the pain had subsided, and Sam was wrapping his arm in a fresh cloth, Nate managed to say, "When did you become such an expert nurse?"

Sam's gaze lifted to his, then dropped back to his arm. "At Simsbury." He said no more, just tightened the bandage and left Nate to roll his sleeve down over it. "I'm going to see about new horses."

Nate watched him stand and stretch his back before making his way across the yard towards the post-boys sitting with their beer. Impossible not to admire the straight line of his shoulders, the confidence of his stride. The glint of sunlight in his golden hair. Lovely. But Nate's pleasure in the moment was shadowed by the mention of Simsbury Mine, where Sam had been imprisoned. And flogged. Perhaps with some of the very men whose names were on the letters Nate had tucked away in his haversack.

Making the most of a few moments alone, Nate fished the letters out of their oilcloth pouch to take a closer look. He'd half feared that the river would have rendered them unreadable, but the oilcloth had done its job and the letters were perfectly preserved. With one eye on Sam, who now leaned easily against the fence while he negotiated with the post-boys, Nate looked at the letters more thoroughly.

They weren't all about Loyalist refugees in London. Most were from Americans, detailing neighbors and acquaintances who might be recruited to MacLeod's cause. All provided lists of names: men and women who'd either expressed opposition to the war or who opposed the growing power of the Continental Congress.

To Talmach, this would read like a list of traitors, but to Nate's mind most of it appeared to be little more than rumor, gossip, and speculation.

He glanced over at Sam — strong, capable, kindly Sam. In his soul, he knew that Sam was no traitor, that he'd never act to harm his country, whatever he thought of the war or its outcome. That was simply a matter of faith.

But how many others on MacLeod's so-called list were the same? Gentle, generous, good men, guilty only of a difference of political opinion, who perhaps now wanted to forget the war and rebuild their lives in America. Did they deserve to be exposed, to be rooted out by Talmach and his men as enemies? Did their single divergence of political thought override every other virtue? Did it make them less worthy, less *American*?

Talmach might think so. Nate did not.

Perhaps, had he never known Sam, he might have thought differently. But he *did* know Sam, and that raised a question: what the hell did he do with the damned letters?

Simply destroying them wasn't an option. Because it was equally possible that some of the people named *did* share the aims of Farris and MacLeod and intended to act on their beliefs. By hiding that information from Talmach, he risked real danger to their fragile new government. But who was he to be the judge of a man's intentions?

He sighed, glanced across the yard, and found Sam gesturing towards the carriage. They were ready to leave. Quickly, Nate slid the letters back into his haversack. But he kept the one containing Sam's name separate, folding it up and tucking it between the pages of his book. That one, he *would* destroy and to hell with the consequences. The others…? Well, perhaps, if he studied them more closely, he'd find a way to determine who posed a genuine threat to America and who did not. Meanwhile, he would keep them all safe.

Deep in such thoughts, he made his way back to the chaise for another long day on the road.

It proceeded very much like the day before. But by midday they'd lost the sun behind a bank of heavy cloud rolling in from the west, and a misting rain floated in the air, spitting at them from time-to-time. They retreated to the comfort of the coach.

Once inside, Sam took Nate's hand, threaded their fingers together and gave a thin smile when Nate glanced over at him in surprise. Sam looked weary. Nate probably did too; neither had slept much in the coach. They traveled like that for some time, their intimacy hidden, and Nate wished the sway of the carriage didn't make it impossible for him to read. He'd have liked to read to Sam. Better still would be reading to him on the sunny banks of the Pawtuxet, with Sam's head in his lap, but for now that remained a distant dream.

And that truth ached worse than Nate's arm.

The hours rattled by and they still saw no sign of pursuit. As far as Nate could tell, nobody was asking questions at the posting inns where they changed horses either. Not that they ever stopped for long. But Nate made a point of asking on his way back from the jakes and was met with blank looks and shakes of the head each time.

Perversely, he grew increasingly concerned by the lack of pursuit. MacLeod wouldn't let an insult go unpunished and their invasion of his home was an insult indeed. If he hadn't sent men after them, what was he doing? Nate brooded on several bleak alternatives as they traveled and tried not to see omens in the darkening summer skies.

On the fourth day they reached St. Albans, rattling over cobbles past a huge old church. Nate wondered at it as they passed. Twin spires soared up beyond the pointed roof, three massive arched doors turned blank faces to the world, and above them rose an enormous stained-glass window. It was everything Marlborough Castle wanted and failed to be: magnificent, imposing, and ancient. He wondered who'd built it, and why a building so splendid would have been raised up here, in such a small town.

He was still studying the church when he realized the post-boy was slowing the chaise to a walk and turning in to the yard of an inn called the White Hart. Nate breathed a sigh of relief, glad of the break. Not that it would be long because Sam wanted to reach London tonight.

Nate stretched his back as the chaise stopped, rolled his shoulders, and winced at the throb in his arm. Next to him, Sam paused in his climb down from the coach. "Are you alright?" he said. "Your arm —"

"It's not bad."

"You look tired."

He laughed. "I *am* tired. We both are. And I'd kill for a good night's sleep, in an actual bed."

"Well, we should be in London by —"

"Or," Nate interrupted, struck by a sudden idea, "we could get ourselves a good dinner and stay here. There's been no sign of" — a glance at the post-boy unhitching the horses — "our 'friend' and there's no harm in spending one more night on the road, is there?"

One last night, he might as well have said.

Sam held his gaze for much too long, a stormy look in his gray-sky eyes. Eventually, he said, "I suppose there isn't," and jumped down from the chaise.

It was as good as a promise and Nate's spirits leaped in response.

The White Hart was an old inn. Not as old as the church, but full of exposed beams and little leaded windows in the Elizabethan style. Some effort had been made to modernize it by plastering the front of the building, but Nate could feel the centuries resting on his shoulders as soon as he stepped inside. Strange, these bygone places, other men's lives sunk into their bones. He'd seen nothing like it at home; there everything was new and looking to the future. Here, places had deep roots.

He waited while Sam spoke to the landlord at some length. Red-faced and jovial, the man had a deal to say, but he made Sam smile and Nate didn't mind watching that. Sam didn't smile much these days, not like he used to. But eventually he escaped and came back with the key for a room — one room for him and Nate — and nobody thought anything of it. Why should they? Nate did, though. Despite his throbbing arm and bone-tired exhaustion, his stomach fluttered in anticipation of the long night ahead. Anticipation and melancholy because this night was their last. When they reached London, everything would end.

As they'd done every evening since leaving Liverpool, they ate in a private dining parlor. No need to risk curious eyes taking note, even if they were only twenty miles from London. The dinner was good, roasted beef and potatoes, and they ate in silence, both lost in thought. Of the evening ahead, perhaps. Or what would come after.

It wasn't even seven o'clock when they'd finished eating, broad daylight still, but Nate was frustrated to find himself yawning.

"Maybe you should sleep," Sam said, studying the table instead of meeting Nate's eye. "You really do look tired."

"Not that tired."

Sam gave a faint smile. But he looked uneasy, his gaze slipping away to stare out through the inn's leaded windows, little black bars crisscrossing the ancient glass. "I'm going to stretch my legs," he said abruptly, pushing to his feet. "Been cramped up in that damn coach for too long."

It was a rejection and it stung. Oh, it was gentle enough, but Nate didn't understand; this was their last chance, their last night. He leaned over the table. "Sam —"

"You see that church? The landlord told me it used to be an abbey. They built it eight hundred years ago, he said, and there's a Saint buried underneath."

"I don't —"

"We could take a look if you're not too tired. Just to see it." He gave a sad smile. "We used to take walks together, remember?"

"I remember." Nate reached for him, his hurt softening to sorrow as they clasped hands. "I miss that, Sam. I miss everything."

For a moment, their eyes met, an aching collision of regrets. Then, blinking too rapidly, Sam gave Nate's hand a squeeze and let go. "Fetch your hat, then."

It was a cool evening, the clouds that had been rolling west all day trailing a buffeting wind. Summer in England was neither one thing nor the other, Nate had learned, and didn't stay the same from one day to the next. But the stormy sky made a dramatic backdrop to the church — abbey, as was — as they approached. "I'm trying to imagine being a medieval monk," Nate said, staring up at the stern portico. This would have been a place of awe for men who believed in an omnipotent God gazing down from his heavenly perch.

Sam gave a hushed laugh. "You'd have made a terrible monk."

"True. I bet those cassocks itched."

They paused in front of the door and by silent consent turned to stroll around the outside of the building. "You'll be interested in this," Sam said as they walked close together, the backs of their hands touching. Nate might have taken Sam's arm in the way gentlemen did if it hadn't felt too intimate. Strange, that their real intimacy made a more casual one impossible. "The landlord —"

"He's quite the font of information."

Sam inclined his head, nudging Nate's shoulder in reproof. "He told me that the Magna Carta was written right here in this abbey."

Nate stared. "Magna Carta. Really?" He stared up at the ancient stones, tried to imagine those old medieval scribes scratching the foundations of the rule of law onto vellum five hundred years ago. And now Nate and his comrades, on another continent, had defended those very rights with their blood. "That's — Yes, that is interesting. *More* than interesting."

"Thought you'd like it."

Sam's eyes were so fond that Nate could hardly stand it. With a quick glance over his shoulder, he pushed Sam into the shadow of the great building, and lost for any eloquence, kissed him. He didn't think the shades of the monks would care because what he felt in that moment was akin to sacred — a pure love that broke his heart.

Sam took his face in both hands, kissed him deeply and then pushed him gently away. "Nate…" He looked like he was trying to say more, as if words were piled up inside and couldn't find their way out. His lips parted and Nate leaned in to kiss him again, but Sam held him at bay. "No. Not here.

It's not safe."

"Then let's go back to the inn." He felt shaky, his fingers flexing against the strength of Sam's arms. "Let's have tonight."

Our last goodbye.

Sam closed his eyes, expression pained, but nodded. After a moment he dropped his hands from Nate's face and smiled. "Hell, Nate, if those monks could see us now…"

He barked a laugh. "I doubt they'd care. What else do you think they got up to between matins and lauds?"

Chapter Eighteen

WHEN THEY REACHED the inn, Nate slipped upstairs while Sam chatted with the gregarious landlord for the sake of appearances. Their room was rudimentary but clean: a bed, a table, and a chair. In other circumstances the bed might have been small for sharing, but Nate felt a thrill as he ran his hand over the counterpane; there'd be no way to sleep with Sam in that bed other than in his arms. And he longed for that almost more than the lovemaking. Though they'd been intimate for years in Rosemont, the times they'd woken together had been few and precious. Tomorrow morning would be one of them.

He set his hat on a hook behind the door and tugged off his coat, maneuvering it over his injured arm with care. He'd have liked to strip bare, to lay himself out on the bed like an offering, but he didn't dare. He had to wait for the door to be safely locked behind them.

Sam was taking an age.

In search of distraction, Nate walked to the window. It looked out over the yard to the tower of the old abbey. Its eight hundred years made Nate feel like a mayfly, his life and struggles fleeting concerns. What did any of his labors matter, he mused, when set against the ceaseless turning of the years? What did his personal sacrifices matter? They would be forgotten as surely as the monks who'd labored to transcribe Magna Carta, or the stone masons who'd toiled to raise the abbey to the heavens. All that was left of them now was their legacy in velum and stone, as his legacy would be left in the founding of a new nation, rooted in principles of law and liberty. Or so he hoped.

Yet each of those men had lived lives. Whether they'd lived wholly, embracing the love and joy they found, or had set aside such things in pursuit of their great undertaking, Nate couldn't know. History didn't record the lives of little men like them. Like him. But one thing he did know was that, however they'd lived their lives, five hundred years later their legacy remained. As Nate's would remain, whether he seized his chance at joy or sacrificed it on the altar of his duty.

And that was a remarkably liberating thought.

Behind him, at last, the door opened. Pulled from his musings, Nate turned and watched Sam lock the door behind him. The heavy clunk of the bolt seemed to shut out the world. Sam set his hat on the hook next to Nate's and paused there, his back turned. Outside, even the noise from the yard seemed muted and all Nate could hear was the restless rush of his own pulse.

"This is a bad idea," Sam warned, his back still turned. "It'll only make parting harder."

Nate thought of those long dead monks and masons, of their forgotten lives, and in two steps he was across the room, slipping his arms around Sam and pulling his back against his chest. He could hear Sam's ragged breathing, feel the tremble of muscles held taut. Nate nuzzled his ear, kissed the soft skin above his collar, breathed him in and held him close. "Don't think about tomorrow," he whispered against his skin. "There's only tonight."

Sam leaned forward to rest his forehead on the door, chest rising as he took a deep breath. Then he moved, turning in Nate's arms until their eyes met. A thousand words could have been spoken between them — every nuance of regret, longing, love, and reproach — but none were needed. The world simply fell away, time contracting to a single night, a single room, a single moment.

Now.

In that sheltered space, they stripped each other with slow and tender care, full of unhurried kisses. It wasn't even dark yet — they had all the time in the world. Sam threw back the sheets, tumbling Nate onto the bed, and it was glorious: the coarse linen, the heat of Sam's body, his weight bearing Nate down into the straw mattress, caressing and kissing, bodies entangled.

Outside, a bell tolled eight and a handful of raindrops rattled against the window. Inside, Sam bathed him in butterfly kisses to his eyelids, lips, to the base of his throat, his chest. Nate buried a hand in Sam's hair, traced fingers over his back, exploring the scars on his shoulders.

God, that they could go back and live unscathed in the world of before.

"Nate?" Sam propped himself up on his elbow, looking down at him. He threaded a hand through Nate's hair, brushing it off his face. "What's wrong?"

He shook his head. "Just thinking."

"Well stop." Sam leaned down and kissed his lips, cupped his face. "There's nothing to think about but this."

Wrapping his arms around Sam's neck, Nate pulled him down until they were flush together, until Sam's weight crushed everything but sensation from his mind. He felt airless, drowning, and he welcomed it. Nothing else in the world existed. He wanted nothing but this.

Pinned by Sam's body, he couldn't move much but managed to rock his hips, his cock pressing into Sam's belly. With a groan, Sam began to move too, lifting his weight onto his arms, settling between Nate's legs. God, it was delicious. Nate ran his fingers down the length of Sam's spine, found his hip, the curve of his ass. They could spend like this and it would be perfect. But tonight, Nate wanted more.

"I have a confession," he said, looking up into Sam's flushed face. "I stole something from MacLeod's kitchens."

"What, in God's name?"

He ran a hand across Sam's chest, rubbed the pad of his thumb over a taut nipple and watched Sam's eyes flutter closed, reveled in his stifled moan. "Salad oil." He grinned as Sam's eyes flew back open.

"Fuck."

Nate gave a slow smile at Sam's rare obscenity and stretched out languorously beneath him, arms above his head. "Only if you want to…"

"Hellspawn." Sam grinned, knotted his hand into Nate's hair and claimed him ungently. Christ, Nate almost spent right then, legs wrapped around Sam's thighs, grinding into his belly. But Sam let go in time, pushed back to sit on his heels, chest heaving and eyes aglow. "Get it." He had a restraining grip on the base of his cock. "Hurry."

Nate slipped from the bed, making something of a show of it as he crossed the room to where his portmanteau sat on the table, bending over to rummage around for the oil.

"Mother of *God.*"

Sam's choking curse made Nate grin and he gave a coquettish glance over his shoulder. "Everything all right?"

With a groan, Sam flopped onto his back. "If you don't damn well hurry, you'll be too late, you gorgeous bastard."

Nate laughed. And hurried. Where the devil had he

put the oil? He dumped out his muddy shirt, stockings, his book — anything that was in the way — until eventually his fingers closed around the little glass bottle. He sent a silent, somewhat profane prayer of thanks to Mrs. Sturge. Then he was back on the bed and straddling Sam's lap, the bottle warming in his hand as he slid forward, chest-to-chest, and kissed him with a languid ease he didn't feel. His blood was burning. "Fuck me," he whispered, biting Sam's ear. "For God's sake, Sam, fuck me."

With a groan, Sam rolled him onto his back. Sitting up, he took the bottle and unstoppered it, pouring a little oil into his hand. Nate watched through the rush of blood in his head, the painful pounding of his heart. Christ, he wanted this and didn't know how to bear its ending.

"Nate."

His gaze had been riveted on Sam's hand, on the glow of the golden oil, and he lifted it to Sam's face instead. His hair fell forward over his forehead, sweat-damp and dark, his flushed lips the same dusky pink as his nipples. But his eyes, they were full of shadows.

"How do you want it?"

In your arms, held close, seeing everything in your face.

But no, that would be unbearable. He swallowed and rolled over, his rigid cock pressing into the mattress. "Hard," he said, voice muffled into his forearm. "I want it hard."

Sam made a stifled sound, paused, then nudged Nate's legs apart with his knees, slick fingers starting to open him with infinite care even as his other hand tightened on Nate's hip. "Hard?" he rasped. "I'll give you hard."

Nate bit his response into his arm, swallowing his groan as Sam's fingers worked him in the way only he could. Christ, but no one had ever known his body like Sam. Every turn of his fingers made him whimper. Sam's breathing grew ragged and then his fingers were gone. For a moment, the emptiness was unendurable, but then Sam was hauling him to his knees, one hand between his shoulder blades, pressing his chest down onto the bed — keeping the weight off his injured arm; the carefulness of that hurt much worse than the wound — while his other hand ran once more over his ass. And then Nate felt a blunt pressure pushing in, slow but unremitting as he buried his face into the mattress and cried out at the intolerable intensity.

Nate horded breath as Sam snugged his hips against his ass and stopped. With one hand, Sam gripped his hip while the other swept a caress along the bow of Nate's spine to seize his shoulder, his name floating on a broken whisper Nate doubted he was meant to hear. And then Sam was moving, slow strokes that pierced Nate to the core. Neither pain, nor quite pleasure, it was simply an overmastering of his senses. His heart pounded frantically against his ribs, lungs burning, throat too tight to make a sound as he strained toward release.

Sam's fingers flexed against his shoulder and he began to move in earnest. Hard, as Nate had said he wanted. Hard, because tender would break him. Hard, because he wanted to be marked, branded. He never wanted to forget.

It went on forever, a timeless building of sensation and need and pressure. Nothing was real but their bodies, the satiny slide of Sam's cock, the bruising grip of his hands on Nate's shoulder and hip, the low grunts of Sam's thrusts, the hot wash of his breath, and the desperate ache of Nate's untouched, rigid stand. The sweat on his skin, the flush of his face. Hovering on the brink of a release he wanted desperately, and desperately wanted to stave off forever.

But then Sam leaned forward, pressing his lips to the nape of Nate's neck and slipped his arm around his waist. Firm fingers closed around his aching cock. Nate bucked and cried out, helpless, as Sam ruthlessly drove him over the edge until he was sobbing his release into the mattress, spilling over Sam's hand. With a stifled shout Sam followed, surging forward with such force Nate's legs gave way and they sprawled together, Sam gasping against his shoulder, mouthing silent words into his skin as his hips jerked and eventually stilled.

In the aftermath, Nate drifted like kelp in the tide, buffeted by wave after wave of emotion. He clung to the only things he could hold on to — Sam's hand stroking his arm, Sam's heartbeat pounding against his back, Sam's love anchoring him to the world.

THEY SLEPT.

Sam knew it was foolish, but he was too wrung out to resist. So, he slept with Nate's back pulled against his chest, holding him close as if that could keep him from leaving. As if loving him had ever been enough to keep them together.

When he woke to the early dawn, Nate didn't stir. He was breathing in the steady rhythm of deep sleep, dark hair sprawled across the pillow. In the thin light, Sam could see finger marks on his shoulders, marks he'd put there, and swallowed a pang of guilty pleasure; Nate had wanted it hard. Sam would have preferred tender, but perhaps it had been for the best.

Today they'd return to London. And this would be over.

He rolled onto his back. Three uneven beams supported the low ceiling, their dark wood black in the gray light. Outside, he could hear the patter of rain and somewhere a rooster was greeting the soggy dawn. By dinner they'd reach the Swan. They were only twenty miles away now, an easy day's travel if the rain let up. And then the job would be over, Nate would sail for Boston, and Sam…

He didn't know what he'd do.

Return to the Bowl, return to the Claims Commission

in hopeless pursuit of compensation? Drift? He turned his head. Nate's bare shoulder caught the light, golden with the summer sun of home, and Sam felt a despairing ache. He longed for Rosemont, he longed to return with Nate, to lay with him on the riverbank and send politics to the devil.

But that wasn't all.

He longed for the life he'd once led, a life of purpose and service to his community. Of respect.

The war was over — the great question of their time decided — and he'd lost. Lost the argument, lost the war. The fight had cost him his wealth, his honor, and ultimately his home.

Must it cost him his future too?

Return to Rosemont would be impossible; he was attainted of treason and banished from Rhode Island forever. But there were other places in America, places where no one knew the name Samuel Hutchinson. The whole open frontier…

A surge of brash hope had him sitting upright.

Who was to say that he and Nate couldn't live someplace else, the arguments of the past put aside, and work together for the future of their country? God knew there was work to be done now that America had embarked on this new and perilous path. Maybe Sam could help; he was still a lawyer, after all. And who better to guard against the tyranny of the mob than a man who'd once been its victim?

His heart raced. Surely it was possible? He was tempted to shake Nate awake and ask him, but he slept so peacefully that Sam decided to let him have his rest. This could wait. Instead, he brushed a kiss against Nate's shoulder and slipped out of bed.

Not even the sodden morning could dampen his spirits now. Dressing quickly, he retrieved the oil — *Nate, you thieving genius* — from the floor by the bed and tucked the incriminating evidence back into Nate's portmanteau. The scattered chaos of his belongings made Sam's pulse quicken with memories of last night's hurried search and he cast a glance over his shoulder, reconsidering waking Nate with more than a kiss. Even remembering that lithesome body beneath him made his prick grow heavy and full.

But, no, Nate needed his sleep and there would be time. He grinned like a fool. Back home, they'd have forever — plenty of time for Sam to love Nate as tenderly as he wanted and as hard as Nate demanded. Still smiling, he started shoving Nate's belongings back into his bag: his shirt, still damp from the river, rolled-up stockings mud-stained from their ridiculous romp in the road. He smiled at the memory. And Nate's precious book. Sam turned the small volume over in his hands. French, by the look of the title. Nate spoke good French and Spanish. Latin, too. That quick mind of his collected languages like dogs collected sticks. Sam didn't have the ear for it, but Nate used to translate as he read aloud. He flicked through the book — yes, it was all in French — and a piece of paper tucked between the pages fluttered to the floor.

Stooping to pick it up, Sam found his attention snagged by familiar words.

…Rosemont, RI.

A hollow drumbeat pounded in his chest as he stared at the letter. The words slithered about on the page, he couldn't quite catch them, and had to read them several times before their meaning sank in. It was a letter addressed to Lord Marlborough and it listed Americans — both refugees in London, and others still living in America — who had opposed the war and were likely to oppose the Continental Congress.

His own name was among them.

For a moment, he didn't understand. Why did Nate

have this? Then realization landed like a punch; *this* must be the document Nate had stolen from MacLeod's strongbox.

Head spinning, his mind darted back to his meeting with Talmach as he reassessed the man's military bearing, his suspicious gaze, and Nate's deference to him. The scales fell from his eyes and he saw the cold clear truth: Nate Tanner was not in England drafting trade deals for the Continental Congress. At least, not only that. Nate was also gathering information about dissenters. Loyalists. Tories. King's men.

Men like Sam.

His throat tightened, eyes pricking. What a cock-led fool he'd been. To think, only moments ago, he'd imagined they could put the conflict behind them and work together for their country's future. He and Nate, side by side.

Now he knew that was impossible.

Because Nate was still fighting the war.

Vivid in his mind's eye, Sam pictured it: the men on this list dragged from their beds in the middle of the night, stripped of their livelihood and property, banished from America. Cast out like Sam had been cast out, condemned by a whisper, by a rumor, by the petty vengeance of their neighbors. Nothing had changed in the years since he'd been gone. Nothing. And Nate was complicit, he was leading the hunt.

Leading the mob.

A cry of anguish caught in his throat and he pressed a hand over his mouth to stifle it, ruthlessly shoving his pain and confusion down deep, burying them beneath the tar and the flames. Only one truth remained clear, as unforgiving as the morning light: wherever Nate's loyalties lay, they did not lie with Sam. And they never would.

He dropped the letter, watched it land atop Nate's open

book. He had to *think*. Swinging away from the table, his heart lurched at the sight of Nate still sleeping — a sprawl of limbs, dark hair spilling across the white pillow, beautiful and treacherous. Sam wanted to punch him. He wanted to shake him and howl *was this a lie too*?

But no, *this* didn't matter. It was over, and Sam had to get away.

He couldn't bear to stay.

Chapter Nineteen

NATE WOKE FULL of hazy pleasure.

From outside came the warm drift of conversation, women's laughter, the bark of a dog and the squeals of playing children. Hoof beats and wheels clattered along the cobbled road beyond the yard and a distant clock chimed the quarter hour.

Peeling open his eyes, Nate blinked in the watery sunlight bathing the room. It fell on the bed next to him, on the space where Sam had slept, and he put out a hand to touch the sheet, warmed now by the sun and not Sam's body. He'd slept in Sam's arms last night, the best and deepest sleep he'd had in years, and couldn't suppress a pang of disappointment that he'd not woken with him too.

A rolling rumble from outside drew his eye to the window, squinting against the brightness. The sun was high, which explained the noise in the yard. How late was it? Normally Sam wanted to be on the road by seven, but it was much later than that. Scrambling out of bed, Nate looked outside. The rumbling noise was a man rolling barrels across the yard and into the inn's cellar. From the height of the sun, it looked closer to nine than seven.

Nate smiled and put a hand to the ring dangling against his chest. Sam had let him sleep, knowing how tired he'd been. The thought filled him with warmth and gratitude. But now his stomach was growling, and it was time to be leaving. Perhaps the landlady could give him something to eat on the road? At least it looked as though the night's rain had passed, the sky a patchwork of blue and gray, clouds drifting on a breeze as languid as Nate felt.

Still smiling, he went to dress. His clothes were where he'd dropped them last night, in a heap near the table. He spared a moment to regret not hanging them up, because he'd look thoroughly disreputable this morning, but supposed it didn't matter. He'd be back at his lodgings tonight and —

Shit.

Hell and shitting buggery.

Splayed on the table was his copy of *Les Liaisons Dangereuses* — terrible for its spine, he thought with manic distraction — and atop it, MacLeod's letter. Unfolded and read.

With sickening panic, he snatched it up and tucked it away, hands shaking as he shut the book around it. "No." It was an airless sound, barely a word. "Please God, no."

For an awful moment, he didn't know what to do. He wanted to go backwards in time and burn the damned letter as soon as he'd found it. Why hadn't he? He wanted to have never concealed it in his book. He wanted to have woken first this morning, hidden the letter away. He wanted — "Concentrate."

Sam.

He had to find Sam and explain. All wasn't lost. He could assure Sam he had no intention of doing anything with the letter but destroy it. He just had to speak to him. Make him understand.

Dressing quickly, barely bothering to tie more than a knot in his neckcloth, he ran out of the room. Downstairs, he found the landlord scrubbing the tables in the tap room, his wife sweeping the floor. No sign of Sam. Nate made himself slow. "Good morning," he said breathlessly, attempting a smile. "I'm —"

"There you are, Mr. Tanner." The landlord looked up with a smile. "And a fine morning it is. I was telling the wife, we've not had —"

"Yes, very good. I'm sorry to trouble you, sir, but I need to speak to my — my traveling companion, Mr. Hutchinson, on a matter of urgency and —"

"Why, he left, sir." The landlord cocked his head, glanced at his wife who was leaning on her broom, watching curiously. "Said you was stopping a while?"

It was all Nate could do not to gape, though he could feel the blood drain to his toes and his head swim. "Yes," he managed after a moment. "I, uh. I'm too late to catch him then…?" He cleared his dry throat. "What, ah, what time did he leave?"

"Before six, sir." He leaned closer, confiding. "Giles weren't too happy to be roused so early — that's our post-boy — but I reckon he was compensated for his time. He'll be back later, more'n like, if you want a word?"

"No, that's…" He lost the thought, everything consumed by the realization that Sam had run from him. Last night they'd been as close as two people could be, but this morning he'd run. He hadn't even wanted an explanation, he'd just gone. And really, Nate shouldn't be surprised. Sam had never truly trusted him.

"You alright, sir? You've gone white as a sheet." The landlord took a step closer. "Maybe you should sit down. Molly, fetch the gent a cup of ale."

"I'm quite well," he said, but sat down anyway. His hands were shaking. "I need to return to London immediately."

"Well, you're in the right place," said the landlord, as his wife bustled over and pressed an earthenware cup into Nate's hand. "All the stages going south stop in St. Albans — either here or at the Bell. You'll be home by supper."

And Sam, who'd left three hours ago at least, would be home before dinner. Plenty of time to disappear into that vast hive of a city. And Nate would never see him again.

Nate would never see him again.

"The next coach to London," he told the landlord. "I must be on it."

COMPARED WITH THE chaise, the stagecoach was a plodding affair and Nate was bone-shaken and weary by the time London's grimy streets closed around them and the coach finally rattled to a halt at the bustling Swan with Two Necks. There'd been no seat inside, so he was crisped from the sun too, which had flitted in and out of the clouds all day. His skin felt tight, his limbs ached, and his heart was a leaden lump in his chest.

For most of the journey, he'd thought of nothing but Sam, wracked with such regret he could hardly sit still. Now that it was too late, he saw that he'd been a fool. A fool and a coward. Because of course he should have told Sam the truth from the beginning — even if it had turned Sam against him.

Even if they'd never reconciled.

Well, Sam knew the truth now. Or thought he did. A version of the truth that painted Nate as a man gathering names of political dissenters. Christ, how Sam must despise him. It turned his stomach just thinking of what he must have thought, finding that letter hidden in Nate's book. And he swore that if he did nothing else before he sailed for Boston, he'd find Sam and make him understand the truth.

It was late by the time Nate rapped on the door of Talmach's rooms on Milk Street. What he really wanted was to return to his own lodgings to bathe and sleep, but first he needed to know what chaos the whole business at Marlborough Castle had caused in London. There was a strong possibility he might not even have a position anymore.

Talmach's limping footsteps approached the door. At the sight of Nate, one dark eyebrow arched. "You're back."

"Evidently." His patience with the colonel was thin.

Talmach opened the door fully to admit Nate and then closed it behind him with a click, leading him into his neat parlor. Taking off his hat, Nate set it on the table beneath the window. Outside, London began to glitter as this dreadful day at last succumbed to dusk.

"Well?" Talmach said, turning to face him. "Did you find the list?"

Nate hesitated, then reached into his pocket and pulled out two letters. Despite his nausea, he'd found time on the slow journey to London to distract himself from thoughts of Sam by studying MacLeod's letters. "A handful of correspondence. These were written by men assuring MacLeod of their assistance in his schemes."

Talmach took the letters, casting his eyes over them. "Only two?"

"The rest were mere supposition and rumor. Nothing that could be considered evidence." They were still in his bag, but the colonel didn't need to know that. Nate braced himself. "I destroyed them."

"What?" Talmach's head shot up. "For God's sake, Tanner, there's value in supposition and rumor when you're looking for the enemy within."

Not good enough. "Perhaps, when we were at war. But the war's over, Colonel. We're at peace now, and we can't police a man's thoughts."

"Don't be so naïve. Some thoughts are too dangerous to be tolerated." Talmach sent him a calculating look. "As are some acquaintances."

For the first time in the colonel's presence, Nate felt a cold clasp of fear. How much did he know? "That's as maybe," he said stiffly. "But there are lines we cannot cross and still call ourselves Patriots."

The colonel pocketed the letters and moved to the fireplace, pouring two glasses of whiskey and offering one to Nate. "A fine sentiment," he said. "Are you finished lecturing?"

Nate eyed the drink for a moment before deciding to accept. God knew he needed to calm himself down before his temper tripped him into saying something revealing. It was good Kentucky whiskey, too, and went down easily. Shame the smoky taste reminded him so painfully of Sam. "You should know that we were discovered," he said abruptly. "And that I was seen by MacLeod." He studied his glass, swirling the amber liquid around. "It was night, and I wore a scarf over my face. I don't believe he recognized me but it's possible that he did, and that he's warned Farris of my involvement."

Talmach let out a slow breath, steepled his fingers and tapped them thoughtfully against his lips. "I'm aware of what happened. Careless, Tanner. I expected better. You could have exposed our whole operation."

Nate noted the two pertinent words in that sentence: *could have*. "I take it I didn't?"

A hesitation, then Talmach moved from the fireplace and eased himself down into a chair, propping his right leg up on a stool. He waved Nate into the seat opposite. "MacLeod arrived in London last night, making wild accusations against Farris. Apparently an unknown man visited the day before the… incident… claiming to be there on Farris's behalf?"

Nate grimaced, but nodded. "That was Hutchinson. He needed to locate MacLeod's study."

"Hmmm. A foolish decision." He brushed his cuff, as if dusting away a spec of dirt. "As you can imagine, I was forced to act. Our case against Farris would have been in jeopardy without his contract with MacLeod. Fortunately, wheels are now in motion to turn the situation to our advantage, despite your… sloppiness at Marlborough Castle."

Nate set his teeth but didn't respond to the rebuke. "If that's the case, I should return to Farris tomorrow. I assume you took steps to explain my absence?"

"I sent an apothecary's note — a bilious fever." He regarded Nate carefully. "You certainly look sick enough. What the devil happened to you?"

"Well, MacLeod shot me, for a start."

Worse, I let my stupid heart get skewered.

Talmach's eyebrows rose. "Do you need doctoring?"

"No. It was a scratch, and S — Hutchinson treated it for me. There's no infection."

The colonel brooded on that and then nodded. "Very well. Go home, get yourself cleaned up. Find Farris in the morning and report back to me in the normal way. With luck we'll be finished here by the end of the week — assuming you can get me a signed copy of Farris's agreement with MacLeod." He smiled in satisfaction. "I'll be glad to leave, won't you? I can see the corruption in the very air of this stinking city. It turns my stomach."

What turned Nate's stomach was the thought of what Sam must be feeling at this very moment. He rose. "I'll take my leave, Colonel. No, don't get up, I'll show myself out."

"No more mistakes," Talmach warned as Nate reached the door. "The mission is everything, Tanner. Don't forget your duty."

"How could I?" he said with a bow.

Duty was all he had left, after all.

Once outside, Nate paused. He was tired and aching from the journey, and leaned for a moment against the building, the brickwork still sun-warmed. He should do as Talmach suggested and go back to his Thames Street lodgings. He should ask the maid for hot water, he should bathe, eat, and sleep. And in the morning, he should try to find Sam and explain himself.

Wearily he set out, walking down to Cheapside. The street was busy, even this late, and he watched two hackneys trundle past before one responded to his hail. Despite having sat in a coach all day, it was a fair step down to Thames Street, and its Billingsgate stench would be ripe after a hot summer's day. The less time spent in that air the better.

"Where to, Gov?" called the jarvey from his perch.

Nate stopped with one foot in the cab. *Thames Street*, he intended to say. What came out was, "The St. Giles Bowl."

He jumped in and sat back against the seat, closing his eyes. Well, and why not St. Giles? Sam had dropped the name that day they'd rediscovered their friendship rolling around in the mud, and Nate had filed the information away as he'd been trained to do. Surely someone in the place would know Sam's name and be able to point Nate in his direction?

And then he'd make Sam listen. Forgiveness might be impossible, but Nate was going to make Sam hear the truth even if it killed him. And it might, he reflected, as the hackney slowed half an hour later outside an extremely unsavory looking establishment.

"Are you sure?" he asked the driver, stepping with care onto the filthy street.

"I am, Gov. Are you?"

"Not entirely." But he paid the driver anyway, with one eye on the sallow, pinch-faced characters slouching nearby.

The St. Giles Bowl — identified only by a rough sign depicting a bowl — appeared half derelict and, behind it, London degenerated into a rat's nest of dark and teeming alleyways. Squalid buildings hunched together, shabby laundry hung from some windows and lewd women, half-dressed, hung from others. The sewage stench was nauseating. Nate resisted the urge to put a hand to his nose, aware of eyes watching him. How far back the slum extended he couldn't tell; he could see flickers of firelight disappearing into the dark and doubted anything would tempt him to set foot into the place to find out.

His skin itched as the hackney pulled away and he abruptly wished he had a weapon. This was the place Sam called home? Good Christ. If the quiet streets of Rosemont were heaven, then this degraded labyrinth was hell indeed. Nevertheless, here he was, and he had a job to do. Straightening his shoulders, Nate braved the menacing looks of the bravos outside the Bowl and pushed open its poorly hung door.

Greasy tallow-light revealed a tawdry tap room. A crude bar ran along one side, behind which stood a slender black man who watched Nate with overt suspicion. Several shabby tables were arranged on the other side of the bar, where men of all types drank or played at dice, and the whole place stank of sweat and gin. When Nate entered, heads turned and didn't look away. After a moment, everyone was silent and watching. Nate swallowed, cleared his throat. "Good evening, gentlemen."

Someone snorted. "Ain't no gentlemen here, mate. 'Scept you, Yankee."

"I'm looking for a man named Hutchinson. I understand that he —"

"And what's he to you?"

The low voice came from behind him and Nate spun,

stumbling back a step in the face of the burly man looming over him. By candlelight it was difficult to make out much beyond a crop of tawny hair and narrowed eyes. "He —" Nate said. "He's a friend."

"Is he now?" The man looked him up and down. "Let me guess. Mr. Tanner?"

He tried not to let his surprise show. "Yes, as it happens."

"As it happens. Bloody hell, this day keeps getting better. It's alright Moses, I'll deal with this." He nodded at someone and Nate looked around to find the bar keeper tucking a cudgel away beneath the bar. "Now, let's you and me have a little talk, Mr. Tanner," said the man, taking Nate by the elbow and marching him over to a table in the far corner of the room. Nate was certain he had no choice but to comply.

The rest of the men lost interest and returned to their business, the rattle of dice and shouts of gaming filling the room. Nate sat down on a stool and the stranger pulled up a chair across from him, elbows resting on the wobbly table between. "Well," he said. "Nate bloody Tanner, as I live and breathe."

"You've the advantage of me, sir."

"Ain't I just?" He grinned. "Name's Cole. I'm a friend of Hutch's. And you'll be the sod what broke his heart."

Nate looked around in alarm, but no one seemed to have overheard. "Lower your voice," he hissed anyway.

"Nah, don't worry. We're all friends of Hal Foxe at the Bowl."

Nate could only guess what that meant.

Cole made a face. "Well, when I say friends, I ain't. Exactly. But that's not the point. The point is: what the bloody hell are *you* doing here? Hutch wants to wring your scrawny neck."

"Does he?" Nate swallowed. "Well. I want to talk to him, that's all. Explain some things."

"Like how you're a conk for the Yankees?"

"A what?"

"A nose. A snitch." He rolled his eyes at Nate's incomprehension. "An *informant.*"

"An agent of the Department of Foreign Affairs, in fact," Nate said. "And one losing patience. Look, it's late and I'm tired. Is Sam here?"

Cole sat back in his chair, rocking it onto its hind legs. "Maybe I don't want to let you see him."

"Let me?" Nate pushed to his feet. "How do you think — ?"

"Oh, get off your high horse, Tanner, and sit down." Cole sighed. "Jesus wept. The way Hutch is bleating on about you I expected a fire-breathing demon or an angel of the bleedin' Lord, not a prickly little bugger like you."

Nate stared. He had no idea what to say to this man, so he sat back down.

"Truth is," Cole went on, "I reckon it would be best all round if you got on a ship and sailed on home, and Hutch gave up on the idea of 'dear friends' and all that bloody molly nonsense. Never got men like us nowhere but hanged."

"I *am* going home," Nate said, meeting Cole's eye. "That's why I'm here. I want to set things straight before I leave, that's all. I —" It hurt to say it, a physical twist in his chest. "I know it's over between us. I'm not here to plead my case, only to tell him the truth about why I'm in London. And then I'll be gone. I won't return."

Cole rubbed a hand over his mouth, thinking. "God knows the bugger's in a state right now. Maybe he does need to hear your truths and make peace with them." He leaned forward and snatched Nate's wrist, pinning it to the table. He wasn't smiling. "Hutch is a decent cove and a good friend. You say your piece to him and leave. Understand?"

"Yes." He licked his dry lips. "Yes. That's all I want."

"Right then. Suppose I better take you over to the Brewery." He released Nate's hand and grinned crookedly. "Welcome to St. Giles, Mr. Tanner."

Chapter Twenty

THE BREWERY TURNED out to be a forbidding building lurking at the back of an untidy yard, its windows dark. Nate's skin crawled with the sensation of unfriendly eyes watching from the shadows. Even Cole hesitated. "I ain't going in," he said. "Me and Hal, we're not exactly on speaking terms just now. But I sent a runner from the Bowl. You're expected."

Expected, in this den of thieves and cutthroats? "You could be sending me to my death."

A flash of white teeth was all he could see of Cole's smile. "I ain't no crook, Mr. Tanner. I happen to believe in the law of the land. Unlike you Yankees, eh?"

"We —"

He held up a hand. "Don't fret. You're under the protection of Hal Foxe tonight, ain't nothing happens in St. Giles without his say so. Now get in there and say your piece."

Squaring his shoulders as best he could while still carrying his portmanteau, Nate stepped into the dark. He was aware of flitting shadows and then two boys appeared on either side of him, grubby but spared the pinch-faced urgency of hunger. "This way, mister," said one of them, shepherding Nate through a door into a large room smelling strongly of hops. It was terrifyingly dark. He flinched at every sound as the boys hustled him along, expecting a blow at any moment despite Cole's assurances. But then another door opened ahead of him and behind it rose a flight of stairs, light streaming down from above. One of the lads scampered up and Nate followed on legs not a little wobbly. God only knew what he'd find in this place.

"You're to wait in there," the boy announced as he opened another door. Nate squinted in the bright light as he stepped into a surprising room. Several shabby but deep armchairs were scattered about, a couple drawn close to an empty fireplace. A table, for cards or writing, stood near the curtained window and — most surprising of all — a bookcase lined one whole wall, crammed with volumes softened and worn from much use.

It was not at all what Nate had been expecting.

The boy disappeared and he was left alone with the slow tick of the clock on the mantel. A minute passed, two. Five. He perched on the edge of one of the chairs, too weary to stand, too tense to relax. He heard the distant sound of raised voices, a door slamming, and then the slow tread of reluctant footsteps. Nate rose, watching the door. The footsteps stopped outside and for a long time nothing happened. Nate's heart beat heavy in his throat. He wiped his sweaty palms on his coat. And waited.

Finally, with a squeak, the handle turned, the door opened, and there stood Sam. He looked as wretched as Nate felt, bruised shadows beneath his eyes, shoulders tensely squared. Nate opened his mouth to speak but found he had nothing to say. He'd not rehearsed this moment.

Sam's gaze flitted away as he pushed the door shut behind

him. "What do you want?"

"To talk. You left before I could —"

"Lie to me?"

"Explain." He balled his fingers into fists. "Christ, Sam. Won't you even listen?"

With a grunt, Sam stalked to the empty fireplace and stood there, fingers tapping on the mantle. "I saw the list of names, the one you stole from MacLeod. The one *I helped you steal.*" He glared. "Don't pretend it isn't what it looks like."

"I won't." Sam frowned and Nate straightened his shoulders, bracing himself to tell him everything. "MacLeod has a network of dissidents in America actively working against the Continental Congress. Paul Farris is one of them, and I'm here to gather evidence to prosecute him for treason." He hesitated, then added, "Colonel Talmach wants MacLeod's list of subversives. That's what you helped me take from his strongbox."

"*Colonel* Talmach…" Slowly, Sam turned from the fireplace to study him. "You're a spy, then."

"I'm an agent of the Department of Foreign Affairs."

Sam looked ashen, lips very thin and pale. "Dragging 'subversives' from their beds, is that it? Seeing men hang for nothing more than their —"

"Farris is —"

"I don't give a damn about Farris! You *lied* to me, Tanner. About everything. And you made me a part of this… this plot to destroy the lives of other men like me." Sam's voice cracked, his eyes shining. "How *could* you?"

Nate's chest compressed. "I'm sorry, but —"

"Sorry?" Sam spun away, arms braced on the mantle, head down. His shoulders shook, breath rattling in his throat. "God in pissing heaven, I'm such a fool."

"You're not." Nate took a hesitant step forward but didn't dare touch him. "Sam, please listen. I'm sorry I didn't tell you —"

"You know, I actually thought we could forget about all this politicking and secret committees. I thought we could live somewhere, you and me. I thought we could… that we could work —" He choked off and fell silent.

Into the airless room, Nate said, "You thought we could live somewhere? You and I together?"

"What a damned idiot."

"No," Nate said urgently. "Sam, none of this business with MacLeod matters. Don't you see? It has nothing to do with us, with what's between us. Nothing at all."

"If that's true, then why hide it?"

"Because I knew you'd react like this!"

Sam turned and Nate flinched from the harrowed expression in his eyes. "And that's exactly why I deserved the truth."

"But I…" His voice shook. "I told the truth about *us*."

"You think that makes a difference?"

"What I think is that I love you." He held out a hand, brushed the tips of his fingers against Sam's knuckles. "Sam, please —"

"Don't." Jerking back, Sam stumbled over the hearth and caught his balance on the mantle, arms splayed behind him. "Don't you say that. Don't you *dare* say that."

For an endless moment, Nate stood there, arm outstretched, nothing between them but distance. Then he let his arm fall to his side, dead as his heart, hope scattering at his feet like ashes. "Well, I guess I shouldn't be surprised. My love was never enough for you, was it? Never enough to change your mind. Not in Rosemont and not now."

Sam didn't yield, his eyes didn't soften. "How could it be? Love's only a word, Tanner. It's what you do that matters."

"Meaning what? I haven't given that letter to Talmach, if that's what you think. I'll burn it. I'll burn them all — they're just rumor and gossip."

Sam shrugged, indifferent. "Thing is, I don't believe a damned word that leaves your weasel mouth."

That was unfair. And it hurt. "It sounds more like you won't even *listen*. I'd never hurt you, Sam. I'd rather die first."

Sam remained stony and unmoved.

"Fine." Nate snatched his hat from the table and ran his fingers along the brim, angry and wounded. "I'm sailing for Boston in a matter of days. I hoped we'd at least part as friends, but if you can't —"

"Go back to your Congress," Sam said, stalking to the door and yanking it open. "Go fight for your cause, Tanner. I hope it makes you happy."

Chapter Twenty-One

BY THE TIME Sam left the Brewery, it was well past midnight. Cole had tried tempting him over to the Bowl for a drink, but Sam was in no mood for company. Heartsore after his confrontation with Tanner, he wanted only to lick his wounds in solitude. And he didn't much care about the risks of walking alone so late at night; his blood was up, and he could use a good fight.

Better to fight than to think.

Because if he thought, it would be about Nate. About Nate dragging dissidents from their beds. About this second, eviscerating betrayal and how Sam should have seen it coming. About how he *had* seen it coming but had blinded himself anyway. It would be about the humiliating stupidity of loving a man whose true loyalties would always lie elsewhere.

Well, that's where sentiment got you: prowling the dark streets of London with your fool heart broken and bleeding on your sleeve.

Heading up to Great Russell Street, he turned east past King's coffee house — still open for those in search of female company. Sam gave it a wide berth as revelers spilled out onto the street amid much drunken carousing.

But as he crossed Duke Street, he heard a sound and slowed enough to peer down the dark road. Was someone there? Nothing moved in the shadows, but nevertheless Sam quickened his pace. It was quieter on this part of the street, away from the riot of St. Giles. Under normal circumstances he might have carried a stick, but tonight he'd been too —

"Samuel Hutchinson." The voice came from behind him and he spun around, fists up ready to defend himself. "Are you Samuel Hutchinson?"

"What if I am? Who the devil are you?" A noise to his left and two other men emerged from Duke Street. Hell. Sam turned in a slow circle. "I don't have any money."

The man who'd spoken took a step closer. It was difficult to make him out in the dark, but he looked reasonably well dressed. Not your usual London rampsman. "Name's Groves," he said. "Of Bow Street."

Sam lowered his hands. He knew that name. Groves was one of Cole's associates. Besides, Hal Foxe had Bow Street in his pocket. Sam offered a smile. "Always happy to help the Principal Officers of Bow Street, Mr. Groves."

"Are you now?" Groves moved closer — he was a moon-faced man, fastidious looking. Cole always said he was a stickler for the rules. He made a slight gesture to one of his men and, to his shock, Sam found his arms yanked hard behind his back.

"What the devil…?" He squirmed but couldn't fight free of the solid grip. "What do you want? I haven't done anything." Someone was cuffing his wrists together, the bite of iron frighteningly familiar. "Hey! I haven't *done* anything!"

"As it happens," Groves said, "we heard different. We heard you was at the estate of Lord Marlborough — up Liverpool way."

"What?" His mind began to race. "I wasn't —"

"Oh, I think you were, Mr. Hutchinson. We've a witness puts you there."

The air stopped in his lungs.

"You and your accomplice."

Nate. A wave of sick dread washed over him. Dear God, had Nate been arrested too? "I don't know what you —"

"Come now." Groves drew closer, studying Sam's face. "No point in lying, is there? We know you broke into his lordship's house…"

Sam could scarcely hear him over the rush of blood in his ears. And all he could think was, *do they have Nate? Did MacLeod recognize him? Have they hurt him?*

Groves went on. "We know you made off with his property…"

But Sam wasn't listening. Wrenching around against the strong grip on his arms, he peered into the shadows behind them as if he might find Nate lurking there. But that was stupid. If they had Nate, he'd be at Bow Street or the Brown Bear. Or Newgate.

His stomach rolled; Nate wouldn't last five minutes in Newgate Gaol.

Turning back to Groves, he blurted, "There's no accomplice."

"What?"

"I had no accomplice."

Suspicion narrowed Groves' eyes. "You admit it, then, do you? You admit you were at Marlborough Castle?"

Sam sucked in a panicked breath. He knew what this confession would cost. He could already feel the earth closing over his head, the crushing darkness of Simsbury Mine stripping away all hope as he climbed down, down, down into that filthy pit. Into that hell. It was an effort to keep his voice even as he said, "I was there." Chin lifted, he met

Groves' eyes. "But I was there alone."

"Our witness says otherwise."

"Then your witness is a fucking liar."

A blow struck the words from his lips. "Watch your mouth."

Sam spat blood onto the ground, tried to shake the ringing from his ears. His heart thundered so hard he thought it might burst, fed by a vicious stream of anger. He clung to that, drank from it, used it to keep his rising panic at bay. "Go to hell."

Grabbing the lapels of his coat, Groves shoved him hard against the man behind him, making them both stagger. "I don't know whether you're brave or stupid, but you'll get nowhere calling the man laying information against you a liar."

Sam spat again. His lip had split. "What man is that?"

"John MacLeod, the Baron Marlborough." Groves bared his teeth in a grimace of triumph. "And it's not just for theft. You stand accused of murder."

Sam jolted backward. "*What*?"

"A footman was shot to death on MacLeod's estate. His lordship named you the culprit…" Groves released him and stepped back, frowning as he studied Sam's face. "I'm sorry, son, because you look properly flummoxed, but you're facing the noose."

Chapter Twenty-Two

THE DAY DAWNED as bright as London's smoky sky allowed, which was to say not very bright at all.

Nate lay in bed and watched the small patch of sky visible through his window slip from gray to hazy blue and felt little incentive to stir. Despite his exhaustion he'd barely slept, and the day stretched ahead without promise. His thoughts had chased each other all night in an endless spiral of misery, and he saw no way to halt them.

If only he'd burned the letter. If only Sam hadn't found it. If only Nate had explained his mission from the start…

But despite the leaden lump in his chest, he made himself get out of bed. He had nothing left but his duty, so he'd better get on with it. He washed and shaved, dressed the healing wound on his arm — and ached at the memory of Sam's gentle ministrations, of the pain of the wound made sweet by the joy of lovemaking. Remembering the tender trust Sam had placed in him, the trust Nate had crushed underfoot, made his throat burn.

Wearily, he dressed in clean, pressed clothes and made

himself presentable. He declined the offer of breakfast from his landlady, his stomach queasy from lack of sleep, but accepted a cup of coffee. It would stir his sluggish blood, at least.

Then he made his way to Farris's shipping office and was admitted by a clerk who made polite inquiries about his health. Nate could honestly answer that he was feeling less than well. Hanging up his coat and hat, he took a moment to gather himself before reluctantly entering the office. Farris sat at his desk by the window but already had a visitor.

Nate stopped in the doorway.

Talmach?

Farris glanced up. "Ah, Tanner, finished shitting through your teeth, eh?" He snorted at his own humor. "You look sick as dog, man. Not infectious, I hope?"

"No, sir." Nate kept his attention determinedly away from Talmach. What the devil was *he* doing there? "Am I interrupting?"

"No, no, you might as well be told. Sit down, Tanner, before you fall. You're as white as a nun's tit."

Nate sat, perched on the edge of a chair next to Talmach and opposite Farris. Talmach didn't look at him, but appeared relaxed, his wounded leg stretched out and his cane resting against his chair.

"This is Wilson. He's a thief taker who's been helping me with a problem." Farris leered. "Solved it now, eh, and to my advantage. MacLeod's in my debt, which is exactly where I want the old bastard."

Nate kept his face blank as he turned to Talmach. "What kind of problem was that, Mr. Wilson?"

Talmach was a true professional, his smile easy and betraying no recognition. "Oh, some bother at Lord Marlborough's estate. A murderous break-in and theft."

"Good heavens." Nate's heart pounded thirteen to the

dozen.

"A footman was killed defending his master from house-breakers. Poor man was shot in the face by the intruder." Nate froze as Talmach added, "Fortunately, I've discovered the identity of the culprit. And last night he was traced to the St. Giles rookeries, enabling Mr. Farris to alert the Principal Officers of Bow Street and have him apprehended. A desperate man, by all accounts, this *Samuel Hutchinson*."

Nate's throat convulsed and he had to cough before he said, "And — And are we certain of Lord Marlborough's veracity?"

Farris snorted. "Well, I'm not questioning him, and you damned well aren't either."

"Hutchinson's a notorious villain." Talmach sent Nate a speaking look. "I think justice will be served, one way or another."

"Be damned to justice," Farris crowed. "MacLeod's so pleased I had the wretch locked up that he's signing our contract today. His lordship's muskets will reach Boston, Congress will be nicely distracted from meddling in the African trade. And I, gentlemen, will be all the richer for it. Calls for a toast, eh? Where's the bloody brandy?"

Nate said nothing. It took all his concentration to keep from screaming. Horror pressed in from every side, worse in each direction he looked. Taylor was dead, his killer would go unpunished. And Sam sat in jail, facing the gallows for MacLeod's crime. *Christ*. He thought he might vomit.

But then a worse realization struck.

This was his fault.

Because of course Talmach had uncovered Sam's past; Talmach uncovered *everything*. And Nate had been an arrogant, selfish damned fool to think he could hide the truth from him. What the devil had he been thinking letting Sam get involved with this business in the first place? He should have warned him off from the start, protected him from Talmach's notice. Because when Talmach said he'd had Sam traced last night, he meant he'd had Nate followed.

He meant Nate had led Talmach straight to Sam.

"Dear God." He hadn't meant to speak, hadn't meant to curl forward in his seat.

"God's balls, Tanner." Farris paused in the act of pouring brandy. "If you're going to shoot the bloody cat, at least have the decency to do it outside."

Outside, yes. Nate lurched to his feet, pressing a hand to his stomach. He didn't have to feign illness. Talmach raised one dark eyebrow, his look a silent warning. Well, he could take his warning to the devil. "Please excuse me, Mr. Farris." Nate backed toward the door. "Forgive me."

Farris ignored him, grinning as he lifted his brandy in salute, knocking his glass against Talmach's. "To trouble and opportunity, sir. Long may they reign."

Nate fled. He stumbled along the docks, blind to where he was going, his thoughts running in ghastly circles. Sam would hang. Dear God, Sam would *die*. He put out a hand, clutched blindly at a railing as he bent double, his hollow stomach emptying bile into the dirt.

Sam would hang. His beautiful, beautiful boy would hang like a criminal. A sob choked his throat and he went to his knees, still clutching the railing. He had no hope. Who would take Sam's word over MacLeod's? Who would believe him? Nobody.

Sam would hang.

And it would be all Nate's fault.

Chapter Twenty-Three

THE HOLDING ROOM at the back of the Brown Bear was empty aside from the vagrant snoring in the opposite corner and stinking of gin and piss.

Sam sat slumped on a wooden bench, leaning his back against cold stone, with his eyes fixed on the room's high window. It looked out over nothing but soot-black brickwork, a heavy iron bar bolted across its cracked glass, but it was all that told Sam that he wasn't back in Simsbury Mine, thrown down into that dark, dank pit.

Forsaken.

He lost track of time. But he'd been there long enough for dawn to come and go. The city clocks had been chiming two when Groves turned the key in the lock, and Sam had heard nothing from him since.

A small mercy.

He wondered why he wasn't more afraid. Death scared him — he knew it did — yet he didn't feel frightened. He didn't feel much of anything. A great deadening fog sat between him and the world. He knew the terror was out there, but he couldn't touch it or see it or feel it. He supposed the numbness was something to welcome; the fog would lift soon enough.

More time passed.

And then the door opened, creaking on heavy hinges. An unfamiliar man appeared. "Oi, Hutchinson," the Bow Street officer said, "you've a visitor."

An unmanning bolt of hope pierced his stupor: Nate?

It wasn't Nate. But it was at least a friendly face. Sam got stiffly to his feet. "Cole." His rusty voice scratched his throat and he coughed to clear it. "Fancy meeting you here…"

Cole rolled his eyes and sat down on the bench, flicking out the tails of his coat. "Groves told me he'd brought you in, but I had to see for myself. Even by his low standards, this is ridiculous."

Against all odds Sam found a shadow of a smile as he lowered himself back to the bench. His jaw throbbed where Groves had struck him. "What did he tell you?"

"That a peer of the realm has laid evidence against you." He sighed and studied Sam's bruised face. "They're saying you'll hang for murder."

His stomach coiled around a nub of anger — the only kernel of life left in him. "It's a lie. MacLeod killed Taylor himself. I saw him do it. He was raging like a madman. And he'd have shot me, too, if Nate —"

He didn't finish the thought.

After a silence, Cole said quietly, "Was it him, do you think?"

"What?"

"Was it Tanner who conked you to Bow Street?" He spread his hands defensively at whatever he saw in Sam's face. "All I'm saying is it's a bloody big coincidence that he comes looking for you at the Bowl, and then Bow Street happen to be waiting right outside the moment you leave St Giles."

Sam shook his head; he couldn't even contemplate the possibility. "Nate wouldn't do that."

"Someone gave them your name, Hutch."

"It was MacLeod. Groves told me."

"Aye. And who told MacLeod?"

"Not Nate." Sam got to his feet, pacing to the other side of the cell and back. "He wouldn't. He despises MacLeod—"

"Last night you told me he was a fucking liar who had your name on a list of traitors. Last night you told me he stood by and watched you get tarred and feathered by a sodding mob. And that don't seem so different from this." Cole huffed out a sigh, his expression pitying. "I'm sorry, Hutch, but a leopard doesn't change his spots."

"No, you're wrong. That *was* different."

"Was it? How?"

"Because he couldn't— If he'd spoken up for me in Rosemont, they'd have—" He lowered his voice, glancing at the door. "Our *friendship* would have condemned us both. Nate had to stay silent."

"That ain't what you said last night."

"I was angry last night."

"And now?"

He dropped back onto the bench, returning his gaze to the window. The sun had risen high enough to penetrate the grimy glass, falling in a thick stripe across the flagstones. "Now I don't care. None of that matters anymore. I just want—" *To hold him, to see his smile again. To say goodbye.* His throat closed, eyes burning. "I just want him to be safe."

Cole gave a low whistle and when Sam looked over, he found his friend studying him. "You're tired. Hungry too, I bet. Here, I brought you some bread." He produced a muslin-wrapped package from his coat pocket and held it out.

It was a searing kindness, lancing through Sam's misery

to touch his heart. He wasn't hungry in the same way he wasn't terrified, but he took the bread anyway. The hunger, like the fear, would come soon enough. "Thank you."

Cole leaned forward, elbows on knees, gazing down at the floor. After a silence, he said, "I've always thought that coves like us should steer well clear of emotional snares. And you're doing a bloody good job of proving why." He looked over at him, lips pursed. "Whether he snitched or not, you do know that you're only in this bloody mess because of Tanner?"

Sam gave a wan smile. "I know. But will you help me anyway?"

"You're a damned fool, and so am I." Cole let out a blustery sigh. "But, aye. What can I do?"

"I think MacLeod recognized Nate. That must be how he got my name." He tried to swallow, but it was difficult around the fear rising in his throat. "MacLeod's a brutal bastard, Cole. If he got his hands on Nate, if he made him talk—" He grabbed Cole's arm, the thought of it too awful to bear. "Make sure he's safe? And if he is, tell him to go. Tell him to run before MacLeod can find him."

Cole covered Sam's hand with his own, squeezing. "You know I don't hold with all this molly nonsense about love and what-have-you. So I wouldn't say this if I hadn't seen it with my own bleedin' eyes, but I met Tanner the night he came to the Bowl. And let me tell you this: his was not the face of a man who'd run."

Sam's grip on Cole's arm hardened. "Then *make him.*"

Their gaze locked but before Cole could respond, the door opened and the Bow Street man poked his head back inside. "Time's up."

Ignoring him, Cole said, "I can't promise to make him do anything. But if I find him, I'll tell him what you said. The rest is his own business." With that, he gave Sam a bracing punch on the shoulder and got to his feet. "Now, keep your pecker up, Hutch. Remember, you've got friends in London."

Sam stared at the door after it closed, listening to the lock turn with a heavy clunk.

Friends in London? Cole meant Hal Foxe, Sam supposed, whose influence stretched to Bow Street but certainly not to Marlborough Castle. Anyway, no amount of grease in the right palm would let Sam slip free this time, because MacLeod needed him to swing for his crime. Just as Taylor had warned, Lord Marlborough made mockery of the law.

As for Nate…

It seemed an age since they'd stood together in the Brewery's library, Nate pale and drawn as he'd tried desperately to explain himself. And Sam not listening. Refusing to listen, the pain of betrayal so fierce it had burned.

Yet not half so fierce as the pain of regret.

How petty that argument seemed in the wake of this second catastrophe. Yes, Nate had lied. Yes, he'd concealed the truth about his reasons for being in England. And yes, the idea of Nate dragging dissenters from their beds touched Sam on the rawest of nerves.

But he saw things clearer now, the world cast in sharp and brutal relief by the shadow of the hangman's tree. And he was forced to ask himself what he'd have done had Nate told him the truth that first day at Salter's. Or before they'd stepped into the chaise together at The Swan. Or at any other time.

Well, he knew the answer. He'd have behaved exactly as he'd done last night, stalking off in a cloud of hurt pride and resentment.

And there would have been no journey to Marlborough Castle. No tender reconciliation. No forgiveness.

No accusation of murder, either. No stinking jail cell, no threat of the noose. Had he walked away from Nate two weeks ago, he wouldn't be sitting here paying the price for another man's crime.

But neither would he have held Nate in his arms again, worshiped Nate's body with his own. Felt his heart overflow with a love that had never died, that had blossomed once more after the darkest and bitterest of winters.

So even facing the gallows, Sam couldn't regret the last two weeks; they had restored him to life.

No, his regrets took a different turn.

He regretted walking out the morning he'd found the damned letter in Nate's book. And he bitterly regretted that the last words spoken between them had been words of anger instead of love.

Christ, why hadn't he given Nate the chance to explain? Why hadn't he trusted him enough to listen? But the truth was that he'd been expecting Nate's betrayal all along. He'd been expecting it since the day Nate stormed back into his life, seized his broken heart with both hands, and set about trying put it back together.

A fool's errand, because Sam's heart was quite irreparable.

Losing his home, his country, his very identity as an American had damaged him beyond healing, rendered him incapable of trusting. No, his heart was entirely broken. And, like a cracked vessel, it was no longer capable of holding tender feelings. So much so that, when Nate had sought him out at the Brewery and offered him his heart, Sam had refused to listen.

He'd thrown Nate's apology back in his face.

He'd thrown Nate's love back in his face.

And now that precious gift was lost to him forever.

Chapter Twenty-Four

"AH," TALMACH SAID as he opened the door to his rooms. "Feeling better?"

Nate didn't wait for an invitation and pushed past him into the parlor. Late afternoon sunlight spilled through the window, opened to catch a breeze that rustled the correspondence strewn across the writing table beneath it. Dispatches from home, Nate noted.

He turned to face the colonel. "You had me followed last night. Why?"

Talmach limped back into the room but kept his distance. Perhaps he thought Nate might punch him. Perhaps he might. "Because Hutchinson's mistake at Marlborough Castle nearly cost us the evidence against Farris." He spread his hands. "Besides, this is for the best. It's justice of a sort."

"Of a sort?" Nate's anger was a slippery thing, barely contained. "Hutchinson is innocent! I saw MacLeod murder that poor man himself. He —"

"MacLeod is necessary. As was my need to divert his suspicion from Farris. Good God, man, he was about to walk away from the whole arrangement —"

"But he'll hang! Sam will hang for a crime that bastard committed. He'll — My God." Nate stared, struck by the cold in Talmach's eyes. "You don't care, do you? You don't care if an innocent man hangs."

"Well." Talmach tugged at his cuff. "Is Hutchinson really so innocent?"

"Yes!"

"Damn it, Tanner, the man's a Tory. We should have hanged them all."

Nate stared, horrified. "No. That is too far."

"Is it? You understand the precarious position our nation's in. Its very survival is at stake. If the Congress can't control Tories, then what *can* it do? Who will take us seriously in the world if we allow the likes of Farris and MacLeod to undermine the authority of the Continental Congress? We'll have anarchy: war between the states, rebellion, invasion. These men must be stopped and publicly exposed. An example must be made of them. And we — the agents of the government — must see it done. So, no, it is not too far. There is no *too far* when it comes to defending our country."

Nate stared at him and it was as if the world had tilted on its axis and he saw Talmach through Sam's eyes. Saw himself through Sam's eyes.

Your liberty is the tyranny of the mob. Don't you see? You've torn down King George, but King Mob will take his place. And God help anyone who dares argue with that *tyrant!*

"There must be limits," Nate said stiffly. "Even when it comes to defending our country, there must be limits to our power, otherwise we're no better than tyrants ourselves."

Talmach cocked his head. "Perhaps it's you, Tanner, who needs limits? The nature of your friendship with Hutchinson —"

"Is none of your concern."

"It is when the man's a convicted traitor."

"Convicted in his absence!" Nate cried, losing his temper. "Which, by the way, violates *habeas corpus* and every law of natural justice. And for what? For refusing to take an oath, for wanting a different future for his country. One no less glorious, no less patriotic. No less *American*." He sucked in a shaky breath, aware that he was exposing far too much. He needed to be careful. Reining himself back, he said, "Colonel, what kind of nation are we building if we call a man a traitor for holding a contrary opinion?"

"A safer one. And you're a fool if you think otherwise. This isn't a Harvard debating society, Tanner. This is war."

"The war's over."

"Tell that to Paul Farris."

Nate held up his hands. "Farris *is* a traitor. *He's* the one who should hang."

"And he will once you do your duty and bring me the signed contract."

His duty. Nate turned to the window, stared down into the street below. It was busy with traffic, the shouts of the drivers and the rattle of wheels rising with the late-afternoon heat. In his pocket sat the evidence Talmach wanted, the evidence of Farris's treacherous deal with MacLeod, signed that very afternoon. Once he handed it over, his duty would be done. He could go home.

And Sam would be left to die, his death the price of defending the Continental Congress. A terrible price. An unjust price.

One Nate refused to let him to pay.

Realization struck like a thunderbolt. Nate might never win back Sam's love, but he could damn well prove himself worthy of his trust. Cost him what it may, Nate would not let Sam hang to please Benjamin Talmach.

He reached into his pocket and retrieved the document.

When he turned from the window, he saw Talmach's eyes alight on the paper with avid interest. "And there's nothing we can do for Hutchinson?" Nate said, just to be sure. "No way to save him now that the deal is signed?"

Talmach's gaze lifted to meet Nate's. He shook his head. "Farris and MacLeod are going to Bow Street tomorrow, to see the magistrate commit Hutchinson to Newgate for trial. Until Farris is aboard ship and we've sailed, we can't risk him realizing he's been compromised. If he knows, he'll stay in London." A hint of sympathy softened Talmach's expression. "This struggle demands a high price, Tanner. From us all."

He gave a curt nod. So be it. "Take it then," he said, offering the contract. "It's done."

Talmach smiled. He had a smile like a wolf. "You've done well — we've averted a disaster. Continue as before with Farris, provoke no suspicion in his mind, and I'll see you both aboard ship in four days." His wolfish smile broadened. "It'll be a fine moment when we reveal the truth to him, eh? After all the indignities he's caused you, I think it's only fitting that you have the pleasure of arresting him yourself."

"I look forward to it."

But he doubted he'd be there to claim that honor. What he knew for sure as he left Talmach's rooms was that he wouldn't go home until Sam was safe. And since no legal redress for Sam's situation remained, he must resort to less than legal methods.

Like Sam, he must become an outlaw.

To that end, he wanted to head straight for St. Giles, find Sam's friend, Cole, and beg for his help. He had nobody else he could turn to, but he'd learned his lesson last night and dared not risk Talmach having him followed again. Instead, he made his way back to his lodgings on Thames Street.

There he placed MacLeod's stolen letters in the cold fireplace, lit a taper and watched them burn, their charred edges curling up as the flames ate every word of rumor, gossip, and insinuation.

When that was done, he changed into a discreet black coat and breeches, waited an excruciatingly long time for night to fall, and then slipped out of the servants' entrance into the cut that ran behind his lodging house. He made his way along the back of the building, turned left down another ally, and emerged one street over. Once certain he wasn't being followed, he hailed a hackney and headed for St Giles.

Unsurprisingly, his welcome there was less cordial than last time.

"I need to speak to Elias Cole," he said, face shoved hard against the damp brick wall of the Brewery yard. "My name's Nathaniel Tanner."

The man who held him in place grunted — a thick-necked bully without much going on behind his eyes. "I know who you are."

"It's about Hutchinson. I need to speak to Cole —"

A snort. "Cole ain't home to the likes of you."

"Please, it's a matter of —"

"It's all right, Bell." Cole's voice came from the other side of the road, accompanied by steady footsteps. Nate twisted his head to see. "Tanner's a friend of Hutch." Cole came into view, holding up a lamp. "At least, so I thought."

"I *am*." He twisted angrily and the bully — Bell — let him go. Rubbing at his wrists, Nate glared at him. "Thank you."

"You *should* thank me, an' all. You nosed us to the tappers. By rights, I should've milled you."

"Well. That sounds bad, whatever it means. Thank you for not doing it." He turned to Cole. Even in the flickering lamp-light, he could see the wariness in his face. No trust there. Nate lifted his hands, palms up. "I'm here about Hutchinson."

"Are you, now?" Cole took a step closer, raising the lantern so he could better see Nate's face. "Did you tell MacLeod where to find him?"

"The devil I did. I was followed here yesterday." He ran a hand over his hair, irritably tucking loose strands behind his ears. His hat had been knocked to the ground and he bent to retrieve it. "Alright, let me explain." He rattled through the details of why it suited the colonel for a notorious Tory like Sam to pay for MacLeod's crime, and how he'd had Nate followed. "I swear I didn't know anything about it until this morning. I'd never —" He lowered his voice, holding Cole's gaze, letting him see the truth if he chose to look. "Sam is my dearest friend. I let him down once before, but I never will again."

After a cold silence, Cole said, "He gave me a message for you."

"You've seen him?" Nate seized his arm. "Is he alright? What did he say?"

"He said you should go. Fuck off back to America, quick as you like."

Nate steeled himself against that stab to the heart. He'd expected it. "I know how he feels about me, but it doesn't matter. I'm still going to save him."

"*You're* going to save him?"

"Yes. Alone if I must, but I'd like your help if you're willing." He glanced around the shadowy yard. "Is there somewhere we can talk?"

For the first time, Cole's expression softened. "You'll never break him out of the Bear."

"I know." Nate allowed himself a smile, a shaky thing perched atop his galloping fear. "I've got a better plan…"

Chapter Twenty-Five

THEY BROUGHT SAM from the Brown Bear to the magistrate's court just after dawn the following day, and he stayed there another few hours, staring at a different wall. At least the air was fresher without the gin-piss stench of his former cellmate. Someone gave him small beer and he ate a little of the bread Cole had brought. He couldn't stomach much.

It was better than Simsbury. There was light and air, and nobody had spat at him or kicked him. So far. Newgate would be different. The prison's name tolled through St. Giles with all the horror of plague, a dozen stories from the louse house on every man's lips. Chances were that Newgate would get him before the hangman earned his coin.

But the thought that consumed him, circling around and around his enervated mind, was that he hadn't said goodbye to Nate. He could write a letter, perhaps, if Cole would provide him with pen, ink, and paper and deliver it before Nate left the country. But dare he risk committing his heart to paper just to relieve his aching soul? If the letter were discovered, Nate would pay the price.

Sam knocked his head back against the wall and closed his eyes.

Sometime later he was roused by a kick to his foot. He opened his eyes to find one of the court officials staring down at him. "On your feet, Hutchinson."

He complied, no point in doing otherwise, and allowed himself to be led into the long, narrow hall that served as the magistrate's court. It was a gloomy place. High windows ran along the left-hand wall, but their sooty glass didn't let in much light. On the right, a raised public gallery plunged everything beneath it into shadow.

Sam was taken to stand at a wooden bar, opposite the man recording the proceedings. Beyond him, at the far end of the court, sat the magistrate. His chair was perched on a low dais and he was in close conversation with a colleague sitting to his left. To either side of Sam, two rows of benches ran the length of the hall, crowded with officials, gawkers, and witnesses. He was too tired to be interested in any of them. He'd not slept in two nights — not since the night he'd slept with Nate in his arms — nor had he shaved or washed. He felt as disreputable as he no doubt looked.

The court was noisy, a babble of voices echoing around its high ceiling. Sam glanced up at the public gallery, at the men and women leering down at him, eager for the next sensation. His eyes felt gritty with lack of sleep, his body ached, and his heart hurt.

Perhaps that's why it took him a moment to notice a shift in the atmosphere of the court, a hush rippling outward from the doorway behind him like a breeze through tall grass. Sam glanced over his shoulder, jolting at the sight of MacLeod strutting into the court, his ruddy face at odds with the pea-green of his coat. Behind him walked a man Sam didn't recognize, bland save the smug smile on his frog-like lips, and behind *him* —

Sam clutched the wooden bar until he thought it must break. Nate. God, Nate was there with MacLeod. What the devil was he thinking? Hadn't Cole warned him to run?

Their eyes met instantly, Nate's dark to the point of blackness against the pallor of his face. There were shadows beneath them, his lips a colorless line of tension as he followed MacLeod and the other man to take their seats at the side of the court.

Someone shouted for order and the hall fell silent. The magistrate pinned Sam with a narrow look along the length of the courtroom. "You are Samuel James Hutchinson?"

It was a struggle to find his voice, a struggle to stop looking at Nate. But Nate's attention was fixed on the magistrate, his fingers knotted together in his lap, and eventually Sam tore his eyes away. "I am, sir."

"You understand that this is not a trial," the magistrate said. "We are here to determine whether there is a case against you to be answered. If I deem that there is, you will be committed for trial at the Old Bailey and sent from this place to Newgate Gaol, there to await your hearing. Is that clear?"

"Yes, sir."

"Very well. You are accused of the murder of one Thomas Taylor, a footman to Lord Marlborough, employed at Marlborough Castle." He glanced up. "A serious allegation. What have you to say to the charge?"

"That I'm not guilty of it, sir. And that the man who accuses me is a liar."

At that, a general murmuring broke out in the courtroom. Speaking over it, the magistrate said, "You are accused by John MacLeod, The Baron Marlborough — a peer of the realm. Are you calling him a liar, sir?"

Sam looked over and found MacLeod staring at him. The last time Sam had seen him, he'd been wearing nothing but his shirtsleeves and breeches, raging like a madman. Now he wore a yellowing old wig beneath which gimlet eyes arrowed in on Sam with murderous intent. His fleshy face over-spilled his cravat and Sam recoiled from the memory of him murdering Taylor in cold blood. Sam straightened his shoulders, refusing to be cowed by this bacon-fed bully. He turned to face the magistrate. "Yes, sir, I am. And that's the least of his crimes."

Uproar. MacLeod was on his feet shouting "Calumny!" while the drudge next to him — Farris, Sam guessed — tried to make him sit back down. Court officials yelled for silence and through it all Sam watched Nate, who sat stock still and stared straight ahead. What he was thinking, Sam couldn't tell.

At last order was restored, MacLeod was persuaded back into his seat and the magistrate said, "Hutchinson, you'll refrain from making accusations against others. We are here to hear the case against *you*." He tapped the sheaf of papers in his hand. "We have Lord Marlborough's account of events. Have you any evidence to prove your innocence?"

"I — No, sir. Only my word."

At that MacLeod snorted loudly and the magistrate favored him with a sharp look before saying to Sam, "Any witnesses in your defense?"

"No, sir. None who can speak freely, at any rate."

The magistrate's eyes narrowed. "Meaning what? Any may speak freely here. At Bow Street, we welcome evidence from the people, from any man — or woman — who has information pertinent to the matter at hand. All witnesses are heard."

"I thank you," Sam said, "but in this case, it's not possible."

Another snort from MacLeod. "And if that don't prove the blighter guilty, I don't know what does, eh?" A few murmured agreements drifted down from the public gallery.

"Thank you, my lord," the magistrate said, "but we are not here to prove guilt, only to determine whether there is a case to answer."

"Well, the blasted footman's dead," MacLeod said. "What more do you damn well need?"

The magistrate gave a terse bow of acknowledgment to MacLeod and turned back to Sam. "If you can provide no alibi, nor any evidence in your favor, nor any witness to speak for you…?"

Helplessly, Sam turned to Nate, just as he'd done that long-ago night in Rosemont. And, like that night, Nate looked back silently. He sat with his jaw locked and his hands clenched in his lap. Motionless. Part of Sam longed for him to leap to his defense, to stand with him as friend and ally, just as he'd longed for it when Amos Holden had him on his knees. But a greater part of him flinched from the idea, horrified by the thought of Nate incriminating himself.

After a pause, the magistrate said, "Mr. Hutchinson, have you a witness?"

"No." He kept his gaze on Nate as he spoke, saw his eyes close briefly, lips thinning. "I prefer not to call any witness."

"Then I am sorry for you, but I cannot dismiss this case. Therefore, Mr. Hutchinson, you will be taken to Newgate Gaol, there to await trial for murder."

Nate didn't react, didn't move an inch. Perhaps, like Sam, he'd expected nothing else with MacLeod as the accuser. The verdict would prove equally predictable.

Someone took Sam's arm, pulling him away from the bar. "Come on, the wagon's waiting."

A sudden rush of panic seized him. Once he left the court, he'd never see Nate again. Never in his life would he see that beautiful, precious face. "No!" He pulled his arm free, opened his mouth to call Nate's name, but stopped himself in time. He dared not betray their connection, not in front of Farris and MacLeod. "Marlborough!" he called instead. "Marlborough, you bastard!"

MacLeod's head turned, jowls wobbling. But Nate turned too, thank God, dark eyes stark in his ashen face.

"Shut your bloody mouth," the guard growled, hustling Sam towards the door.

Helplessly, he struggled, desperate to go to Nate, to hold him one last time. To say goodbye. But it was impossible. In agony, their gaze met across the court — *Oh God, this is it, this is the end* — Sam's eyes filled, Nate blurred in his vision, and then he was out through the door and Nate was hidden from him.

An unmanly sob choked out, burning his chest. He scarcely knew where he was being taken, soaked in misery and his face wet with tears. Oh God, Nate was gone. He'd never see him again. Someone bound his hands with rope, and he was led out into the yard behind the court. Blinking in the daylight, he saw that a prison wagon awaited, other convicts slumped sullenly within its iron cage. He recognized Groves perched next to the driver, but Sam didn't have time to say anything before he was bundled roughly up the steps and into the wagon. The guard locked the cage door behind him.

Then, finally, the first sliver of fear penetrated his misery. He swallowed hard, wiping his eyes on the cuff of his sleeve. God, would he ever see sunlight again? The suffocating memory of Simsbury Mine swept over him and he began to panic, his lungs tightening, guts turning to water. Not again. He couldn't endure it again. He'd go mad in the dark.

The wagon lurched forward, jolting him as the driver turned the horses toward the wide gate that led out to the street. Sam had to grab the bars with both bound hands to keep from falling.

A crowd had gathered outside the court, drawn as people were by the entertainment of their neighbors' misfortune. Ruthlessly, Sam tamped down his dread and kept his head held high, staring down anyone who jeered at him, refusing to give the gawkers their pleasure. He could easily bear the mocking taunts of strangers. Last time he'd been driven away in the back of a wagon, the mob had been his neighbors, their anger had been deadly, and Nate had been watching.

He thought of it now, but for once the terror and shame of that night didn't return. No tar stench filled his nose, no flickering reminder of flames danced before his eyes. For a moment he was surprised, but then he realized that something had changed; he'd forgiven Nate his silence that night. More than that, he understood that sometimes the best a man could do for the one he loved was simply to bear witness to their suffering and not flinch away.

As Nate had done in court today.

They made slow progress along Bow Street, the lumbering wagon trundling past the entrance to the court just as a familiar figure emerged through its doors. Nate. Sam's heart flew. It felt like a reprieve, a last chance to drink his fill. Nate came to stand with MacLeod and Farris, who turned to speak with him, but Nate was watching the wagon instead — watching Sam. Although still pallid, he looked nervy, bouncing on his toes. Even from yards away, Sam could see his nervous energy. Nate looked as though he were about to start a fight, and Sam's pulse quickened in response. Shifting a step or two in the cage, he tried to keep Nate in sight as the wagon rolled on, cursing when a woman's feathered hat blocked his view. He coveted every moment he could see Nate and —

"Whoa!" The driver yelled and the wagon lumbered to a halt. Sam didn't look around to see what was happening, just counted his blessings and kept his eyes on Nate. He was walking away from Farris now, shoving his hand aside when Farris tried to stop him. Sam stared, unsure what he was seeing, his heart racing ahead of him in hope he barely allowed himself to feel.

From ahead came the sound of arguing and a man's raised voice. American. Moses? Startled, Sam glanced over his shoulder. Through the bars of the cage he saw a coster-monger's handcart overturned in front of the wagon, fruit and vegetables spilling across the street, and Moses yelling and fussing and making no effective effort to clear the way.

Sam's pulse started galloping in earnest. What the devil? He looked back to Nate and found him cutting through the crowd at a fast but steady walk, focused entirely on the wagon. Sam maneuvered his way as casually as possible to the locked door of the cage.

"Here, Groves, got a minute for a word while you ain't going nowhere?" To Sam's astonishment, Cole swung him-self up onto the front of the wagon, effectively blocking Groves' view of what was happening behind him. "Reckon I've got a lead on Wessex. Heard he's started doing business with Dick Radcliffe. You know him? Fence up at the Red Lion…"

Sam turned back to Nate. He was running now and launched himself up onto the back of the wagon, jamming a heavy iron key into the lock.

"Oi, watch out!" yelled a voice from the crowd.

Through the bars, Nate's urgent gaze met Sam's. "Run," he said as he yanked the door open and half-jumped, half-fell back onto the street. Sam threw himself out after him, stumbling to his knees thanks to his bound wrists. Nate grabbed his arm, hauled him up, and then they were pelting down the street. The rest of the prisoners spilled out after them, adding to the confusion, while the crowd looked on in delight, hoots of laughter and shouts of encouragement chasing after them.

"Tanner!" MacLeod loomed out of the crowd, swinging his walking cane like a weapon. Its silver knob flashed in the sunlight, a hair's breadth from Nate's face. He ducked, stumbled in the muddy street and went down in the dirt. MacLeod lifted the cane for another blow.

"No!" Sam barreled into him with a savage cry and MacLeod staggered, lost his footing, and fell hard. Breath exploded from his lungs, his cane skidding away. Sam snatched it up with both his bound hands. Raising it, he took aim.

A firm grip on his wrist stopped him. "Don't." Nate, wild and frightened, glanced past Sam. "Christ, just run."

Sam hesitated, stared down at MacLeod's wheezing hate-filled face, and dropped the cane. Nate was right. He was no murderer, and he wouldn't let MacLeod make him one.

Lighter on his feet than Sam, Nate pulled ahead. But he didn't know London like Sam did. "Nate, this way!" Sam darted right, along the alley leading to the Theatre Royal. The theatre was quiet at this time of morning, not even the whores were open for business, and Sam staggered to a stop halfway along the alley to catch his breath. Two nights in jail, with little food and no sleep, had taken its toll.

"Keep moving." Nate put his hand on Sam's shoulder and pushed him on. Together, they made their way around the back of the theatre and from there toward the noise and bustle of Covent Garden.

Neither spoke. With so much to say, Sam didn't know where to begin and he imagined Nate felt the same. But as they got closer to the open expanse of the market, Sam glanced over his shoulder. Seeing no sign of pursuit, he drew Nate to a halt and glanced down at his bound wrists.

"Do you have a knife?"

Wordlessly, Nate reached into his boot. Sam held out his arms and Nate sliced the rope, letting it drop to the ground at their feet. He rubbed at his wrists, aware of Nate standing close, aware of the last angry words that had passed between them. Aware he was unshaven, and prison soiled. "I, uh, thank you. For saving me…"

Nate kept watching the marketplace, which hummed with life under the hazy morning sun. "Contrary to expectations, I know."

"Nate —"

"We should go. Come on. I said we'd meet the others at the Bowl."

"The St. Giles Bowl?" Sam gave a soft laugh. "We'll make an outlaw of you yet." Nate didn't answer, but Sam caught the hint of a smile curling his mouth and his spirits lifted.

Covent Garden, with its covered stalls, hawkers, acrobats, peddlers, and footpads was as good a place as any to get lost. Sam wove a meandering path around the crowded edges of the market where the stalls were packed together in the shadows of the great buildings behind them, the light muted by grubby canvas awnings. Carefully avoiding the open expanse at the center where livestock grazed on hay bales, Sam ducked out along James Street and from there led Nate through all the dark alleys and yards up to Seven Dials. Hal Foxe's protection didn't extend so far south, but nevertheless Sam relaxed — the squalid streets of Seven Dials were hardly friendly territory for Bow Street, either. After another half hour walking in silence, they crossed Broad Street and reached St. Giles proper.

Something of a hero's welcome awaited them at the Bowl. Cole, smiling, pulled Sam into an embrace, while others slapped his back and Moses yanked shut the door, barred it, and sent a couple of boys out to watch for tappers.

There were back ways out of the Bowl that meant everyone would be lost in St. Giles' warren of alleyways long before Bow Street got through the door.

Sam let out a breath — he was safe.

And it was only then, as the threat finally lifted, that the true horror descended: the scaffold, the noose, and the terror of the great unknown beyond. He'd seen men die at Simsbury, legs kicking and face purpling, tongue lolling. And that might have been him. It would have been him…

"Oh God."

Panic ambushed him. Everything he hadn't felt in the jail overwhelmed him in a great wave. Struggling to catch his breath, he reached blindly for a table as the world went gray around the edges, his knees buckling.

"A chair!" Cole barked, catching him. "You there, move back. A chair — Thank you, Tanner."

Sam sat, head down and eyes screwed shut as he struggled to master his spiraling fear and force air into his cramping lungs. Someone gripped his shoulder, steadying him, and slowly, slowly his breathing became easier and the panic receded. He was safe. Nate had saved him.

When he could sit up again, Moses pressed a cup of good whiskey into his hand and one of his girls set a chunk of greasy pie on the table before him. Sam ignored the pie and stared into his glass, breathing in the heady aroma, and watching the liquid gleam amber in the lamplight.

It reminded him of home, of Nate and all that they'd shared in those golden days before the war. And for the first time since he'd left Rosemont, those memories brought him comfort.

Lifting the glass to his lips, he took a long, deliberate swallow, relishing the flavor of home as he scanned the crowd and found Nate hovering near the door, talking to Cole. He had the look of a bird sensing the approach of a cat, about to take flight.

Sam couldn't blame him. Nate had saved him; he'd risked everything to save him from injustice. That was all Sam had ever wanted and more than he had any right to ask. But now Nate would go home to the new country he was building, he would go home and save it from men like MacLeod and Farris who wanted to shape it in their vile image.

And with startling clarity, Sam knew that he wanted it too. Not just for Nate but for himself. He wanted to help build an America where men like Amos Holden and John MacLeod could hold no sway. A land of law and justice.

Which left one question: was there a way to go home?

Chapter Twenty-Six

ON THE ORDERS of Hal Foxe, Nate and Sam were escorted back to the Brewery. It was for their own safety, Foxe said, lest Bow Street come looking. But Nate suspected that, had he preferred to go elsewhere, his escort would have become less friendly.

As it was, he had no objection. It suited him to keep his head down. Farris would be livid, MacLeod apoplectic. But neither of them scared him half so much as Talmach. Nate would have to face the colonel at some point, but he'd rather wait until the heat of the moment had passed. If he were lucky, none of this would affect Farris's prosecution and, so long as that was intact, he suspected Talmach would forgive him in the end. If not…? Then so be it. He glanced at Sam, trudging wearily beside him, and received an uncertain smile in return. God only knew how things stood between them, but Nate didn't regret saving Sam any more than he regretted drawing breath. Both were necessary for life.

The Brewery was a place of mystery, Nate soon realized. The snug library he'd seen on his first visit was just the start of it. While he and Sam were shown to two comfortable rooms not far from the library, Nate caught a glimpse through a half-open door of a much larger and private establishment beyond — and none of it at all like the building's decrepit exterior. Curious, indeed.

But, for now, Nate was too tired to do more than smile his thanks to the young girl who showed him to his room. "You can rest here, sir," she said. "There's water to wash and you're to go to the library when you're hungry and someone will bring food."

The room itself had a good size bed, a washstand, and an ewer of water. When he put his hand to the jug, it was warm. Wonderful. Outside, a hazy white sky spread above the tattered rooftops and chimney pots of St. Giles, a bowl of dried lavender on the windowsill perfuming the room and masking the pervasive rookery stench.

Nate eyed the bed, tempted to just lie down and close his eyes. Until that moment, he hadn't realized the depths of his exhaustion. Now that Sam was safe, the tension that had kept him on his feet was rapidly unraveling. He found it an effort even to strip off his shirt and wash, but the water felt good on his sweaty skin and he sighed as he sluiced a jug-full through his hair, scrubbing it dry with the towel set next to the basin.

The room was warm, a stripe of hazy sunlight crossing the bed, and Nate could resist no longer. He slung his shirt back on and flopped down onto the mattress. He had a few moments to consider Sam, alive and safe, before the softness of the bed, the sun-warmed sheets, and his utter exhaustion dragged him down into a leaden sleep.

He woke sometime later with a start, disoriented. Propped up on his elbow, heart pounding, it took a moment to remember where he was and to understand what had woken him. Someone was knocking on the door. The girl from before, most likely, with food. Nate blinked, rubbed a hand over his face. "Come in," he rasped, swinging his legs over the side of the bed. The light had changed, taking on the golden hue of evening, slanting into the room from an entirely different angle. He must have slept for hours.

The door cracked open, but it wasn't the serving girl whose head poked around it.

"Did I wake you?" Sam was carrying two gently steaming cups.

"You did," Nate said, "but that's alright. What time is it?"

"Past seven." Like Nate, Sam had washed—and shaved, too. He was dressed in clean clothes, the dark green of his coat complementing the gray of his eyes. "I brought you some tea."

"Tea?" Despite his patriotic duty to prefer coffee, Nate had never shaken his love of tea. "I haven't had a decent cup in years." He took the mug and breathed in the steam with pleasure. "Thank you."

Smiling slightly, Sam walked to the window and stared out, sipping his own tea. Nate didn't know how to fill the silence—everything between them was so tangled. He wished he could just walk up behind Sam, slip his arms around his waist, and tell him he was loved and that nothing else mattered. But the world had never been that easy for them.

"You'll be sailing for Boston this week," Sam said at last, turning to face him.

Nate tried for a smile. "Probably in the brig the whole way."

"Because of today?"

"Small price to pay. I'd rather that than see you come to harm." It was the bare and painful truth. "Look, I know you don't believe me, but—"

"I do." Sam watched him, evening sunlight gilding his

skin. "I do, Nate. I — Hell." He set his tea on the windowsill and scrubbed his fingers through his hair. "I wish I'd talked to you when I found that letter."

Nate sighed as he bent to set his own cup on the floor. "There are a thousand things *I* wish I'd done different, Sam. I wish I'd never told you we couldn't be friends back in Rosemont. I wish I'd spoken out against Holden from the start. I wish I'd stood with you that night —"

"I wish I'd stayed." Sam spoke to him across the small expanse of the room, but it felt to Nate that he spoke from across the years. "I wish I'd sworn the damned loyalty oath and stayed in Rosemont. I think I could have done good there. More good than I've done here. Maybe we could have done good together. And I —" In two strides he was across the room, kneeling next to the bed. He took both Nate's hands in his, looking up with a face stripped of everything but honesty. "Hell, Nate, I want to be with you. That's the truth. I know you need to go back to America, and I agree. You *must* go. It's not that I've changed my mind — I still fear for our country's future, I'm still afraid of men like Holden, of what they could do with a mob at their back — but I see now that you need to stop them. And I want to help you. I want to help build a country ruled by laws, not demagogues. I want to go home. And I think there's a way I can do it. I spoke to Hal and he knows a good scratchman, someone who could get me false papers in a different name. I couldn't go back to Rosemont, but maybe we could go somewhere else? Somewhere I'm not known. And we could be together, Nate. Work together. If…" His grip on Nate's hands tightened. "If you still want that?"

Nate's throat was too tight, his eyes blurring. He leaned down and pressed his lips to Sam's knuckles where their fingers tangled together. "Christ, Sam. I've never wanted anything more."

Sam made a gruff noise, bent his head to kiss Nate's hair. Then, freeing his hands, he cupped Nate's face and lifted it up to look him in the eye. "You mean the world to me, Nate Tanner. You always did, I was just too hurt and angry to admit it."

Helpless to do anything else, Nate slipped off the bed and into Sam's waiting arms, all but sobbing in relief as Sam gathered him in. "I'm so sorry," he breathed, holding Sam tight. "I'm sorry for everything you lost. I'm sorry for everything you suffered. And I'm sorry I couldn't stop it happening." He pulled back, looking at him deeply. "I *love* you, Sam. I always have and I always will."

And then they were kissing, Nate pressed back against the edge of the bed and Sam's arm around his waist holding him up until it all got too awkward and they sprawled in an undignified heap on the floor. Nate laughed, burying the sound against Sam's shoulder.

"Bed," Sam said, untangling himself. He stood, offering Nate a hand, his happy grin untarnished by the bleak years between them.

With leaping joy, Nate let Sam pull him to his feet and back into his arms. They kissed deeply, Sam tracing glorious paths with his lips across Nate's collarbone, the open neck of his shirt slipping off his shoulder. It was damned unfair since Sam was still fully dressed. Laughing, Nate ducked away, pulling his shirt over his head, and delighting in Sam's heated gaze. "Clothes off," he ordered, and glanced behind him at the door. "Hurry."

While Nate threw the bolt, Sam took off his coat and waistcoat. Nate helped with the neckcloth, eager for the taste of his skin, and then Sam's hands were on the buttons of Nate's breeches and Nate was hauling Sam's shirt over his head.

"Damn, you feel good," Sam growled when they pressed

together, naked from chest to toes. Sam's cock was a hard pressure against Nate's belly, and he rolled his hips with a grunt that made Sam whimper.

Nate grinned and pushed Sam back, toward the bed. "Lie down," he said, and Sam flopped back onto the mattress, pulling Nate down on top of him. Warm clean skin, golden sunlight spilling over them both: it was unbearably perfect. Nate paused, framed Sam's face in his hands to see him better — this face he'd been without for years, this beloved face he'd so nearly lost forever. "I'll never leave you," he said, eyes filling. "I swear on my life, Sam. We'll never part again."

Sam's smile was emotional as he lifted a hand to palm Nate's cheek. "You're the love of my life."

"And you, mine."

Laughing, Sam wiped a hand over his shining eyes. "Hell, never let Elias Cole hear us talking like this."

Nate grinned. "Well, that's unlikely."

"He'd say we were fools." His smile dimmed. "He'd say love isn't possible for men like us. He'd say it's too dangerous."

Leaning down, Nate kissed his forehead. "Then I say he's the fool." He kissed one eyelid, then the other. "I'd say Elias Cole doesn't know what he's talking about." He kissed Sam's lips. "I'd say he doesn't understand that it's worth risking everything for this. For you."

"For us." And Sam kissed him again, warm, languorous, and with all the time in the world.

TWO DAYS LATER, Sam watched from the window as Nate left.

They'd spent a blissful couple of days holed up at Hal's, where nobody cared what two men did together behind closed doors. They'd slept and eaten and fucked with abandon, they'd talked and kissed and thoroughly ignored the world outside.

The world would intrude, however, and on the third day Nate had gotten dressed, kissed Sam on the forehead, and gone to see Colonel Talmach. Sam had wanted to go with him, but Nate had forbidden it and Cole had suggested locking him in his room if he tried.

Even Moses had voiced an opinion. "Don't go courting trouble, Hutch. It'll find you easily enough without handing out invitations."

They were right, of course. MacLeod's accusation against him had only gained more weight since his flight from justice, and God knew Colonel Talmach was no friend of his. But plenty of wanted men lived among Hal Foxe's brethren, and while Sam stayed under his protection, he knew he'd be safe.

The same couldn't be said of Nate, out alone on London's streets.

To distract himself from his worries, Sam headed down to his workshop at the back of the Bowl. He was pleased to see that several pieces of jewelry had been set aside for his assessment in the time he'd been away. Nice pieces, too.

"Wessex?" he asked Moses.

"That's right. He came in twice last week. Says it's urgent he gets his money."

"Wessex always says that." Sam picked up his loupe and began to examine a rather elaborate silver pocket watch, the case inset with a garish arrangement of gemstones. It was a display of wealth rather than taste, but in this place all that mattered was the price. He angled the watch to the light. Wessex was in luck; the gems were genuine rubies and diamonds. Wessex was usually in luck, Sam had noticed, and suspected he chose his targets well. He certainly brought in fine pieces.

Alongside the watch sat a gentleman's ring and a lady's chatelaine. Ignoring the chatelaine, he picked up the ring. It was an elegant rose-cut emerald and the simple oval setting reminded him of the ring Nate still wore about his neck. He'd like to see that ring on Nate's finger again, Sam decided with a smile so giddy it made him blush. Hell, he was as love-struck as a milkmaid — and nervous as a cat when he thought of Nate off to make peace with the colonel. Smile fading, Sam set the ring aside. He needed to concentrate on his work, or the wait would be unbearable.

Pulling out his stool, Sam reached for pen, paper, and ink. He'd start with the watch and make a few notes to assist with the assessment. The design, he thought, looked French, although the maker's mark was obscured by the latch which appeared to have been badly mended some years after the piece was made…

"Hutch?"

He glanced up, blinking at Moses who'd poked his head around the door. "Hmm?"

"Tanner's back. He's gone to speak to Mr. Foxe in his study."

"Already?"

Moses raised an eyebrow. "It's past noon. You've been in here all morning."

He rubbed at the back of his neck, not surprised it was stiff. Hours disappeared when he was deep in his work. Losing himself like that was a joy he'd missed over the past couple of weeks, and it came as something of a surprise that this room felt like home. He'd miss it when they were back in America. "I'll be up shortly," he said, reaching for his loupe again. Whatever Nate needed to say to Hal, he wouldn't want Sam butting in. Besides, he didn't want to look too much like a faithful hound sitting at the door awaiting his master's return. Even if that was exactly how he felt.

Nonetheless, he made short work of the last piece he had to examine — the chatelaine was pretty but, unfortunately for Wessex, only pinchbeck. He made notes for Moses and told him to offer Wessex three hundred pounds for all three pieces together. He'd get more from a jeweler, but if Wessex could sell his ill-gotten gains to a respectable dealer he would, wouldn't he?

Slipping out of the workshop through the Bowl, Sam hurried across Bainbridge Street to the Brewery. He walked with his hat pulled low and one eye over his shoulder until he could duck into the safety of the yard's shadows.

Weaving his way through the busy mash room, the air full of hops, Sam ran up the stairs and past the library, slipping through the door into Hal's private rooms. Only intimates were admitted to the study, which Nate hadn't been until now. What that meant, Sam didn't know. Perhaps Nate was asking about Sam's false papers?

The study door stood ajar and Sam slowed, not wanting to intrude.

Hal Foxe sat behind his desk, immaculate in his black coat, watching Nate with his bright hawk's eyes. When they'd first met, Sam had tried and failed to judge Hal's age; anything between thirty and fifty could be right. In some moods, younger even than that. In others, old as old stone. Hard and unyielding. Hal kept his guard high and, as far as Sam knew, nobody had ever glimpsed what lay behind his walls. Rumor had it that his heart had been broken, long ago, by a beautiful young lordling who'd toyed with him and cast him aside. Rumor had it that Hal had faced the noose while the boy floated away unscathed. Rumor had it that's why Hal had founded the Brethren, why he provided shelter for men like Sam who found themselves in trouble with Bow Street.

But who knew whether any of that was true? Hal Foxe never spoke of his past. Not even deep in his cups.

"When a man hangs for stealing bread to feed his children," he was saying in his gravelly voice, "I say that the law is unjust. And not worth following."

"Perhaps." Though Nate sat with his back to the door, Sam could hear the smile in his voice; Nate dearly loved to debate. "But isn't the injustice really that the government refuses to provide for the poor, and so leaves them no choice but to steal or starve? The law against theft protects us all."

Hal spread his hands. "I've even less faith in government than I have in lawyers, Mr. Tanner."

"In this government, perhaps. But, to paraphrase Mr. Jefferson, whenever any form of government becomes destructive of life, liberty, and happiness, it is the right of the people to alter or to abolish it."

For a moment, Hal said nothing, but his eyes shone, and his lips ticked towards a smile. "If you're spreading your revolution to London, Mr. Tanner, then I say all power to you. There's plenty in St. Giles who'd rally to your cause."

Sam's pulse skipped at the notion of Nate leading a mob against Westminster Palace. But Nate only laughed, shaking his head. "The British will have to start their own revolution. All I want is peace, for me and for Sam. I think we've earned it."

"Then I hope you find it." Hal rose to his feet, his gaze flicking over Nate's shoulder and landing on Sam. He gave a slight nod, then looked back at Nate. "You're welcome to stay in the Brewery as long as you need; I dare say I'll find a use for you."

Nate stood too, gathering papers into a folder. "Thank you, Mr. Foxe. I'll endeavor to be useful."

They parted with a polite bow, and Sam stood away from the doorway as Nate left Hal's office. His last sight of Foxe was of him sitting back down at his desk and reaching for pen and ink.

Then Nate was before him, closing Hal's door behind him. It had only been three hours since they'd parted, yet

Sam's heart swooped like a swallow at the sight of him. He smiled and suddenly didn't care how besotted he looked. "Is it foolish that I missed you?"

Startled, Nate fumbled the papers and then laughed at himself as he turned around. "If it is, then we're both fools."

Grinning, Sam strolled closer. "I see you survived your meeting with Talmach. How was it?"

"Difficult. He wasn't happy, of course."

"Is he ever? I never a saw a more sour-faced man."

"He has his reasons to be sour, Sam. Besides, you can't dislike him too much. If it wasn't for the colonel, we may never have found each other again." Nate smiled and shook his head. "I'll never forget walking into Salter's and seeing you both sitting there, *tête-à-tête*. I thought I was dreaming."

"I thought something else." Hell, but he'd been angry. Angry and hurt. "And I don't like to think of what I said to you."

Nate set down his papers on a console table and stepped closer. With a cautious glance toward the door behind him, he touched Sam's cheek. "I'm only grateful we met at all."

Sam briefly covered his hand and then let go, clearing his throat. "So, what did Talmach say? Clearly he didn't clap you in irons."

"All he really cares about is clapping Farris in irons. Luckily, he's still set to sail on Friday, despite my behavior. It seems that men like Farris, men who think the world is there for their pleasure, can't conceive of losing."

"I'm sure you'll enjoy setting him straight."

Nate didn't answer, just walked back to the console table and fiddled with his papers. "About that," he said.

Sam felt a pulse of unease. "About what?"

"Going home." Nate looked up; his expression was serious. "Sam, I don't think you should go. Not yet. Talmach's truly angry. And he *knows* you. He — He's not without influence at home and he's certainly not the only one in power with strong opinions on Loyalists."

Sam's skin flushed cold. "But Hal's scratchman can give me a new identity: a loyalty oath, a citizenship certificate, and—"

"I'm not saying you can't ever go back," Nate said, tucking the folder under his arm. "I'm just saying not yet. In a few years, maybe it'll be safer?"

"A few *years*?" His chest tightened. "And you'll… What? You'll wait for me?"

Nate came to stand before him, his head tipped as if surprised by the question. "Of course."

"For years? Nate, I don't want to be apart—"

Nate's fingers pressed against his lips, stopping him. "Sam, I'll wait here. I'll wait right here with you." He smiled at whatever he saw in Sam's eyes. "I don't want you sneaking home like a thief cracking a house. I don't want you denying who you are, or what you believe. I don't want you hiding from people who know you. I want us to go *home*, Sam, to Rosemont. Together and with our heads held high."

"But…" Sam was speechless. "It could be years. And what about your work, your position? *Our* work."

"We can serve our country here. God knows there's enough for the Department of Foreign Affairs to do in London. Besides" — Nate tapped the folder under his arm — "Hal Foxe knows merchants willing to trade with America despite the British embargo." He flashed a grin. "Off the books, of course, but they'll still need contracts drawing up. Plenty of work for a couple of outlawed lawyers. And if we must wait a few years to go home… Well, then we'll wait together."

Sam stared at him, his dearest friend, and doubted he'd ever loved Nate more. "Come here," he said, tugging him closer. Nate smiled, lips parting in anticipation of a kiss, but that wasn't what Sam had in mind. Instead, he lifted his hands to Nate's neckcloth, ignored his flustered protest — "Sam!" — and snagged the leather cord about his neck, tugging the ring free from his shirt.

Turning it over between his fingers, Sam smiled. It was a fine piece; he'd been specific about the design. Their woven hair sat within an oval setting of warm gold, its shoulders enhanced by delicate *repoussé* work that merged into a sturdy band that suited Nate's slim fingers. And inside, the inscription AETAI: *Amicus est tamquam alter idem.*

A true friend is a second self.

Sam traced his fingers over the shell of Nate's ear, the line of his brow, his cheekbone, his face as familiar to Sam as his own reflection — the other half of his soul. Then he reached up to hook the leather cord over Nate's head, untied it and freed the ring. Nate watched in silence as Sam took his hand and slipped the ring back onto Nate's finger where it belonged.

"Always together," Sam promised.

Nate curled his fingers around Sam's hand, bringing his knuckles to his lips even though his eyes never left Sam's. "Always and forever."

Epilogue

**Six months later – February 20th, 1784
London, England**

FOG SAT HEAVY in St. Giles, creeping up from the river on stealthy feet. Sam drew his muffler closer around his neck and hurried across the street from the Brewery, glad to see the yellow light of the Bowl bleeding through the murk. He'd be gladder still when Nate got back. Nights like these were made for footpads and Nate was still green in the ways of London. At least he'd taken to carrying a heavy stick at night.

And Sam should learn to stop worrying. It was difficult, though, when your heart and soul were walking about on the sleeve of another man. Sentimental tosh, perhaps, but the truth nonetheless: six months after they'd found each other again, he and Nate were absurdly besotted, and Sam had never been happier.

Still, the friend he was meeting tonight would knock that sort of nonsense out of him and he wasn't sorry for the distraction. In fact, he found himself smiling at the prospect as he shouldered open the door to the Bowl.

He was met by the distinctive fug of a warm public house on a cold night, one-part damp wool coats and three-parts gin. Welcome, nonetheless. From behind the bar, Moses lifted a hand in greeting. He had a good listening ear and gave plain-spoken advice. Sam had noticed more black faces and American accents in the place too, these past few months, exiles drawn together in search of friends in a strange land. Sam approved. He felt increasingly at home in this wretched, wonderful corner of London. And business at the Bowl had certainly never been better, as evidenced by the crowd playing dice this Friday night. Over their heads, Sam mimed a drink and Moses nodded.

Then he searched the room and found Elias Cole lurking in a dark corner at the back. As usual, Cole preferred to keep to the shadows. He wasn't exactly welcome on Hal Foxe's turf, although nobody here would ever do him harm. Why, Sam didn't rightly understand and didn't plan to find out. Every man was entitled to his secrets.

As Sam approached, Cole nudged a chair towards him with his foot. "Looking well, Hutch. How've you been?"

Deliriously happy, foolishly in love. "Well enough. And yourself?" Sam cocked his head as he sat down. "You look… excited?"

Cole grinned, sitting forward. "Maybe I am."

"Will you tell me why, or is it a secret?"

"Let's just say six months of bloody hard work are about to pay off. And when I say pay off, I'm talking about three hundred quid's worth of pay off." He made a face. "Less what I'll have to split with Bow Street."

"That's a decent reward." Sam smiled as Moses came over with his whiskey. "Thank you. Another for you, Cole?"

"No." He tapped the half-drunk jug of ale at his elbow.

"Need to stay fly tonight."

"Let me guess," Sam said, when Moses had left them. "Tonight's business involves the elusive Mr. Wessex."

"Guess what you like." Cole grinned. "I ain't likely to tell one of his known associates, am I?"

He snorted. "Hardly an associate. I've bought a few baubles from him, that's all. Never even seen his face — he's careful to stay hidden." Sam lifted a teasing eyebrow. "Pretty blue eyes, though."

"Sod off. The man's a bleedin' menace. The nobs are terrified of crossing the heath, even by day, for fear of being spiced by the bugger."

Nobs like John MacLeod. "My heart bleeds for them."

Cole flashed a grin. "Aye, well. If they want to pay me three hundred quid to nab the bloke, I ain't complaining."

Behind them, the door opened, letting in a draft of cold air. Sam turned, hoping to see Nate, disappointed when it was a stranger. Damn, but he wished it weren't such a foggy night.

Cole gave an exaggerated groan. "Bleedin' hell, look at you." But when Sam turned back around, he saw the end of a melancholy smile fading from Cole's lips. "Expecting your 'dear friend'?"

"He's been hours."

"Must be nice to —" Cole checked himself with a shake of the head and leaned forward. "Listen. I hope you're being careful. No mushy love letters with your name signed to 'em, alright? Nothing damning."

"Cole…" He spread his hands. "I've got nothing to fear from Nate."

"Aye, that's what everyone says until they're up before the beak and their 'dear friend' is running the other way, or claiming they was forced against their will. Just ask Hal Foxe."

That was the last thing Sam would ask Hal, but the point

was moot. "I guess you won't understand until you meet your own…dear friend. But believe me, when you do, you'll know why it's worth the risk."

"I hope I ain't so unlucky." He jerked his chin toward the door. "Speak of the devil…"

Sam looked around again, smiling in relief at the sight of Nate weaving his way through the tables toward them holding a suspiciously book-shaped package under one arm. Standing, Sam greeted him with a brief embrace, and even that fleeting contact set him grinning. To hell with Cole's despairing shake of the head, Sam was happy, and he didn't care who knew.

Nate dragged a chair over, pulling off his muffler and greatcoat. His hair was fog-damp, his cheeks pink from the cold. Sam could have kissed him right there, but he could feel Moses' eyes on them from the bar. A certain degree of decorum was required, even at the Bowl. "Sorry I'm so late," Nate said, draping his greatcoat over the back of his chair and setting his books on the table. "I got a little, uh, distracted."

"Don't bother me," Cole said with a smirk. "Hutch was panicking, though."

"I was not." But Nate's fond smile, his hand squeezing Sam's knee in apology, made him add, "It's a filthy night."

"Couldn't see two yards in front of my face in Finsbury Square," Nate agreed, "even with a link boy showing me the way. Took forever to get back."

"A link boy?" Cole looked horrified. "Don't trust those little buggers on a night like this, Tanner. They'll lead you straight to a rampsman's crew."

Nate lifted an eyebrow. "And yet, I live."

Beneath the table, Sam took Nate's hand. "Next time, I'm coming with you. And no argument."

Nate didn't argue, he just smiled, Sam smiled back and for a moment the room was empty of everything else. Nate's eyes were darkest brown tonight, lit by a golden flicker of candlelight. A lock of his damp hair had come loose, and Sam pushed it back from his face, unthinking.

With a noise of disgust, Cole got to his feet. "There's only so much billing and cooing a decent cove can take."

"Apologies," Nate said. "Don't go, we —"

Cole held up a hand to stop him. "I must. I've business of a lucrative nature to be done tonight." He grinned. "With luck, I'll be back tomorrow to celebrate the unmasking of a certain gent of our mutual acquaintance."

"I wish you luck, then," Sam said, "although Wessex has been a good client of Hal's."

"I dare say Hal's empire will survive his loss." Cole took a final swig of his ale and set the jug down. "Gentlemen, enjoy your evening of soppy poetry, or whatever it is you get up to together." He gave Sam a smile, rather more wistful than teasing. "I'll be seeing you around."

Nate lifted a curious eyebrow as Cole wound his way between the tables and slipped out into the fog. "Poetry?"

"He's teasing, or — You know, I think he might be jealous. Not of you," he said, smiling at Nate's look of surprise, "of us. Of this. I suppose it isn't so usual for men like us to have… To have what we have."

"I suppose not," Nate said, finding Sam's hand again. "And I'd say we were lucky, only I don't think we've ever had much luck. And, anyway, it's not so much about luck as about wanting this more than anything else the world put between us."

"Including a revolution, a war, and the Atlantic Ocean."

Nate smiled. "Talking of which, there's news from home. First, Talmach has his conviction in Farris's trial. Second…" He hesitated before pulling a folded newspaper cutting from his coat pocket and handing it to Sam. "He sent me this."

Unfolding the cutting, Sam read the headline: *Treaty of Paris ratified by Congress, January 14.* He looked up. "That's it, then."

"The war's officially over."

It wasn't any kind of shock. But seeing it in print and knowing what it meant—that the country he'd grown up in was gone forever—tolled heavily inside Sam's chest. "Congratulations. I guess you won."

Nate plucked the newspaper from his hand, folded it up and set it aside. "I think maybe we all won, and maybe we all lost too. God knows what the next years will bring, Sam, but America's on this path now whether we like it or not. We have to see it to the end."

"At least there's peace," Sam conceded, "and a chance for reconciliation. Perhaps, one day, I'll be able to go home."

Nate took his hand again, holding it between both of his. "The future's unknowable, Sam, but I think you will. I'm hopeful."

He looked so earnest sitting there in a grimy London pub, trying to reconcile Sam to the future he'd resisted for so long, that all Sam felt was an intense rush of affection. The world had spun beneath his feet, and God knew Sam hadn't wanted this new direction, but he had Nate's love and he had his respect. And that was enough. "I'm hopeful too," he said, tracing his thumb over the *repoussé* band of Nate's ring. "But you're wrong about the future, not everything is unknowable. For example, I know I'm going to spend my life with you."

Nate's eyes shone as bright as his smile. "That's true."

"I also know I'm about to take you home." He leaned in and grazed his lips against Nate's ear. "And to bed."

Nate laughed. "I'm in awe of your prescience."

Grinning, Sam got to his feet and held out his hand in invitation. "Come on then, Nate Tanner, let's go find our future."

The End

Author's note

BACK IN 1998, I completed a master's dissertation on the treatment of American Loyalists during the American Revolution. Ever since, I've wanted to write about the Loyalist experience but struggled to find a way to frame the story. That changed in 2016, when two things happened: I discovered male/male romance, and the UK voted for Brexit.

King's Man is the result.

The agony and bewilderment of Loyalists, who felt just as American as their Patriot neighbors, has always touched me. These men and women found themselves ostracized, accused of treachery, and even exiled for holding political opinions that had been mainstream for their whole lives. Should anyone want to explore this from a serious historical perspective, I highly recommend Bernard Bailyn's *The Ordeal of Thomas Hutchinson* as a place to start. It's one of the few academic books to have brought me to tears.

But it wasn't until the Brexit referendum, and the political vitriol thrown around by both sides of the debate, that I understood the Loyalists' pain on a personal level.

I wrote *King's Man* as a catharsis back in 2016, and to explore whether a people riven by opposing visions of their nation's identity and future could ever come back together. And, because I'm a romantic, I framed it as a story of two men — lovers — torn apart by the great political question of their day.

In the years since I wrote the first draft, much has changed about the story and in the real world, both in the UK and the US. The debate Sam and Nate have about the dangers of demagogues and mobs has recently become especially pertinent in America, and both our countries are still deeply divided in how we see ourselves and our future.

I'm not sure whether *King's Man* offers any answers, but I hope it provides some hope that — on a personal level — it's possible to reconcile our differences, understand each other, and move forward together in love.

Rebel

TO FIND OUT how Sam and Nate first met and fell in love, check out Rebel, the prologue to *King's Man*.

Rebel is available free to my newsletter subscribers. Sign up here to claim your copy: https://bit.ly/3cYKCQ9.

Or find Rebel in the Amazon store.

Rebel (An Outlawed Story)

SAMUEL HUTCHINSON HAS lived his whole life in Rosemont, Rhode Island. And as far as he's concerned, his future is fixed: complete his legal training, marry a respectable woman, and settle down to raise a family.

But Sam never counted on meeting Nathaniel Tanner.

Clever, urbane, and dazzling, Nate has been banished to Rosemont by a father determined to remove him from the rising political tension in Boston. The last thing Nate expects to find in the sleepy Rhode Island town is a man who's not only interested in Nate's radical ideas, but who interests Nate in return.

In every conceivable way.

Over books and conversation, their friendship deepens.

But when Nate dares to confess his true feelings, Sam faces a stark choice—reject his friend and continue to live a lie, or rebel against everything he's been taught and embrace his heart's desire…

This short story is approximately 12,000 words and comes with a guaranteed HFN.

The Outlawed Series

Rebel (An Outlawed story)

1774: Clever, urbane, and radical, Nate Tanner's been banished from Boston by his father. The last thing Nate expects to find in the sleepy Rhode Island town of Rosemont is a man who's not only interested in his free-thinking ideas, but who interests him in return. In every conceivable way…

King's Man (Outlawed 1)

1783: Had there been no war, Sam Hutchinson and Nate Tanner would have lived their lives together, as friends and secret lovers. But when the revolution convulsed America, it threw them down on opposite sides of history…

Thief Taker (Outlawed 2)

1784: Elias Cole doesn't believe in love. It's not for men like him. What he believes in is his work. Elias is the best thief

taker in London and always gets his mark—except when his mark is the elusive highwayman known as 'Wessex'...
Coming Winter 2021

Libertine (Outlawed 3)

1785: After being abandoned to the pillory by his aristocratic lover, Hal Foxe will never trust the honeyed words of a gentleman again. But he's happy enough to take their money. When a Peer of the Realm asks him to make his dissolute brother respectable enough to marry, Hal is glad to pocket his coin.

He doesn't expect to like the scathing, prickly young viscount. And he certainly doesn't expect to fall in love...
Coming 2022

Also by Sally

Historical

The Last Kiss

When Captain Ashleigh Dalton went to war in 1914, he never expected to fall in love. Yet, over three long years at the front, his dashing batman, Private West, became his reason for fighting — and his reason for living…

Contemporary

Perfect Day

Finn's spent a long time forgetting Joshua Newton. He certainly doesn't plan to forgive him.

Between the Lines

No mushy feelings, no expectations, and no drama. That's the deal. And it suits them both just fine…

Love Around the Corner (novella)

Real life enemies, online lovers. Two lonely men, destined for each other — if only they knew it.

Twice Shy

The last thing struggling single dad Ollie Snow needs is to fall in love…

About the author

SALLY MALCOLM WAS bitten by the male/male romance bug in 2016 and hasn't looked back. Her stories are emotional, romantic, and always have happy endings. She lives in South West London with her American husband, two lovely children, and two lazy cats.

To connect with Sally, sign up to her monthly newsletter at https://bit.ly/3cYKCQ9. Or find her on Facebook and @Sally_Malcolm on Twitter — she loves to talk to readers!

Scan this QR code to sign up to Sally's newsletter!

Printed in Great Britain
by Amazon